KNIGHT OF HER LIFE

MARISA CHENERY

CONTENTS

CHAPTER ONE

Isle of Wight
Carisbrooke Castle
July 1389

"Give me one good reason that I cannot go. That is all I ask."

"You know very well I have my reasons. I will speak of this with you no further, Jacqueline."

Jacqueline Montacute repressed the urge to stamp her foot in frustration. Her mother was being stubborn, but Jacqueline could be just as stubborn when pushed.

"I know why it is you do not want me to go, Mother. *He* is going to be there, is he not?"

Elizabeth Montacute, Countess of Salisbury and Lady of Isle of Wight, sighed deeply. "Aye, your father will be at Windsor. That is the main reason I forbid you to go to the tournament with your brother."

Her father, William Montacute, Earl of Salisbury, and the absent Lord of Isle of Wight, was seven and ten years older than her mother, who hadn't been her father's first choice for a bride. His first marriage had been to Lady Joan Plantagenet, who was also known as the Fair Maid of

Kent. In 1349, William married Elizabeth, eldest daughter of John, Lord Mohun of Dunster. After impregnating her, her father had left her mother on the isle and never returned, which suited her mother very well. Theirs was no love match, by any means.

Jacqueline felt nothing but disgust at the mere thought of her father. The stunt he'd pulled two years before still left a bitter taste on her tongue.

Thinking to further himself, he had contracted marriages for both his children. With her brother, William, and herself being twins, their father decided, at the age of nine and ten, they were of an age to wed. William's marriage had ended up being a blessing. Her brother loved his young wife dearly. and Beth FitzAllen was devoted to William.

The earl had contracted the marriage of his only son with Beth's father, Richard, Earl of Arundel, without the knowledge of his wife. He had done the same for his daughter. The match had not been to her liking, nor had Jacqueline's mother been prepared to meekly accept what her husband had done.

Her chosen bridegroom had been thirty years older than her nine and ten. He was Forwin De La Mare, Earl of Somerset. Besides being older, Forwin was obese and known for his cruelty to his past wives. All four of them.

Jacqueline was exactly what he preferred in a wife— beautiful and in the peak of health. With her waist-length dark brown hair, vivid turquoise blue eyes, and a perfect face to match, Forwin had found her ripe for the picking. He practically licked his lips in anticipation when he had come to look her over before signing the marriage contract. That Jacqueline, at five feet nine inches, towered over him by three inches had not concerned him at all.

She had felt physically sick when Forwin had presented himself at the castle. She had known in that instant she would never bind herself to such a man.

So her mother had come up with the ruse to foil her husband's plans. It had been drastic, but it assured Jacqueline would never be bothered by any such goings on again.

They faked her death, even going so far as to place a headstone in the family cemetery with her supposed date of death inscribed upon it. It was assumed by all concerned that Forwin would want proof, and they had been correct in their thinking. A week after receiving word of Jacqueline's supposed demise, he had arrived at the isle to see for himself. It had not taken much effort on her part to avoid him. The man took one look at the headstone and then had promptly left.

Now, to the rest of the world off the isle, Jacqueline Montacute was no more.

"Mother, I can do what I have done in the past when I have been to other tournaments with William and Beth. No one has ever questioned whether I was Beth's maid or not." She had never been to Windsor and was determined not to miss out on experiencing it.

"Jacqueline, I know you have been forced to miss so much of life outside the safety of the isle. What was done, is done and cannot be undone."

Reaching out, her mother tucked a wayward strand of hair behind Jacqueline's ear and stared into her eyes. Jacqueline knew that look. It meant her mother would not be swayed, no matter how much she tried to push her to do just that.

"You look so much like I did at your age. You and your brother look so much alike. I still remember the stunt the two of you pulled by switching clothes to see if anyone would notice, and how delighted you both were when no one did." Her mother sighed. "Jacqueline, no more of this. The discussion is pointless. The other tournaments were different. Your father was not present, and they were only small affairs compared to what Windsor will be. Now

3

leave me in peace for a while."

She left her mother in the hall and went in search of her brother and his wife. If they could be swayed to her side, maybe the three of them could change her mother's mind.

* * * *

Carisbrooke Castle was the only home Jacqueline knew. The castle itself was seven acres, including the earthworks surrounding it, and had been built atop earlier Roman and Saxon defenses. Inside the walls were a keep, chapel, and a one hundred and sixty-foot deep well, situated in the middle of the bailey.

Jacqueline now skirted past the well, and knowing where her brother and his wife were, she headed straight to the tilting grounds. Sure enough, as she drew closer, she could make out Beth, standing on the sidelines.

Moving to stand next to her sister by marriage, Jacqueline watched William take a run at the quintain. He hit the target with his outstretched lance. He must have landed the blow squarely, if not, the weighted arm would have swung around with enough velocity to unseat him. He went past still firmly seated in his saddle as it swung harmlessly aside.

Both of them cheered for him as he turned about and rode to where they watched. After dismounting, William pulled off his helmet and chuckled.

"No luck with mother I see."

Jacqueline huffed and shook her head in response. "She will not be moved by any of my reasons for going with you."

William flashed a brilliant smile. "I wonder why not. Maybe it is because she knows you never think far enough ahead to see the trouble you get yourself into."

She fisted her hand and punched her brother in the arm. She instantly regretted it when she made contact with the steel plating of his armor. Shaking her bruised knuckles, she glared at him as he chuckled once more.

"Are you saying you agree with her, William? I thought you of all people would take my side in this."

William wrapped his arm around her shoulder and pulled her to his side. "Jacqueline, mother is right. Windsor is too risky. There will be too many people there. All it would take would be one of them to see how closely my wife's maid and I look alike."

Jacqueline could not argue with that. Though he was male, William only stood an inch taller than her. They had the same turquoise blue eyes and dark brown hair. She wore hers to her waist. Her brother kept his trimmed to the nape.

Being twins, they were very close. When younger, they had been inseparable. Whatever the one did, the other had to try as well, with Jacqueline being the more adventurous of the two.

At one and ten, she thought nothing of putting on William's clothes and taking part in lessons in swordplay. Such activities had come to an end the year before. Lady Elizabeth could no longer abide her only daughter dressing as a man or acting as a knight would.

"You, Beth, do you agree with William and mother?"

Beth, only ten and eight, could make Jacqueline feel much younger than she was. All it took was a certain look Beth used when she thought Jacqueline was being unreasonable. One most mothers seemed to develop in their dealings with their offspring. Though Beth and William had no children, Jacqueline could only guess how her sister by marriage came by it. Standing at only five feet four inches, Beth seemed not to care that she had to look up at Jacqueline to give her such a look, either.

"Jacqueline, there will be other tournaments. Think of how your mother would feel if anything happened to you."

"Must you do that, play upon my emotions like I am some thoughtless child?"

Beth's tinkling laughter filled the air. "If not me, then who else would?"

Jacqueline could not help but join in Beth's laughter. She could never bring herself to be annoyed with William's wife. She was one of those people who were just as beautiful on the inside as she was on the outside. Jacqueline loved her as a true sister, and had from their first meeting. Just as William had. He had not been able to stop staring at her beautiful heart-shaped face, small pert nose, and ruby-red lips. Massive amounts of long, light blonde hair and pure green eyes made up the rest of Beth.

In exasperation, Jacqueline threw up her arms. "Fine, you all win. I will stay on the isle with mother. I will miss you both terribly."

William once more pulled her to his side and kissed her lightly on the cheek. "It is not as if we will be gone forever. It is only for a fortnight."

"Just promise me you will be careful. I have a feeling not all will be as it should. If anything happens to you —"

He placed a finger on Jacqueline's lips, silencing her before she could complete the sentence. "I am coming back. I promise you."

"You swear?"

William kissed the tip of her nose. "I swear."

* * * *

She knew something was wrong. It was just a gut feeling she had, but it would not go away. Jacqueline had felt on edge ever since the day William and Beth had left the isle. In the beginning, she had come to the conclusion this feeling was caused by the separation from her twin. Now, almost two weeks into her brother's absence, it was even stronger.

Trying to quell the foreboding sensation, she climbed up to the top of the castle walls. William was to have returned home two days ago. With the hope of catching a glimpse of his return, she walked the walls for hours at a time.

Pacing in a gown was not a particularly easy thing to do, either. Jacqueline missed the freedom of the male clothes she wore during arms training. Every time she turned, she had to push the skirt out of the way or she would become entangled in its length. If given the choice, she would gladly never wear a gown again—ever. She much preferred the tunic and hose in which William, and every other man, garbed themselves.

After completing her first circuit of the walls, she stopped at one of the twin towers attached to the gatehouse. She searched for any sign of travelers approaching the castle. Jacqueline squinted against the sun's bright rays and focused intently on what were slowly becoming discernible shapes in the distance. Once she realized her eyes were indeed not playing tricks on her, she raced down the steps.

She set off at a run and crossed the bailey before she went to find her mother, who was inside the hall. Lady Elizabeth smiled. "William has returned?"

Jacqueline took a few deep breaths, trying to still her rapidly beating heart. "I did not see for sure, but who else can it be? We are not expecting visitors."

Lady Elizabeth took Jacqueline's hand. "Now you will see all your worrying was for naught. William was more than likely delayed for a very good reason."

"I suppose you are right, Mother."

"I know I am."

After releasing Jacqueline's hand, they left the hall and went to stand in the middle of the bailey. They did not have long to wait. A few minutes later, the men-at-arms who had accompanied William to Windsor passed through the raised portcullises. Beth followed them. William was nowhere to be seen.

Jacqueline grabbed the bridle of Beth's horse and pulled it to a halt. "Where is William? Is he back with the baggage cart again, making sure his precious armor is not getting scratched?"

Her sister-in-law did not respond, causing Jacqueline to look up into the other girl's face. There was a trail of tears streaming down Beth's cheeks. Her gut clenched. Her feelings had not been so unfounded, after all. Something had happened to William.

"Where is William, Beth?" The girl remained silent, and Jacqueline released the bridle and took hold of Beth's leg and squeezed. "Answer me! Where is William?" she shouted.

At the rumbling sound of the baggage cart entering the bailey, Jacqueline released Beth and rushed to it. The closer she came, the more intensified the feeling of having lost a part of herself became.

Her whole being centered on the covered form lying in the middle of the cart. It felt as if the world had fallen away with only her and it in existence. Jacqueline vaguely noticed her mother had come to help Beth dismount and then pulled the girl into her arms. She barely heard her mother softly crying. All that mattered was what lay in the cart.

With a shaking hand, Jacqueline pulled back the blanket that completely covered what the cart carried. As William's face was revealed, she knew he was dead. He was too pale. It showed none of the laughter he was always so quick to share. Feeling as if her heart were being ripped from her body, she slowly backed away. She could not accept this. That could not be William.

"Nay...nay, William cannot be gone. He promised to come home to me. He has never broken his word to me—ever."

Her mother tried to take her into her arms, to offer comfort, but Jacqueline roughly shrugged out of her embrace. Seeing Beth standing, she grabbed her by the shoulders and shook her.

"Tell me! Tell me how this happened!" Beth did not answer promptly, so Jacqueline shook her again.

Her mother stopped her. "Enough, Jacqueline! Can you not see she is distraught? She just lost her husband. She grieves as much as we do."

"I need to know, Mother." Jacqueline was very close to falling completely apart. She found it hard to breathe, and her heart seemed to beat painfully.

"Beth, I think it best you tell Jacqueline." Lady Elizabeth once more held her daughter by marriage in her arms.

Beth wiped away her tears, only to have more flow. "William was unseated when his competitor's lance shattered. A large piece of it managed to enter his neck just where his helm and the collar of his breastplate met." She swallowed as if she fought back the urge to dissolve into a fit of weeping. Once she seemed to get some control, she continued. "A physician removed the piece of broken lance, he even said William would recover, but wound fever soon set in. As William's condition deteriorated even more, I had him placed in the baggage cart. I thought if I could just get him home to the isle all would be well again." She said no more as her grief overtook her. She turned in her mother-in-law's arms and buried her face in Lady Elizabeth's shoulder, weeping in earnest.

Jacqueline had stood dry-eyed as Beth related the details of William's death. She still could not shed a tear. If she did now, she would never be able to stop. Someone had to be the strong one. Someone had to keep their head. Even though it seemed Beth had told the whole tale, she had neglected to tell the most relevant piece of information — against whom had William tilted with and paid with his life?

"Beth, who did my brother tilt with?" she asked in monotone.

The girl brought her weeping back under control once more. Beth looked into Jacqueline's eyes, and said, "William tilted against the earl, your father."

Lady Elizabeth gasped as all the blood seemed to drain from her face. It was as much a blow to Jacqueline as it was to her mother. The earl had to have known who William was. How could he have jousted with his son, his heir? She could understand William wanting to meet the earl in the list, wanting to prove to their father that he was a man, but the earl was another story. He had nothing to prove. He already held sway over William.

Jacqueline kept her face as still as a mask. With no inflections in her speech, she finally spoke in a low voice. "He will pay for this. By god, I will make him pay."

Her mother shook her head. "Jacqueline, let it go. There is nothing you can do. No matter what you might plan to do to the earl, William will still be gone from us. It will not bring him back. You must accept this."

"I know that, Mother, but I will still have my revenge."

"Just how do you expect to do that? To your father, you are dead and buried." A look of worry settled on her mother's face.

"It is quite simple, Mother. I am going to meet Father in the lists myself."

Lady Elizabeth shook her head once more. "It is not possible. How could you survive going against a seasoned knight? You have never jousted with a mounted man. Besides, they would never allow a woman to compete."

"Oh, I will compete. From what Beth has said William was still alive when they left Windsor. No one knows of his death yet. So I will become William. As for surviving against a seasoned knight, training for the earl's next tournament will now be my life. There is nothing else that matters anymore. The earl killed a part of me when he took William's life. My only reason for living now is making the earl pay for what he has done."

Her mother and Beth wore shocked expressions. Jacqueline received no response from either woman. She turned her back on them and headed to the hall. There were plans to be made, and there was no time like the present to begin.

* * * *

Two days later, William's funeral service was held. Only those who dwelled in the castle were in attendance. Jacqueline's mother and Beth had tried to steer her from her course of revenge, but she had to do this. Standing at the open grave as William's body was lowered into it firmed her resolve even more.

The priest said the final words in the service, and those in attendance slowly walked away. Soon, only the three women of them were left as mourners.

Elizabeth gave her daughter by marriage a hug and motioned for her to head to the keep without her. William's grave was slowly covered with dirt by two of the castle's men-at-arms. Jacqueline did not look up as her mother came to stand next to her.

"Is there nothing I can do or say to make you change your mind? I fear I will lose my daughter. I have just lost my son. Must I go through this pain again?"

Jacqueline met her lady mother's gaze and found her eyes red and puffy from crying. Her own showed no marks of mourning. She could not, would not, let such weakness take hold of her. It would assuredly defeat her.

"You know my answer to those questions. I will not be put off. I would save you from the pain you feel now, Mother. I cannot think of how me taking William's place might affect you should I fail. Please understand, I will do this."

Her mother sighed as if she knew she wasted her breath with Jacqueline. "Fine. I can see there is no changing your mind. If you are set on doing this, I will bother you no further about this matter. You are no longer a child. I have to respect your decision, even though it kills me to think what can happen to you. I will keep William's death a secret from the mainland, and from your father. I only ask you do not attempt to go against him until you are deemed ready by Sir Guy. He will oversee your training."

"I will gladly have Sir Guy train me, but I will decide when I am ready."

Her mother's voice was tinged with anger. "If you do not allow Sir Guy to decide, I will stop you in any way possible. All it will take is a missive sent to your father, informing him of William's death."

"How could you do that knowing how I feel?"

"Quite easily, my girl. I will not stand by and let my remaining child commit suicide, because that is what it would be. Now, do I have your word?"

Not liking it one bit, Jacqueline allowed her mother that small victory. It would not change anything. She would go and no one would stop her. "You have my word. Sir Guy will have the final say when I go."

* * * *

The next day found Jacqueline on the castle's tilting grounds. Once more she donned a man's clothing. Today was her first day of training with Sir Guy, the castle's castellan. He had trained William in the knightly arts. He had even trained her in the limited amount she had been allowed to learn.

Sir Guy was fifty, but was built as sturdy as any oak tree. At just slightly over six feet, he was formidable-looking even without his armor. He possessed piercing hazel eyes, which did not miss very much. His midnight black hair was slightly peppered with gray, making him look distinguished. Not that Jacqueline would ever tell him. He had been more of a father to William and herself than the earl ever would. She loved Sir Guy. His gruff exterior hid a soft-hearted man, one who had taken pity on the fatherless twins and treated them as his own children.

At that precise moment, he was very much playing the role of father figure, pacing back and forth before Jacqueline, a deep scowl upon his face. He made her edgy, and well he knew it.

"Stop looking at me like that. You can give me menacing looks all day if you wish, but I am not going away."

Sir Guy stopped his pacing, and clasping his hands behind his back, he rocked up and down on his toes. "I am just trying to see if you are as mad as I think you are. Planning to pull this stunt would qualify you as exactly that."

Jacqueline could not help but roll her eyes. "I am not mad. You of all people should know what I am capable of."

"I will give you that. You do excel at riding at the rings, but catching a suspended ring on the tip of your lance is nowhere the same as hitting a fully armored and mounted knight."

"I am not exactly some weak, pathetic female."

"No, you are not, Jacqueline." Sir Guy's words were spoken with affection.

He had been proud of what she had accomplished in the previous training sessions. If she had been born a man, he had said he could have easily completed her training. He would have arranged for her to be knighted when she had reached the age of twenty.

Sir Guy fell silent once more and intently studied Jacqueline. "Come, I have your armor for you. Some is from what we used in the past and some pieces were William's." He turned on his heels and headed to the quintain. Under it sat a pile of armor.

Jacqueline cleared her throat, pushing back her emotions. Raw pain shot through her with the knowledge she would be using parts of William's armor. She swallowed back the lump in her throat as she ran to catch up to Sir Guy. How could she possibly fail now? She would have something of William with her when she faced her father. Hopefully, William would be with her in spirit.

CHAPTER TWO

Every bone in his body ached. He felt as if there was no part of him not bruised and battered. Sir Terric Aubrey felt older than his six and twenty years. What else did he expect with the type of life he had chosen? As a landless knight who made his living following and competing in the tournament circuit, he had picked a hard road. At times, a painful one.

Terric released a groan as his squire, Edwin, rubbed his bruised left shoulder. As Edwin attacked the area in earnest, Terric groaned in protest. "Easy, boy. Are you trying to maim me?"

The squire relented and stepped away. They were in Terric's pavilion, the only home both had known for the last three years, the length of time Terric had been on the road.

"You need to get off the circuit for a while before you kill yourself. Today was too close for my liking."

Edwin was correct. Today had been a very close call. During his last run in the list, his competitor's lance hit him in the helm, missing blinding him by a scant half-inch. The mark of the blow was still on his helm, making it easy to see how close it had come.

Standing, Terric stretched his six foot four inch frame. He rolled his left shoulder a few times, then heard it pop as it settled into place. A dislocated shoulder was quite common on the circuit. He had firsthand experience on how painful one could be. As a result, his shoulder popped and cracked after each tournament.

"Do not remind me how close I came to ending my career as a tournament knight. Luck was on my side today."

Edwin scoffed. "I should say it was more your great skill than luck."

Terric smiled. "Well, thank you, squire. I gladly accept your compliment."

A wet cloth hit Terric squarely in the face. Edwin laughed. "There will be no more compliments from me. I would not want you to get a big head. We would never be able to get your helm on."

Wisely, Edwin ducked out of the pavilion after issuing those words, leaving Terric alone. He shook his head in amusement with a chuckle. Edwin was always good for such comments.

Their relationship was not solely based on that of a knight and his squire. Edwin was his companion as well. At aged eight and ten, Edwin had seen, and done, more than he should have at his young age. Being a child alone on London's streets had a tendency to do that. To this day, Edwin still claimed a guardian angel had been watching over him when he had encountered Terric.

It could have been an angel who led Terric to him, or he had just been in the right place at the right time. No matter how he had happened to stumble across the badly beaten ten-and-two-year-old Edwin, he was thankful he had been the one to be there when the boy had needed help.

After Edwin had been dumped into an alleyway behind the alehouse Terric was about to enter, the commotion had drawn his attention. If he hadn't been found, Edwin would have surely died in the filth. He still had no memory of who had beaten him or why.

Terric rubbed the wet cloth across his chest. He had to make himself presentable for the feasting, which would begin shortly. It could be a hard, lonely life, but the meals sometimes helped to make up for a few shortcomings. In particular, the ladies who would be in attendance. A little flirtation with the ones who tried to gain his attention was one of his favorite ways to unwind after a battering in the list. He was not ugly, far from it. Knowing what his face did to the ladies, he used it to his advantage.

His eyes were an unusual violet color. Hair the color of wheat worn shoulder-length, a strong chin, straight nose, and sculpted lips were what drew women to him. Edwin took full advantage of Terric's luck with the fairer sex. He had no problem finding a woman for himself amongst his master's admirers. The boy was no slouch himself in the looks department with his shaggy dark blond hair and green eyes.

Though women flocked to Terric, he did not take up what they offered most times. He did not want or need a woman to be a part of his life. Not while he was in the circuit. Spending just one night with one was not something he made a habit of doing. Flirting was more his forte.

Once dressed in a tight-fitting, mid-thigh, dark blue tunic and black hose, he pulled on his boots and exited his pavilion. The feast was being held at the castle. To be perfectly honest, Terric could not remember the name of the castle or the lord's name, for that matter, only that they were in Devon. After attending so many tournaments, they tended to blur one into another, especially smaller ones like this. Though it was small, he had managed to take enough ransoms to make it profitable. That was all that really mattered at the end of the day.

* * * *

"Come on, girl, give me your hand. Let's give it another go."

Jacqueline reached up and clasped Sir Guy by the hand, allowing him to pull her up onto her feet. Landing flat on her back and not being able to get up she found to be a humiliating experience. Being encased in full armor, helm and all, she was too weighted down to gain her feet on her own.

The quintain proved harder than it looked. After a week's worth of training behind her, Jacqueline was still being knocked off her steed, but she refused to give up. She would not allow a damn sandbag to get the better of her.

"Up you go." Sir Guy cupped his hand for Jacqueline to step into so he could help her back into the saddle. "Remember to get your lance aimed for the center of the quintain. Any deviation from that point and the sandbag will get you."

"Thanks for the reminder, but I have found that out myself already, a number of times." Jacqueline accepted her lance once more, set it in place, then prepared to run at the quintain one last time before ending the training session.

She took a couple of deep breaths to help clear her mind, then focused all her attention on the quintain. Satisfied with her grip on the lance, she shoved her heels into her horse's sides and barreled toward her target.

As her lance hit the quintain, Jacqueline braced for the inevitable feel of the sandbag whacking her from behind. It never came. She looked over her shoulder and found herself now past it, and miraculously, she was still in her saddle. With a loud whoop, she turned her steed around and headed to where Sir Guy watched.

She yanked off her helm and waited for him to speak. She dismounted and stood before him. "Well, are you at least going to say something?"

To her complete surprise, he wrapped his arms around her, holding her in a bear hug. Sir Guy lifted her off her feet. Once he set her down, there was a large grin upon his face.

"Well done, my girl, well done. I knew you had it in you."

Jacqueline basked in the older man's approval and quickly kissed his cheek. "I had a good teacher, don't you know."

Feeling light of heart, more than she had for the last few days, she spun on her heels and walked in the direction of the hall. Now that she had managed to best the quintain her mother could finally stop worrying about her so much.

CHAPTER THREE

Having completed six months of intense training, Jacqueline was now ready to test her newfound skills. With winter drawing to a close, the tournament circuit would resume the following month. A smaller tournament would be the ideal opportunity to test herself in the list. The only foreseeable problem would be her mother.

Lady Elizabeth had been supportive of her during her training, but it was not hard to see she did not totally approve, either. Jacqueline would have a small battle on her hands. Not so much because her mother did not think she would do well, but that she would be taking the final step in assuming William's identity.

Much to Lady Elizabeth's chagrin, Jacqueline had already taken to wearing a man's short tunic and hose all the time. She had put aside her gowns when she had started her training, not once donning one since. She had yet to take the final step — cutting her hair. To participate in a tournament, it was what she must do.

She headed to her mother's solar and hoped to convince Lady Elizabeth to allow her to go. Sir Guy seemed to think she was ready, though he had not said as much, but he would stand by her. He had given his word. He could not back out, not when she had mastered the quintain. She could beat it now with every run she made.

Lady Elizabeth's solar was full of bright sunlight, which shone through the large windows running the length of the chamber. The windows overlooked her mother's walled garden. Beth and her mother were sewing. Beth sat before a tapestry frame, stitching while her mother worked on a tunic. Clearing her throat, Jacqueline announced her presence.

Her mother looked up and smiled. "Have you come to join us, Jacqueline?"

Jacqueline shook her head. "Nay, Mother. You know I prefer the lance to a needle these days."

Frowning, her mother sniffed, and said, "It did not hurt to ask. I have missed your company these past months."

Jacqueline groaned to herself and pushed on. This was not a good sign. Getting her mother to agree to her wishes would not go without a fight it seemed. "You know why I have not had the time to sit with you like this."

Her lady mother sighed. "Aye, I do. I am reminded of it every day seeing you dressed like that."

Jacqueline self-consciously pulled on the hem of her tunic, then abruptly stopped herself. She had nothing to be ashamed of. "Be that as it may, I need to discuss something with you. Something of importance."

Her mother put aside the tunic and motioned her to sit in the empty chair next to her. "Sit. Tell me what is on your mind."

Jacqueline took a deep, cleansing breath, deciding it was best to get right down to the point and not drag it out any longer than it had to be. "The tournament circuit starts soon. I want to attend one of the smaller tournaments, one in which the earl will not participate."

"You mean to observe it only, am I correct?"

"Nay, Mother. I mean to participate. It is time I see how

I handle myself in the list."

Her mother quickly glanced at William's young widow. "Did you know about this?"

Beth guiltily looked down at her tapestry. "Jacqueline has hinted such to me."

"You did not think to mention it?"

"I had no idea she wanted to go so soon."

"Do not worry, Beth. I will not hold this against you. You are not responsible for Jacqueline's ideas." Once more focusing her full attention back on Jacqueline, she spoke again. "I do not think you are ready. You have only been training for six months."

"Ask Sir Guy. He thinks I am. I think it is you who are not ready, Mother."

Elizabeth gave her a frosty glare. "Forgive me if I'm not ready to take the chance of losing my last child. Why must you persist in this? It is a mad scheme, which will only end badly."

Jacqueline cringed at her mother's words. She had known her lady mother was not a great supporter of what she did. "Try to understand. I will not be put off. I am going to this tournament with or without your consent."

Lady Elizabeth picked up the tunic she had been stitching, letting her know she would not speak further. Eyes downcast, her needle flashed in and out of the material she worked.

Jacqueline turned to Beth and beseechingly looked at her. "Do you feel the same? If I am to really do this properly, I need you by my side. As William's wife, you will make it more believable."

The younger woman took a quick look at her mother-in-law as if to mentally apologize for what she was about to say. "I will help you, Jacqueline. A part of me wants to see William revenged as much as you do."

* * * *

The tournament chosen to be Jacqueline's final test before facing the earl was being held at Portchester Castle on the mainland. The castle was situated near Portsmouth's harbor, one of the more used landing spots when leaving the isle. It was a royal castle, but neither King Richard nor his queen would be in attendance. The constable would be presiding over the tournament.

Now with the day of the event there, Jacqueline was second guessing herself. Was she capable of really doing this? It had not helped her nerves any when her mother had refused to see them off, a blatant show of her disapproval. Getting Beth to cut her hair close to how William wore his had been the last straw for her mother. She now chose to ignore Jacqueline, as if she were not even in the same room.

Jacqueline reached up and pulled at her hair, which now just brushed the tops of her shoulders. Only to herself would she admit she did in some small way regret having to cut it, but it would grow back, after she completed what she set out to do.

The ferry transporting them across the water to Portsmouth bumped against the landing. Waiting for the rest of her company to disembark, Jacqueline took a deep breath to steady herself, then followed.

She was not alone. Including the two men-at-arms as protection, Beth and Sir Guy traveled with her. Having Sir Guy accompany her had been an unexpected surprise. She just hoped her mother would not make it hard for him upon their return. He did not seem worried about what Lady Elizabeth's reaction would be, though. He had simply stated he would not allow Jacqueline to compete in her first tournament without him at her side. William had had no squire. So Sir Guy decided to fulfill some of the duties one would be expected to perform, not trusting the men-at-arms to do a proper job of it.

Upon reaching Portchester Castle, their small party slowly converged on the area that had been set up where the tournament was to be held. After picking an empty space amongst the already pitched pavilions, the men-at-arms unloaded the baggage cart. After theirs was taken from the cart, Sir Guy directed the two men as to where it should be erected, and where to picket her steed.

With not having much to do but wait, Jacqueline scanned the other pavilions. Each one had a standard with the knight's coat of arms standing before it, showing who presided within. She did not recognize any who were close by, which was understandable. She had only been to a couple of tournaments in the past.

Beth quietly came to stand beside her. "I am here for you. If a knight William was acquainted with confronts you, I will make sure to be by your side. At present, it should be no real concern. William did not know any who are camped near us."

"If you had not agreed to come, I am sure I would have made a complete fool of myself."

Jacqueline jumped as Beth looped her arm through hers. Beth gave her a pat. "Remember, you are William, and I am your wife. You cannot jump at a mere touch from me."

Jacqueline smiled. "You caught me off guard. I have not yet thought that far ahead."

"Well, start acting the part of William—now. You are about to go through your first test."

Beth was correct. A squire from the pavilion across from where they stood headed in their direction. He smiled and seemed not able to take his gaze from Beth.

"Good day to you." The squire bowed. "Can I have your name, sir? My master might wish to engage you in the list."

Jacqueline cleared her throat and tried to make her voice as deep as possible. "I am Sir William Montacute.

May I inquire who your master is?"

"Sir Terric Aubrey, and I am Edwin." He grabbed Beth's hand and placed a kiss on the back of it. She quickly yanked it away.

Settling into her role, Jacqueline warned the squire away. "I would appreciate it if you would keep your hands off my lady wife."

To give him credit, Edwin blushed while he backed away, only to be brought up short as he stepped into the knight standing behind him. The knight grabbed the boy's shoulders to steady him and gently moved Edwin aside.

"I see my squire has introduced himself. I hope Edwin was not bothering you too much." Sir Terric sent his squire a meaningful look.

Jacqueline's jaw dropped. She could not tear her gaze from Sir Terric. The man was too handsome for his own good. She found his blond hair and unusual colored eyes, a beautiful shade of violet, appealing. It was his height that drew her the most. Being taller than most men, finding one she actually had to look up at was a novelty. Even though she was supposed to be acting a part, she could not help but rake Sir Terric with her gaze. The man was all muscle. She had to stop herself before she reached out to see if his body was as hard as it looked.

Realizing Terric watched her, waiting for some kind of response, Jacqueline mentally gave herself a shake. "No harm done, Sir Terric."

He flashed a smile, which caused her to take complete leave of her senses, and said, "Good. I could not help but overhear your name. I am glad to see you have recovered from your wound. I was at Windsor when your father unseated you."

CHAPTER FOUR

She froze, her mind drawing an absolute blank. Jacqueline had not expected to face that particular question so early on in her deception. Luckily, Beth sensed her dilemma and took control of the conversation by drawing Terric's attention to herself.

"My husband's recovery was faster than we had anticipated. This is his first tournament since receiving his wound in Windsor."

"I must say Sir William has made a speedy recovery. I had thought a wound to the neck would have laid him up much longer. I am happy to see he is well enough to grace the list once again. If you will excuse me, I will leave you to finish your camp preparations." With a nod, Terric motioned for Edwin to follow him, then left them alone.

Jacqueline let the breath she held out in a rush. "He is going to be a problem."

"He can easily be avoided. Just carry on as you have planned. If you let Sir Terric get to you, you will fail. Ignore the man."

"If only it were that simple."

Beth looked at her. "Jacqueline, you are attracted to

him, are you not?"

Feeling her face turn red, Jacqueline tore her gaze from Sir Terric and looked at Beth. If only her friend knew what ran through her head concerning that particular knight.

With a shrug, she replied, "It is of no import if I am. It is not as if I can do anything about it, now can I?"

"Just remember that. We do not need you losing your head over that one. I remember Sir Terric from Windsor, though I did not know his name at the time. He flirts with anything in a gown."

Jacqueline chuckled, then acting the part of a husband, offered Beth her arm. "Have no fear, dear wife. There are bigger stakes here. Much more important than any passing fancy I might have. Let us see how the men-at-arms are doing setting up the camp."

* * * *

Thankfully, a pavilion was quite an easy thing to erect. The men already had the center and inner support posts grounded and the wooden, spoked wheel set upon it. They were fitting the canvas over the whole thing, spreading it to the ground and pegging it down when Jacqueline and Beth returned.

Sir Guy awaited them inside the pavilion. After they entered, he rapidly fired questions at them. "Who was the knight? Did he ask to challenge you? Did he accept you as a man?"

Jacqueline held up her hand and shook her head, halting his barrage of questions. She could not help but find humor in his query. "If you would let me answer one question before asking the next, I will tell you all that passed between us."

Sir Guy crossed his arms, and said, "I was just curious, lass. It is no test run here. If you do not pull this off at this tournament, there will be no other one for you."

"Will you stop your worrying? As you can see, no alarm was raised. To answer your questions, the knight is Sir Terric Aubrey. He did not mention anything about a challenge, and he believes I am William."

"Jacqueline has neglected to tell you one other small thing about her meeting with Sir Terric," Beth said oh, so casually. Having gained Sir Guy's attention, she grinned. "She forgot to tell you she is smitten with him."

Sir Guy rolled his eyes. "Besides that utterly useless piece of information, do you have anything else to say about him?"

Beth grew serious. "Aye, there is. Sir Terric remembers William was wounded at Windsor. He was there and saw it all."

"Then we will all have to be cautious around him. It might be best to keep our distance from him entirely."

Knowing she would be questioned if she did not agree, Jacqueline nodded. If opportunity did arise to get to know Sir Terric better, she would not openly shun him. The mere sight of him caused her body to ache and wetness to form at her very core. She had finally met a man who she wanted in the most intimate of ways, and as fate would have it, she had to make him believe she was just as male as he.

* * * *

The next day the tournament began. Jacqueline had not gone to the castle the previous evening. It had seemed prudent after the questions Sir Terric had posed to her.

The list was set up just outside the castle walls. Bleachers had been erected on the sidelines for the ladies and men of rank who were not participating. There, they could watch the competitors make runs at each other. Beth was seated amongst them.

Jacqueline had to admit her nerves were getting the

better of her. She stood in the middle of her pavilion as Sir Guy helped her don her armor. The crowd outside roared. She resisted the urge to wipe her sweating palms on her thighs, which were already encased in steel.

After he finished fastening her breastplate and backplate, Sir Guy attached the plate armor worn on her arms. Jacqueline accepted the metal gauntlets from the older man. She tried her best to hide her nervousness as he placed her helm upon her head, which she, of course, failed miserably. He put his hand under chin, forcing her to look at him. It was hard to see him clearly through the eye slits.

"You will be fine, Jacqueline. Just remember what I taught you. Ignore the crowd and focus on your opponent."

"I will remember. I just have to get through my first run. It is the unknown that is making me feel this way. I have never jousted against a real knight. I know naught of what will happen."

"It is not all that much different from the quintain. Only with this, the object you are aiming for is moving as well."

"I beg to differ," Jacqueline said gruffly.

Laughing, Sir Guy passed her shield to her. "You are correct. I am only trying to make you feel better." Growing serious again, he strapped her sword around her waist. "You will get through this, my girl."

She adjusting her shield, which had been her brother's and was painted with the Montacute coat of arms. The background completely white, it had three large red diamonds in the center. There were three black circles, above the first and third diamond and a third just below the second diamond. The sword strapped around her hips was her own, having been especially made for her a few years before.

Jacqueline took a deep breath for courage, then stepped out of her pavilion. Her steed, also armored, stood patiently nearby. The man-at-arms who held the animal's reins walked it to where she stood. Sir Guy helped her mount, then after passing the reins up to her, he took hold of the horse's bridle and led it to the lists.

Her first competitor was Sir Hugh Blakely. All Jacqueline could see was an armored knight who sat upon his horse opposite her with a lance in his hand. Allowing her mind to go blank, she accepted hers from Sir Guy. Everything—the roar of the crowd, the jingle of her horse's harness—fell away.

Once the flag was lowered, signaling the start of the charge, Jacqueline shoved her spurs into her steed's flanks and barreled toward her opponent. They met, and her lance shattered as it came into contact with Sir Hugh's shield. She hit it squarely in the center. His lance grazed her shield, but remained intact. The first point was awarded to her. She turned her horse about and then returned to her end of the field. After accepting another lance, she prepared for her second charge.

This time both lances shattered, but her hit was hard enough to fling Sir Hugh backward over his horse's rump. He landed with a loud *clang* as his armor-clad body hit the ground. The crowd called her name, William's name, and Jacqueline slowly became aware of her surroundings. She turned her horse about and rode to her fallen opponent. His squire had come to his aid and helped Sir Hugh to regain his feet. He appeared not to be injured.

Seeing Jacqueline, Sir Hugh spoke as she went past. "I will have the usual ransom money sent to your pavilion at the end of the tournament."

She turned in her saddle, and replied, "That is acceptable."

Once she reached Sir Guy, he led her horse back to her pavilion, then followed her in after she dismounted. "How do you feel?"

After putting her shield down and pulling her helm and

gauntlets off, Jacqueline wiped the sweat from her face. The armor was hot as well as heavy. She would be happy to have it removed. "My left shoulder feels a bit numb after that last charge. Other than that, I am fine."

"Get used to it. There is more to come. I must say you have acquitted yourself quite admirably, my girl. You would have made William proud."

She beamed from the older man's words and smiled. "Thank you, kind sir. One down and only four more to go."

"Did Sir Hugh make arrangements for paying the ransom? If he has not, his armor, sword, and horse are yours."

After taking a swallow of water from a skin, she nodded. "Aye, he did. I do not want his armor or horse. I am not here to make money."

"I know, but it would look strange if you did not accept the ransom. You did win the match, and it is customary to take such."

"I know that. How long until I face my next opponent?"

Sir Guy unbuckled her armor, and answered, "You have a half hour. Rest. By the time you face your last opponent, you will feel bruised from head to toe."

* * * *

Sir Guy had not stretched the truth when he had said she would feel bruised. Her whole body ached. Her left shoulder was already a beautiful array of colors. Just getting herself dressed for the feast that evening was proving to be a challenge.

Beth seemed to take pity on her and finally helped her pull her tunic over her head. "What do you think, Beth? Do I look enough like William?"

Beth took a step back and checked her handiwork. She blinked back tears. She still felt the loss of William greatly.

"Aye, you will do. Too much really." She pulled herself together. "You will do as long as no one looks too hard at you. With your short hair and bound chest, you can pass for a young William. There is no disguising the feminine curve of your hips. At least the cloak will shield them from behind."

Jacqueline moved closer and put her arm around Beth's shoulders. "If this is going to be too much for you to bear, we can bow out of the feast."

Beth shook her head. "Nay, you have to go. You need the practice. I will be fine."

Not wishing to upset her any further, Jacqueline offered her arm to Beth. "Then let us face the lions together."

The great hall in Portchester Castle was just about filled to capacity by the time they arrived. Sir Guy had arrived earlier. Upon seeing Jacqueline enter the hall with Beth on her arm, he motioned them over to where he sat. He had managed to save them each a seat.

They squeezed onto the bench and accepted a trencher from a passing pageboy. After filling them with food, they settled down to the business of enjoying the meal. Before they could finish eating, a voice from farther down their table interrupted them.

"I am glad to see you could attend the feast, Sir William. This is the best part of a tournament."

Jacqueline leaned slightly forward to look down the table and found Sir Terric staring back at her. She silently groaned. "How could I pass up such good food? After a day in the list, it is much welcomed."

Obviously, taking her reply as an invitation, Sir Terric stood with trencher and goblet in hand. He walked to where Jacqueline sat. Smiling politely at Sir Guy, who sat to one side of her, he squeezed in between them, which in turn caused everyone else on the bench to shift down, filling the empty space Terric had created by leaving his seat.

He placed what he held on the table in front of him, then motioned for a pageboy to refill his goblet with wine. "Hope you do not mind my intrusion, but I would rather be in your company."

Not sure how to respond, Jacqueline nodded and did her best to keep her gaze on her food. Sitting so close to Terric, having her thigh and hip plastered to his, did funny things to her insides. Her heart beat erratically while her stomach was so jumpy her food sat like an uncomfortable lump. The scent of sandalwood and man was something she found she could not ignore. For the first time in her life, she felt a longing a woman had for the opposite sex, the kind that would only be satisfied in the arms of that person. Much to her shame, she found it hard not to stare at his handsome face.

Oblivious to how she reacted to his presence, Terric continued to make idle conversation. "You did well in the list today, Sir William. Though only able to unseat two of your opponents, you made a fair profit."

Jacqueline took a sip of wine, trying to still her rapidly beating heart. "I am not here to make a profit. I compete because I enjoy the sport."

"Well, some of us do not have such luxury. This is my livelihood."

Meeting Sir Terric's gaze, Jacqueline noticed a touch of regret in the violet depths of his eyes. She could imagine that depending on success in a tournament to determine one's lifestyle would not be an easy life. "I did not know you had to be here."

Terric laughed. "Don't feel sorry for me. It is not that bad of a life. There is always lots of good food to eat, well, most of the time. The ladies can be very accommodating when they wish to grant you their favors."

As if to prove the truth of his words a lady, who Jacqueline very much doubted was such a thing, came and draped herself over Terric's shoulder. Much to Jacqueline's disgust, he did nothing to remove the woman.

Terric warmly smiled at the woman. "My Lady Rose, I see you managed to escape your husband yet again."

The woman laughed gaily at his words. "Not at all hard to do, especially when he is so far gone in drink. You know I would take you over him any day."

"Your words bring joy to my heart, my lady."

Jacqueline turned to Beth, who sat on her other side, and rolled her eyes at Sir Terric's words. Beth quietly chuckled. Since the couple seemed to be more involved in each other than those around them, she continued to make Beth laugh. She batted her eyelashes much in the same manner as Lady Rose had done to Terric. Getting into her role-playing, Jacqueline added some of her own faces, making Beth laugh all the more. She placed the back of her hand to her forehead and sighed deeply, pretending to feel faint.

"I hope I have entertained you enough this evening."

Feeling her face turn a bright shade of red, Jacqueline turned to look at Terric. Lady Rose was nowhere to be seen. From the look upon his face, he had been watching her antics for some time.

"I do apologize, Sir Terric. It was not my intent to make jest of you."

Terric seemed to be trying to keep a straight face, but in the end, the smile that tugged at his lips turned into a full-fledged laugh. At the sound of his laughter, Jacqueline and Beth added their own to his.

Terric brought himself back under control and clapped Jacqueline on the shoulder. She stiffened. It felt like being touched by fire. All the laughter left her as she stared into his eyes. Her mouth went suddenly dry, and her breath caught in her throat. She had thought only silly-headed girls acted so foolishly around a man they found appealing, but she could not tear her gaze from his face. She peered at his firm lips and unconsciously licked her own.

He shifted uncomfortably on the bench, the first to break the spell. He quickly snatched back his hand and cleared his throat. "Apology accepted, Sir William."

Terric lifted his goblet to his lips and drained it in one large gulp. He appeared slightly unnerved by what had just passed between them. Jacqueline had the feeling she had been staring at him like a lovesick girl. She could see it would disturb him. She was disgusted with herself as she attempted to get him to overlook what had just taken place and started a new conversation. Something on a less stressful subject.

"So, Sir Terric, where is the next tournament you go to from here?"

Terric jumped on the change as he quickly answered Jacqueline's question. "The next tournament is to be held in Lymington. Are you going to be attending as well?"

Jacqueline shook her head. "Nay, I had not planned to."

"Why not? You claim to love the sport. Why not attend? Lymington is not too far from here. It is to be held in a week. Plenty of time to travel at a leisurely pace."

"I had not thought that far ahead."

"You should attend. If anything, it will be a good place to practice for the tournament the king has planned in May. It is going to be a grand tournament with many knights competing. Not just English knights, either. They are to come from all over."

Terric had Jacqueline's full attention now. The king's grand tournament could be what she had been waiting for. "I had not heard of this tournament."

He gave her a surprised look as if to say that information was known by most of the knights on the circuit. "King Richard heard news that Queen Isabella is to make a public entry into Paris. You know how our monarchy does not like to be outdone by the French. So the grand tournament is to be held in London and will take place on the Sunday after Michaelmas day. On the following Monday, the knights will compete as well. I am sure it will last longer than two days. Anyone who is anyone will be there."

Jacqueline stiffened in anticipation. "My father, the earl, should be in attendance?"

"I would be very much surprised if he was not." Terric gave her an odd look.

"Perfect. It will work out perfectly," Jacqueline said distractedly. Plans already swirled inside her mind.

"I guess you could say that."

Beth gave Jacqueline a warning jab in the ribs, and Jacqueline chose to ignore Beth's reaction to the news of the tournament. It might be a bigger one than she had originally planned to face the earl, but it was an ideal situation. She could not have planned it better.

Terric was still looking at her strangely. "So, do you plan to go to Lymington now, my friend?"

Jacqueline shifted her foot under the table so Beth could no longer stomp on it in agitation and smiled. "I think I have changed my mind. We shall meet again at Lymington."

* * * *

The following day they made the short trip to the isle. As the ferry took her party across the water, Jacqueline used the time to think of what to say to her mother. She would be greatly distressed with her decision to participate in another tournament. That was a given, because she had not been at all pleased with this one.

Sir Guy and Beth were not at all happy with her decision either. They felt she would be taking too much of a risk. Each tournament Jacqueline participated in offered a greater chance a knight acquainted with her father could tell him what she was up to. Not that they would recognize her as a woman, but the number of tournaments "William" attended would still be suspicious. William never went to more than one or two at the most in any given year.

Once they reached the landing, Jacqueline still had not planned exactly what she would say to her mother. The only merit she could push on her mother would be the money she had made in the list. Jacqueline had to keep reminding herself that she was only using it as an opportunity to perfect her performance. There was no other reason, really.

Jacqueline was only fooling herself. It was one reason, a very good one at that, but not the main one. It was the chance to see Terric again that drew her to make that choice.

She mounted her horse, then steered it onto the road leading to Carisbrooke. She hoped this homecoming would find her mother in good humor. If not, Jacqueline could find herself with an argument on her hands.

CHAPTER FIVE

Lymington did not have a castle, but it did have a fairground. It was not a large port, though it was well known for its salt making. It imported French wine and exported cloth, which was woven in Salisbury too.

Jacqueline led her small party down High Street to the fairground. The tournament was to be one of the events of the fair. Lymington had two fairs a year. The lord of the manor would be presiding over the tournament and fair.

Upon reaching the fairground, Jacqueline casually searched the multicolored pavilions already erected. She spotted a standard that sported Sir Terric's coat of arms — a white falcon in flight on a dark blue background — and motioned to her men-at-arms to set up her pavilion right beside his.

Her party was one person smaller than she had had at her first tournament. Sir Guy was absent. Lady Elizabeth had been greatly distressed with Jacqueline's decision to attend another tournament. In a fit of pique at the last moment, she forbad Sir Guy to leave the isle. She had not been able to stop Beth from going, for which Jacqueline was grateful.

Once she was all settled, Terric called on them. Even though only a week had passed since they had parted company, Jacqueline had not been able to stop thinking about the man who stood before her. He even haunted her dreams. Ones that left her restless once awake and aching for his touch in the most intimate of places on her body. She was being a fool, but she could not ignore the attraction she felt for him. Beth, giving Jacqueline a sly grin, nodded to Sir Terric and then left the two of them alone.

"I hope I did not make your wife feel as though she had to leave. I know you have just arrived. I wanted to renew our acquaintance."

"Nay, you did nothing to bother my lady wife. She more than likely has gone to see what items are for sale at the fair."

"Ah, a pastime many woman enjoys." Terric chuckled at his quip, but when he did not get the same response from her, he slowly let it die. He took the conversation in a different tract. "I see you lost Sir Guy. Who will act the part of your squire while you are here?"

"He could not join me this time. He has his duties to attend to at Carisbrooke. I will have one of my men-at-arms attend me."

Terric shook his head. "That will not do."

Jacqueline was a little taken aback by his denial. Was there some rule she had not heard about? One that said who was allowed to act as squire? "Why will it not do?"

Terric laughed. "Have no fear, William. You do no wrong by having a lowly man-at-arms attend you, but I will personally not hear of it. Edwin will be happy to squire for you, along with myself. We are not going to be tilting against each other, so he should be able to keep up."

She opened her mouth to refuse his offer, then shut it again. He would think it strange for her to say nay. He was doing her a great favor by offering her the use of his squire. There were some drawbacks, though. For her. There would be no problem with Edwin helping her at the tilting ground, but assisting her to don her armor was a completely different story.

Terric waited for her answer. Feeling decidedly unsure about the whole thing, Jacqueline did what she had to do. She accepted his offer. "I would be happy to have your squire assist me."

"I will inform Edwin of his additional duties. I ride first, so he can come to you after."

With that decision made, they fell silent. Jacqueline noticed how close Terric had come to stand in front of her. As at Portchester Castle, her body responded to his nearness. There was no denying it. She was very attracted to this man. She could not seem to tear her gaze off his mouth. All she had to do was lean slightly forward, take his face in both her hands, and pull his lips down to meet hers. Her body stirred with desire just thinking about it.

She did not realize she acted out what she thought until Terric took a step back before she could reach for him. He stared at her more than a bit strangely. Flustered by what she had just about done, Jacqueline stepped back even farther than he had.

Terric acted as if he did not know how to respond to her strange behavior and loudly cleared his throat. "Ah…well, I will leave you now. I will make sure Edwin assists you."

"I thank you, Sir Terric."

* * * *

Needing time to mull over what had taken place, Terric returned to his pavilion. Edwin was already there, busily polishing his armor. He looked up from his work at his arrival. "Did you speak to Sir William?"

Absentmindedly, Terric said, "Aye, I did."

He did not go into any further details of the meeting.

Edwin put down the armor and confronted Terric. "You have the most peculiar look upon your face. Just what took place at Sir William's pavilion?"

"That is what I am trying to figure out myself. I have offered your services to him for this day, by the way. When you attend him, I want you to watch very carefully what goes on there."

Edwin laughed, but stopped after Terric glanced toward him. "You are serious? You want me to spy on Sir William?"

"Aye, I do. There is something not quite right with Sir William. It is a gut feeling I have, and usually they prove to be correct."

"All right," Edwin said haltingly. "I will see what I can come up with."

"Good."

Terric plunked himself down into a camp chair as Edwin once more went back to the business of polishing his armor. What happened in William's pavilion would not leave his mind. He had not missed the flush of desire on William's face. Nor the way the younger man had stared at his mouth. At first, he had found it unnerving, but to his disgust, he had felt himself drawn to William. The more he had stared at him, the more he had responded. It had been very much like when he found a woman attractive. The manliest part of himself had stirred to life before he had gotten a hold on himself and tapped it down. That did not sit well with him at all.

There was nothing for it, though, except to hope Edwin found the clues he needed. An answer to why he felt this attraction to another man, to William in particular, formed in his mind. All he needed was the proof.

* * * *

Surprisingly, Jacqueline found Edwin's help not so

trying as she had first expected. Donning her armor with his assistance went smoothly, mostly because he spent a great deal of time looking at every item in her pavilion. If she did not know the squire, she would have thought he searched for what he could easily steal.

Now, facing her opponent, she prepared herself for her first run. She sent up a silent prayer, then set off. She was able to make the first hit. After accepting a new lance from Edwin, she started on her second run.

Jacqueline knew as soon as her opponent hit her shield she was not going to leave the field completely unscathed. The hit she received had enough power behind it to throw her back onto the rump of her steed. She was able to keep her seat, but unable to get out of her prone position. Mostly the weight of her armor held her back, but it was the pain that left her weak. She had taken the full force of the strike on her left shoulder.

Unable to see, nor control her horse, she was thankful Edwin was there to grab her steed's reins and halt its movements. She groaned in agony and allowed the squire to help her slide off her mount.

Edwin, being of the same height as herself, took her good arm and put it around his shoulders. "Let me get you to your pavilion, Sir William. Then I will see to your shoulder."

Jacqueline furiously blinked back the tears of pain that threatened to fall. She could not give way to them. No knight would put on such a womanly display. Luckily, she still wore her helm, hiding her features from all those she passed.

Upon reaching her pavilion, Edwin helped her onto a stool and carefully disarmed her. Once free of her breast and back plate, he removed her armoring doublet that she wore beneath. With her upper body free of all armor, the squire examined her shoulder.

"Looks as if it is dislocated, Sir William. I will have to

pop it back into place for you. Then most of the pain will leave you. I will have to ask you to remove your tunic."

As Edwin reached out to lift the hem of her tunic, Jacqueline shot to her feet. "Can you not fix my shoulder with my tunic still on?"

Edwin blinked at her behavior and shook his head. "It must come off. It will be easier to move the shoulder back into place with it removed."

As the squire advanced on her again, Jacqueline retreated, only to back into something that felt very much like a solid wall.

"What goes on here?" Terric asked. "I can hear the commotion all the way in my pavilion."

Edwin let out an audible sigh of relief upon seeing his master. "Sir William refuses to remove his tunic. His shoulder is dislocated, and I need to fix it."

Before Jacqueline realized his intent, Terric knocked her feet out from under her and lowered her to the ground. Holding and then lifting her left arm, he put his foot into her underarm, which rendered her virtually helpless. She was already in enough pain. The hold he had on her made it worse.

"All right, Edwin, I want you to put your hands on William's chest and hold him down. This might take a couple of tries to get the shoulder into place."

Beginning to feel frantic, Jacqueline tried to avoid Edwin's hands, but her movements caused a sharp shooting pain to race up her left arm all the way to her shoulder. She finally ceased moving, and he placed his hands where he had been instructed.

Terric did not move. He looked at Edwin expectantly, who had frozen in place with a shocked look upon his face. "Well? Can we get on with this or not?"

Jacqueline closed her eyes and waited for all hell to break loose. Though her chest was bound, she did not bind it as tightly when she wore armor. It was too constricting.

Not being able to take proper deep breaths made her feel faint while wearing full gear. Besides, it really was not necessary with the plating.

The sound of Edwin's gasp filled the pavilion. "I cannot do this."

"Why ever not?" Terric asked gruffly.

"Sir William is no man. The proof is there." Edwin's hands abruptly left her chest.

Terric released Jacqueline's arm, squatted beside her, and placed one of his hands in the same place Edwin's had been. He chuckled. "I think you have some explaining to do."

Jacqueline opened her eyes and found Terric's face a few scant inches from her own. "I...I know. Fix my shoulder, then I will tell you all."

"Anything to please a lady."

Terric signaled Edwin to once more hold her down, then again took his place at her shoulder. With a firm twist and a hard pull to her left arm, the shoulder audibly popped into proper position. Jacqueline yelped at the pain of it, but as Edwin had predicted, with it now back in place, the hurt slowly receded.

Terric helped her to her feet and made Jacqueline sit on the stool. No sooner had she sat than Beth rushed into the pavilion. Upon seeing both Terric and Edwin, she searched Jacqueline's face for any sign of trouble.

"Is everything all right, William?"

Before Jacqueline could respond, Terric took Beth by the arm, secured the pavilion opening, and led her to stand beside Jacqueline. "There is no need to continue your ruse with us, Lady Beth. We know *William* is of the fairer sex."

At Jacqueline's nod, Beth confronted the knight. "What do you plan to do with this knowledge, Sir Terric?"

He smiled politely. "It entirely depends on what I am told."

"If we feel we need not make any explanations? What

then?"

"Then I have no qualms about revealing who Sir William really is. Now, I want to hear what your *husband* has to say about the matter."

Jacqueline stood. She would not defend her actions to Terric while having to crane her neck to look at him. She made sure their gazes met. "Even though I feel I do not owe you any explanation, I will give you one. William was my brother, my twin, to be exact."

"Therefore, the great resemblance between your brother and yourself."

"Aye. William died from the wound he received at Windsor. Though Beth did all she could to bring him home to us alive, he succumbed while on the road. Now I take his place."

"Why? Does your family need the money won at tournaments?"

She shook her head. "Nay, not at all. You were present at Windsor. You know who delivered the killing blow. I want revenge. The earl took away the one person who made me whole. He did not have to accept William's challenge. He could have refused, but he did not stay his hand. Now I intend to strike back at him. I want to ride against my father. I despise the man."

Terric searched her face before he asked, "What is your real name?"

Blinking at how fast Terric had changed the subject, she answered, "I am Jacqueline. What does knowing my name have to do with your decision?"

"Nothing. I just wanted to know what to call you. Other than a mad woman."

After all she had already gone through this day, Jacqueline did not let Terric's insult go by lightly. She raised her right hand to deliver a slap to his face only to have him grab it before she made contact. Growling in fury, she jerked her hand free.

"Jacqueline, that will do nothing to sway me to your side, but I do beg your forgiveness for the slight I gave you. It was unfair of me, but you are no match for your father. You have obviously never seen the earl in the list. Very few can defeat him."

"I do not care. I will face him."

Beth interrupted them. "Sir Terric, can I speak with you privately in your pavilion?"

Terric agreed. He and Beth left her and Edwin to go to Terric's pavilion next door.

* * * *

It was not hard to tell that Sir Terric had some concerns about Jacqueline, so Beth strived to make him understand why it was so important to her sister-in-law that she do this.

"You have to understand how William's death affected Jacqueline. It is as if a part of her died with him. The only thing that has kept her going has been her burning need for revenge. Until she faces the earl, she will not let herself accept the loss of her brother. She has not shed one tear in all this time. She will not grieve."

Terric ran his fingers through his hair. "Before I make my decision on what to do, I need you to truthfully answer one question."

"I will try."

"Jacqueline has so much hatred for her father. I have seen it in her eyes. I know what happened to William was just the catalyst that pushed her to this point. What has the earl done to her in the past?"

Beth laughed, but it held no humor. "You are correct in your thinking. William was the last of many wrongdoings by the earl. The only difficulty is knowing where to start. The list is many and varies greatly. The earl basically abandoned his pregnant wife on the isle and never had any interest in his children once they were born, or his wife, for that matter. He already had his heir so there was no need. What really made Jacqueline despise him was the marriage he arranged for her. Without her consent or her mother's."

"I take it the bridegroom was not to her liking?"

"Hardly. I think you have heard of the man the earl chose for her. The Earl of Somerset."

Letting loose a low whistle, Terric shook his head. "I would not even contract a marriage with that devil, Forwin, to my bitch hound. The bitch being too good for him. Obviously, Jacqueline somehow stopped the marriage."

"Not so much Jacqueline as her mother. Lady Elizabeth was dead set against the marriage so she took matters into her own hands. To make a long story short, she faked Jacqueline's death. Therefore, the marriage contract became void."

"Lady Elizabeth sounds like a very intelligent woman, one well able to look after her children on her own."

"That she is. She is not at all happy with what Jacqueline is doing, but she has kept her promise to keep William's death a secret from the earl." Taking both his hands in her own, she looked at him beseechingly. "I have told you enough, Sir Terric, of what goes on. I implore you not to reveal Jacqueline as an impostor. She has worked so hard to reach this point. If she cannot proceed, I am very much afraid it will break the fragile thread she desperately holds on to."

Terric remained silent for a few seconds before he answered. "You and Jacqueline win. I will say nothing." As Beth started to thank him, he stopped her. "I am not finished yet. I have some conditions. Firstly, Jacqueline competes in no more tournaments until the time she faces her father. Secondly, she goes home to the isle, where I will accompany her."

"Why do you want to come home with us?"

"If she plans on facing the earl and survive the experience, she needs me. I am one of few who have won a ransom from him. I will train her. She is nowhere near ready to go against her father. Do not ask me why, but I do not relish the idea of Jacqueline doing this without me."

CHAPTER SIX

Jacqueline had not bargained on having Terric and his squire going with them to the isle. She was thankful he had held his tongue about her, but she was not all that certain she liked his being in such close proximity.

After dismounting in the bailey, Jacqueline braced herself for her mother's reaction to unexpected guests. As predicted, her lady mother noticed the strangers in their midst and headed directly to confront her.

"What goes on here, Jacqueline? Who are these men?" Her mother whispered her questions. Jacqueline was pleased she remembered to keep her real identity a secret.

"Sir Terric is my friend. The other man is his squire, Edwin. There is no need to whisper, either. Both know who I really am."

"You told them who you are?" Her mother gasped.

"Nay, Mother. When I was injured at the tournament, they helped me and found out for themselves."

"You were injured?" Lady Elizabeth's words were spoken so loudly everyone looked in their direction.

"Calm down. I am fine. I just had a dislocated shoulder. Terric fixed it for me. You know it happens more than not in the list. William sustained the same injury at one time."

"That might be so, but you are not your brother. I cannot fathom why you persist in this foolishness."

Unable to deal with her mother any longer, Jacqueline stalked away.

Terric raised his brow in question when she approached. "Is everything all right?"

Jacqueline nodded, trying to rein in her temper. "Aye. Do not worry yourself. My mother was just expressing her disapproval is all."

Hearing her mother's steps behind her, she made the introductions. "Mother, this is Sir Terric Aubrey. Terric, this is Lady Elizabeth Montacute, my mother."

Playing the gallant, Terric took Lady Elizabeth's hand and kissed the back of it.

"I bid you welcome, Sir Terric."

"Thank you for your warm welcome, my lady."

"May I ask how long you plan to stay on the isle?"

"As long as it takes to train Jacqueline. Since she is determined to challenge her father, I plan to make sure she learns enough to survive the encounter." Terric's gaze met Lady Elizabeth's worried one. He leaned in closer, and whispered, "Have no fear, my lady. I will not let anything happen to Jacqueline. I promise you that."

Lady Elizabeth continued to hold Terric's gaze, and replied dryly, "Do not think I will release you from that promise, Sir Terric." Terric inclined his head in acknowledgment. "Now, if you will excuse me, I will see about having a chamber prepared for you and your squire. Jacqueline will show you around."

Even though she was right there, it was obvious she would not be allowed any say in the matter. Since her mother had conceded so easily, she thought it best to let it go.

After Lady Elizabeth departed, Jacqueline motioned for Terric to follow her. Her mother kept the main hall well looked after and inviting. The rushes upon the stone floor were fresh, and the trestle table was polished to a high gloss. Once a servant brought Jacqueline and Terric some ale to quench their thirst, Jacqueline looked toward the stairs that led to the floor above.

"I hope our coming here has not caused too much upset for your mother," Terric said.

Jacqueline dismissed his concerns with a wave of her hand. "Nay. My mother is more upset with me. It will upset her more when I tell her where I intend to confront the earl."

"You have not told her about the grand tournament yet?"

"Nay, I have not. I have been delaying that particular battle."

Terric smiled. "Your mother does not seem to be a woman who misses anything that concerns her family."

"You are quite right. Mother does not like being ignorant about any goings on."

Lady Elizabeth appeared at the top of the stairs. Once she reached the bottom, she joined Jacqueline and Terric at the table. "Your chamber is ready now, Sir Terric. If you wish to see yourself settled, you may do so at any time."

Terric looked between Jacqueline and her mother, then said, "I think I will do so right now. I will collect Edwin from the bailey."

After Terric disappeared through the hall doorway, Lady Elizabeth spoke. "I heard what you and Sir Terric were talking about. He is a very astute man. He was correct. I already know about the grand tournament, Jacqueline."

"How did you find out?" she asked softly.

Lady Elizabeth reached out and gently brushed a lock of hair from Jacqueline's brow. "It was not so much me finding out as being told. You see, I have a secret I have been keeping from you as well. One I now feel I am ready to tell."

"What is it?" It had to be something serious to cause her mother to keep it to herself. Her lady mother was not the type of parent who kept her children ignorant for their own good.

"I received a missive a fortnight ago from your father. In his letter, he requests William and I attend the grand tournament to be held in London. It was worded as a command, really. So you see, if we do not go, your father will more than likely come to the isle and personally make sure we do not disobey him."

Jacqueline felt the blood drain from her face in shock. When her father sent missives, it usually portended a change to their everyday lives, and they were never good. "Did he give a reason he had demanded our presence in London?"

"Nay, but I like it not. He is up to something, no question about it. We will go, you along with Beth and myself. There will be no thwarting him. We will have to be very careful, Jacqueline. If your father uncovers our ruse, he will not be pleased, to say the least."

Jacqueline picked up her mother's hand and gave it a reassuring squeeze. "I will not let that happen. Having you and Beth with me will make it more believable. With Sir Terric now training me, I will be better prepared to face the earl in the list. What could possibly go wrong?"

* * * *

The following morning Terric began Jacqueline's training. He had to admit she was very skilled at the quintain, but it was only a poor substitute for facing another man on horseback. Deciding it was best to start the training minus it, he motioned for her to come to him. She had just completed a successful pass.

"I think your skill cannot be any furthered with the

quintain, Jacqueline. For now, I will be your target. To begin with I will not ride at you. I want you to hit me with your lance only. That way I will be better able to see just where you hit with each pass."

"I do not think that is a good idea, Terric. You are going to be getting hit full force. I do not want to hurt you."

Terric flashed her one of the bone-melting smiles he knew won over the ladies. "I had no idea you cared so much for my welfare, my lady." Accompanied by the clanking of his armor, he bowed in her direction.

"I am not playing games, Terric. I would feel dreadful if I injured you."

Even though Terric could not see Jacqueline's face with her helm shielding it from view, he could tell from the tone of her voice she would not let this pass easily. Becoming serious, he tried to lay her mind to rest. "There is no need to worry. My armor will protect me. I know how much it can handle."

"Fine, I will do as you say. You are more knowledgeable about this sport than I. So I will acquiesce to your greater experience," she said sassily.

"Enough of that. Go to the other end of the field, and I will signal you when I am ready."

Once in place, Edwin, who had been recruited to assist Terric and Jacqueline at these training sessions, handed her a lance. After she took possession of it, he quickly ran across the field to Terric.

As Edwin helped Terric mount his horse, he quietly whispered, "Do you think it wise what you do here? I am not like yonder lady over there. I am not quite so beguiled by your charms that I lose my senses."

Busily adjusting his shield on his left arm, Terric absently replied, "I did not ask your opinion on the matter, Edwin. Jacqueline's aim is very erratic. This is the best way for me to see what she does when she runs the list."

Edwin shook his head. "Suit yourself. Just do not come

to me to have your shoulder fixed. I hope the lady knocks you on your ass."

"Such kind words, squire."

Still shaking his head, Edwin stepped out of harm's way. "Be a fool then."

Seeing she was ready, Terric motioned for Jacqueline to come at him. She kicked her heels into her steed's sides and brought her lance up into position. He had a split second of misgiving about this mode of training. It was an eerie feeling sitting still while a fully-armored rider raced toward him, lance at the ready. When it hit his shield at full speed, he seriously thought he had lost his mind to have ever come up with that suggestion. The impact was twice as hard, harder than when he was in motion and able to ride past the other rider. He kept his voice even as he told Jacqueline to take another run.

After she had completed three more such runs, Terric had reached his limit. Having found out what she was consistently doing wrong, he signaled the end of it. His shoulder could stand no more.

With her last run completed, Jacqueline returned to Terric's side. "No more, Terric. I refuse to do it again."

"There is no need. I found what I was looking for. On the morrow we will focus on correcting it."

Jacqueline removed her helm. Using his right arm, Terric did the same. He did his best not to let any appearance of pain to show on his face. He must have pulled it off, because she seemed to let herself relax. Each time she had hit his shield, it had taken all his strength to remain in the saddle.

"What am I doing wrong then?" Jacqueline asked.

"You are over-compensating your aim. You start off fine, but halfway down the list you think you have to correct it. If you had just held steady, you would have hit the center of my shield each time."

"All right, I will work on not over-correcting. Now let

us go to the hall. I have worked up an appetite with all this." She set her horse into motion and slowly headed toward the stables. Terric did not move to follow her, and she pulled her horse to a halt. She turned in the saddle to look at him. "Are you coming or do you plan on sitting there for the rest of the day?"

"Go on ahead. I will be along shortly."

He made no further response. She shrugged and then continued on to the stables.

* * * *

Sweat profusely poured off him by the time he entered his chamber. It was not caused from wearing heavy armor on a hot spring day, either. It was from the strain of ignoring the painful mass his left shoulder had become.

Not wanting to give Edwin the pleasure of knowing he was right, Terric had dismissed him once Jacqueline had left the field. So now, for the sake of his pride, he suffered.

Luck must have been on his side, because the hall had been virtually empty when he had entered it. Only a few servants had been about, setting the trestle table for the evening meal. They had paid him no notice as he had slowly, painfully, ascended the stairs to his chamber.

Terric shut the door behind him and leaned heavily against it, trying to catch his breath. Though it had been hard getting this far, the most painful part was still to come. He had to divest himself of his armor, without Edwin's assistance.

After what felt like hours, he managed to unbuckle his breast and back plates. A knock sounded on his chamber door just as he was about to reach up and start working on removing his chain mail. He stilled, waiting to see if whoever was there would go away.

The knock came once more, and this time the person on the other side spoke. "Terric, are you in there?"

The one person he did not want to see him like that, of course, had to be the one knocking. Realizing Jacqueline would not leave him to suffer in peace, he answered her. "Aye, I am."

"The evening meal is going to be served in a few minutes. Are you coming down to the hall?"

"I will be along shortly. I have not finished changing."

"Fine, but do not be long."

* * * *

Thinking Terric had sounded a bit strange, Jacqueline went to the hall. Beth and her mother were seated at the trestle table. Sir Guy stood beside Lady Elizabeth, quietly talking with her. They looked up at Jacqueline expectantly.

She shook her head. "He is changing. He should not be much longer."

Her mother frowned. "What is keeping the man? He has been up there for over an hour. The servants saw him when he returned to the hall after your training. We can hold off on serving the food for a short time, but I will not have it ruined by his lateness."

"Have no fear, Mother. Terric will be down in good time."

Jacqueline took a seat beside Beth and gazed toward the stairs. The uneasy feeling of all not being right with Terric just would not leave her.

Beth noticed her agitation. "What is taking him so long? In past conversations, he said a good meal was a favorable way to pass an evening."

Jacqueline thoughtfully tapped her finger on her chin. "That is what I have been thinking. He would not be absent unless something was wrong."

"Did the training not go well today?"

"It did go well. At least Terric thought so, but he has a very unorthodox way of going about it. Let us just say he wanted me to treat him like a quintain."

"Please tell me you did not agree to do it." At Jacqueline's sheepish look, Beth groaned. "Oh, Jacqueline, you could have refused."

"Do not look at me like that. He is the one who has the most experience in this. I just did what he asked."

"Well, I think he got more than he bargained for. Why else would he still be upstairs in his chamber, alone?

It was Jacqueline's turn to look surprised. "Where is Edwin? I thought he was with Terric."

"He is at the barracks, taking his meal with the men-at-arms."

The uneasiness she felt increased tenfold. Her mother tapping her fingertips upon the table in impatience was enough to make up her mind. Jacqueline stood and headed for the stairs.

* * * *

She stood before Terric's chamber door, raised her fist, and pounded loudly upon it. "Terric, open this door!"

The sound of rustling came from the other side, but Terric did not open it. "I will be down momentarily."

"No more. Either you open this door right now, or I will get the key from my mother. Which will it be?"

The unmistakable sound of Terric cursing met her ears. She thought she heard him say, "Plague the woman."

Jacqueline had not counted on having Terric open the door only clothed in his hose. The sight of all that bare male flesh left her speechless. She had never seen a man without his tunic on before. Not even William. Although she had had a relatively isolated upbringing on the isle, her mother had made especially sure Jacqueline was kept ignorant of men. As any respectable unwed daughter should be.

Right now, the large expanse of bared chest was enough

to keep her fascinated. He was solidly built, well-padded with muscle. There was a light sprinkling of hair on it as well. Seeing it was not only on his chest, but also arrowed down and seemed to disappear past the top of his hose caused Jacqueline to gulp. That tiny line made her think wicked thoughts about what could be found beyond that point, about what that particular part of Terric looked like. She might be ignorant when it came to a man's body, but that did not mean she was not curious. Quickly, she raised her gaze back up to his chest and saw his left shoulder.

CHAPTER SEVEN

"**D**id you plan to sit up here all night and suffer?" Terric stepped away from the door and returned to the bed. He sat heavily and looked at Jacqueline. "That was not entirely how I saw my evening developing."

Jacqueline closed the door behind her before she walked to him. There was no missing that colorful array of bruises on his shoulder. Nor the way he held his left arm close to his body. "It is dislocated. Correct?"

Terric casually tried to shrug, which caused him to hiss in pain. He kept his gaze averted. "It is nothing. Once you have had it happen, it can happen again quite easily."

Jacqueline shook her head. "You call me the fool."

Her words caused him to look at her. "Are you going to scold me like a child or help me?"

Taking advantage of having him at her mercy, she decided to toy with Terric a bit. She pretended to think over his question, and said, "I do not know. After all, it was your idea for me to pummel you today on the training field. Maybe you should suffer the consequences for your stupidity."

Before she knew what he intended, Terric grabbed Jacqueline around her waist and threw her onto the bed. He laid his full weight atop her. He must have seen her shocked expression at having her advantage so quickly taken from her, because he smiled. "Now, what were you saying, saucy wench?"

She squirmed a little, managing to free her hands and placed them on his chest. She gave a shove, but he did not budge an inch. Intending to plead for her release, she lifted her gaze to his face. The look of teasing, which had been there a minute before, was gone. What Jacqueline saw made her shiver.

It was not from fright, but something else entirely. He looked as if he wanted to devour her, and she had to admit she found it exciting. The vein in his neck quickly pulsed, a match for his rapidly beating heart, and licked her lips. With a groan, Terric lowered his mouth and claimed her lips.

To Jacqueline, nothing existed but Terric and herself. She found the sensations his kiss caused thrilling and a tad bit scary all at the same time. She had never been kissed like that before. It was like being consumed by fire. Her whole being became focused on the joining of their mouths. He licked her bottom lip. She gasped at the mere brush of his tongue, which allowed him access to her mouth.

His tongue gently sweeping hers made the delicious sensations swirling in her body intensify. She moaned. She craved something only Terric could provide. She ached, for what she had no idea, but she felt it prominently at the apex of her thighs.

She tried to relieve some of the ache by pressing herself against Terric's strong body. That only intensified it as something large and hard come in contact with her mound. Jacqueline rubbed herself against the hard ridge of his sex. Pleasure shot through her, causing wetness to pool between her legs.

Her small movement seemed to bring Terric back to reality. He twisted his head away, breaking contact with her lips. Jacqueline opened her eyes and found him looking at her. Her face felt flushed with desire, and her lips bruised from his kisses. The look he gave her was filled with passion.

"We cannot do this, Jacqueline. I am sorry. I let things get out of hand."

Blinking, she finally became aware of where she was. The feel of him lying flush atop her, settled between her legs, sent ripples of pleasure through her. Now that he no longer kissed her, her common sense took over. She realized her hands were still pressed to his chest and gave Terric a push. This time he released her by rolling onto his side. Jacqueline quickly slid off the bed and turned to face him.

"I know we cannot. Do not take all the blame for this. I could have stopped you if I chose to."

Terric, having moved onto his back, groaned and stared at the ceiling. "Are you trying to torture me? Do not say such things. Or you might very well find yourself back under me on this bed."

She felt her face grow hot, and a shiver of pleasure ran up her back. "Then I had best say no more." Flustered, she walked toward the chamber door. Terric stopped her before she could reach it.

"Jacqueline, wait. You have to help me with my shoulder."

Turning, she nodded and returned to the bed. "Would it not be better for me to just get Edwin?"

"Nay. I am in no mood for him to berate me. I will hear more than enough from him on the morrow as is. You can do it. Just as I did for you."

With a deep breath, Jacqueline removed her boots and climbed up onto the bed. She took hold of Terric's left arm and placed her foot in his underarm. When he had done that to her, it had only taken him a couple of tugs. For her, she found it no easy task to perform. She was hurting him. He groaned with each attempt she made to right the shoulder. After a half dozen tries, they were sweating from the effort.

"Terric, I do not think I am strong enough to do this."

"Do not give up now, Jacqueline. It is just about back into place. One more good yank should be all it needs."

Jacqueline wiped her sweating palms on her tunic, adjusted her grip, then pulled for all she was worth. At that instant, two events happened. The chamber door was thrown open by her mother and Terric's shoulder loudly popped back into place.

Jacqueline and Terric froze as her mother barreled into the chamber. Looking from one to the other, she demanded loudly, "What goes on here, Jacqueline?"

Feeling much as she had as a small child when she had been caught doing something her mother had disapproved of, she dropped Terric's arm and jumped off the bed. Her mother stood stiff as a board, which meant she was furious.

"I was only helping Terric."

"Helping him to do what exactly? I expected better from you, Jacqueline," her mother snapped back.

Knowing what her mother thought had happened between her and Terric, Jacqueline quickly defended herself. "It was nothing inappropriate, Mother. Sir Terric had dislocated his shoulder during our training. So I was only returning the favor he did me. I simply fixed it."

Her mother did not appear to be happy with her explanation. Her eyes seemed to be shoot sparks with anger. "This will not do. Do you think I am a fool? What I heard being said behind this closed door did not sound in any way appropriate."

Jacqueline recalled what she and Terric had been doing

before and could not stop the guilty flush that heated her cheeks.

Terric rose off the bed to stand next to Jacqueline. "Please do not be angry with Jacqueline. It is entirely my fault for her being here. I convinced her to stay, even though it went against her better judgment. I can assure you, it will not happen again."

"It will not, Sir Terric. For if I find my daughter in your chamber while you are only half-dressed again, you will no longer be welcome here. I suggest the next time you injure yourself, have your squire attend you and not my daughter."

Terric bowed. "You have my word, my lady. I will not put Jacqueline in such a position again."

"I am glad we have reached an understanding, Sir Terric. Now, I am having the evening meal served. Come, Jacqueline. Let us leave Sir Terric alone so he can garb himself decently."

Not giving Jacqueline any chance to refuse, her mother took hold of her arm and pulled her from the room. Jacqueline had just enough time to throw an apologetic look over her shoulder at Terric before her mother roughly yanked her through the chamber door.

The meal was a very strained affair. At least that was how Jacqueline found it. Her gaze was drawn to Terric time and again. She still felt the sensation of his lips claiming hers, his powerful body surrounding her. He seemed not to notice her watching him, but he was not totally oblivious. For each time she averted her eyes, she felt the sensation of being watched. She had no idea if things would go much further with him, but she wanted the chance to explore the possibilities, especially after what had happened in his chamber. The only question was — did he feel the same way about her that she felt about him?

* * * *

They ganged up on him. Much to his disgust, he had had to give ground.

After the slight injury to his shoulder the day before, Jacqueline and Edwin decided training had to be put off for a few days. Terric had told them his shoulder was all right, but they would not listen. The rest would do him good, or so they had told him.

He would rather be on the training field. The idleness gave him too much time to think, too much time to remember. The incident that had taken place in his chamber the evening before still haunted him. So much so, he found he could not be in the same room as Jacqueline for long stretches of time without his body betraying what he felt. His cock grew hard the instant she entered his thoughts. So he had escaped to walk the castle walls.

Even up there, the memories would not leave him. Just closing his eyes brought the taste of her lips and the feel of her body pressed flush against him flooding back. As if to bewitch him more, Terric spotted the object of his desire crossing the bailey below. Jacqueline conversed with Edwin as they walked toward the stables. He did not bother to hail them.

How he could have believed her to be a man was beyond him. Jacqueline was every inch a woman. Even with her cropped hair, it did not detract from that overall perception of her. If anything, it enhanced her features. Soft dark hair framed her face. Terric would have loved to see her with it long, falling to her waist.

Jacqueline and Edwin disappeared into the stable. A few moments later, she stepped back out. She appeared to be searching for something. She scanned the bailey, turning her head to look in every corner.

Terric knew when Jacqueline finally spotted him standing atop the walls, staring down at her. A radiant smile broke across her face. She waved, then came up to join him.

"So this is where you have been hiding yourself."

"I am not hiding. I am only enjoying the sunshine," Terric replied.

Jacqueline laughed and shook her head. "If that is what you want to call it. I get the distinct feeling you are trying to avoid me." As if to prove her point, she moved to stand right next to Terric. With her arms resting on top of the walls, the same as he, their bodies almost touched. He moved farther down, increasing the space between them.

"What is it, Terric? Have I done something to upset you?"

"Nay, you have not. It is I. I am the problem."

Jacqueline took a deep breath. "If you are worried about what happened the other night, do not. I know how you feel about that. It was a moment of weakness. We will just have to put it behind us." She squeezed his hand before she left him alone again.

Terric released the tight grip he held on himself. Just the simple touch of her hand on his had almost been too much. It had taken all, everything he possessed, not to pull her into his arms. If he had given in to his impulse, he would not have let her go. It mattered not that they were atop the castle walls. He would have taken her then and there. He would have pulled her down onto the rough, cold stones and sunk his throbbing cock into her moist depths.

Terric brought himself back under control. He would not be able to put the kiss they had shared so easily behind him. For better or worse, Jacqueline was now in his blood.

* * * *

Having left Terric to his brooding, Jacqueline decided to seek out Beth. She needed some advice. As luck would have it, she found her alone in the solar, sitting before her embroidery frame. She looked up when Jacqueline entered the chamber.

"If you are looking for Mother, she is with Sir Guy."

Jacqueline shook her head and pulled up a chair to sit next to Beth. "Nay, I am not. I came looking for you."

Beth placed her needle down and turned to face Jacqueline. "Well, you have found me."

Unsure of exactly how to broach the subject, Jacqueline spoke hesitantly. "All right. I was wondering if you could give me some advice."

Beth smiled. She glanced to where Jacqueline nervously dug the toe of her boot into the rushes. "You want some advice about Terric. Correct?"

Jacqueline smiled sheepishly. "How did you know?"

"I have had my suspicions. It is not hard to miss the longing glances the two of you give each other when either of you is not looking."

Jacqueline groaned. "Is it that obvious?"

"Nay. Only to me."

"Since you have noticed, tell me what I should do. Terric avoids me. No matter that he says otherwise. He thinks the kiss we shared was a grave mistake."

"You do not agree with that?"

Unable to sit any longer, Jacqueline stood and paced. "Of course I do not."

Beth patted the chair beside her for Jacqueline to sit. Once Jacqueline complied, she nodded. "Now, if you want to win Terric, do what I say. Let him think you feel the same as he, that nothing has changed between you two."

"How is that going to win me him?"

Beth shook her head, then continued. "There is more to it. Along with acting as if it is nothing, do your best to never let him forget it either."

"What do you suggest I do?" Jacqueline leaned in closer.

Beth smiled conspiringly. "Take every opportunity you

get to touch him. A simple brush of your hand will suffice. Make sure to put the least amount of distance between you. The closer the better. Do not give him any chance to ignore you."

"It sounds as if you are suggesting I seduce Terric."

"Of course I am. If left to him, he will avoid you like the plague. Use what you have. Women through the ages have. No man can resist the lure of a woman he desires. Use his weakness to your advantage."

Jacqueline stood once more and absentmindedly nodded while she mulled over Beth's words. It could work. "Thank you. I will do as you say. Starting right now."

With renewed purpose, Jacqueline left the solar. Terric would not know what hit him.

* * * *

He was going out of his mind. Everywhere he went Jacqueline was there, and she drove him mad. Terric noticed the change in her during the meal the evening before. Having sent her away after she had spoken to him on the walls, he had assumed she understood how he felt. He seriously doubted she had.

She had seated herself beside him at the table. As they had eaten, he had not been able to ignore her closeness, especially when she had kept touching him. Her thigh had brushed against his as she had shifted in her seat. Once she had stretched and seemingly caressed the back of his neck. She had not been overly pointed about it, but the slightest touch still affected him.

Terric was unable to tell if Jacqueline had known what she had done. She had spent a large part of the meal acting as though he was not there. Much to his chagrin. By the time the meal was over, Terric had found himself wanting Jacqueline all the more, which resulted in his spending half the night tossing and turning, aching for her. When sleep had claimed him, she had filled his dreams.

Waking to a sun-drenched chamber, Terric groaned. His head pounded like a battering ram from lack of sleep. He had slept longer than usual. He dragged himself from the bed, then pulled on a plain tunic and hose. After slipping his feet into his boots, he strapped his sword around his waist and left his chamber.

Having slept so late, Terric had missed the morning meal. Everyone would already be about their daily business. Hopefully, Lady Elizabeth had arranged to have a meal set aside for him. At the hall, he was surprised to find Jacqueline still seated at the trestle table. If he did not know any better, he would swear she was there waiting for him to show up. He was not sure how he felt about that.

She had her back to him. Not wanting her to think he snuck up on her, Terric loudly clomped down the last remaining steps. "Jacqueline, what do you here? I thought I was the only slug-a-bed this morn."

She turned in her chair and smiled brightly. "It is about time you came down. No, I did not laze about in bed all morning like you. Did you not sleep well?"

How innocently she asks. Jacqueline's turquoise eyes seemed to sparkle with amusement. "I slept well enough."

"You missed eating your morning meal, but I made sure there would be something for you once you came down to the hall."

Standing, Jacqueline indicated that he should take her chair. A platter of bread and cheese sat on the table. Thankful for that small courtesy, he did as she had suggested.

Jacqueline remained standing by the chair. Expecting her to step back, he made to slide into it from her side. She did not move aside as he had expected. Almost intentionally, she turned to face him at the last moment, causing him to literally walk into her. Her breasts lightly pressed against his chest. It took all his willpower not to pull her to the floor and under him.

*

Terric stiffened as their bodies met. A shudder ripped through him a second later. There was no question about it. She was getting to him — badly. Beth's advice was working better than Jacqueline had anticipated. All that was left to see would be how long it would take him to admit defeat and do what they both wanted.

Deciding to make him squirm all the more, Jacqueline tilted up her head. This brought her lips a hair's breath away from his. Terric sucked in a sharp breath through his clenched teeth. She moistened her lips with the tip of her tongue. His violet eyes darkened with desire.

It was the slight movement of Terric's head as he began to lower his lips to hers that brought Jacqueline back to reality. She quickly jumped away, disturbed that she too had fallen under some sort of spell. "I will leave you to finish your meal. I have dawdled enough in the hall." Before he could respond, she beat a hasty retreat.

* * * *

Bright and early the following morning, Jacqueline once more faced Terric on the training field. He had assured her his shoulder was not the worse for wear from their training two days before. He did not appear to be favoring his left arm so she made no further comments.

At least this day, Terric had no-out-of-the-ordinary training techniques planned, which suited Jacqueline just fine. He said would not break lances with her, but he would go through the motions as if he were.

At his signal, she set her steed into motion. Terric did

the same. Keeping in mind what he had told her, not to correct her aim once she was on her way down the list, Jacqueline barreled toward him. They met in the center of the field, and her lance hit his shield dead in the middle. It shattered on impact.

Jacqueline turned her mount around, then headed to Terric, who had halted his steed beside Edwin. The squire had another lance ready to hand up to her when she reached them.

"You did well, Jacqueline," Terric said. "I see you remembered what I told you. You did not change your aim. Now, let me see you do it again."

She spent the next hour breaking lance after lance upon Terric's shield. Not once did she miss her mark. When he suggested they take a rest, she could not keep the foolish grin from her lips, even after she removed her helm. He helped her dismount and must have noticed her expression since he smiled back.

"Now do not get too smug, Jacqueline. This is just the start."

"You must admit, Terric, I have proven myself this day."

"I admit you are a fast learner. I am happy with your progress so far."

"Thanks for your kind words, sir." Buoyed by her success, she stepped closer. "I have found a good teacher."

The smile slowly left his lips as he looked at her. Jacqueline sensed the change that came over Terric. The way he stared so intently caused all the new sensations he had awakened in her to come rushing back. Unable to stop herself, she leaned closer as if an invisible string pulled her to him. He slowly bent his head toward her.

Their mouths were a mere breath apart, and Jacqueline closed her eyes. As his lips softly brushed hers, she sighed. She reached up and wove her fingers through the hair at the nape of his neck, pulling him closer still. He obligingly increased the pressure of his lips.

Edwin very loudly cleared his throat. When that did not gain their full attention, he did it again, adding a barking cough. They jumped apart. Terric had a guilty look upon his face, and she imagined she did as well. Jacqueline, embarrassed about having lost her head so completely, grabbed her horse's reins and swiftly left the training field. Terric seemed to be getting to her as much as she was getting to him.

* * * *

Terric watched Jacqueline's retreating back as he struggled to bring himself back under control. He thrice damned himself for a fool. He always prided himself on having control over any given situation that he found himself in, but his so-called control had utterly deserted him when she had leaned nearer. She had looked so kissable at that precise moment. He had had to taste her lips once more.

Edwin moved to Terric's side and cleared his throat again. "Just what are you playing at? Trifling with the Lady Jacqueline is likely to have us booted out of Carisbrooke Castle faster than you can spit. Lady Elizabeth is not the type of woman to allow her daughter to be toyed with."

Terric snorted. "You think I do not know that."

"You could not have been too worried a moment ago. That was quite a display you two put on."

"Shut your mouth, Edwin. I am well aware of what occurred between us. It was not very well done of me—again. When it comes to Jacqueline, I have no control. I just cannot stop myself."

"Then you have a bit of a dilemma on your hands."

Terric ran his fingers through his sweaty hair and nodded. "You are indeed correct, Edwin. So there is only one option left — I will have to leave."

"What!"

Terric turned to stare at Edwin, and said, "We leave on the morrow. I will inform Lady Elizabeth at the evening meal."

"What of your promise to Lady Jacqueline? The grand tournament is still a couple of months away."

"Sir Guy can take over her training. She now knows what she was doing wrong. Besides, I did not plan to stay here until the grand tournament took place. Each one I miss lessens my chances of earning coin. We leave come first light."

Dejectedly, Edwin shook his head. "I will see that everything is ready. I just hope you do not break Lady Jacqueline's heart with this decision."

Under his breath, Terric said, "So do I. So do I."

CHAPTER EIGHT

Jacqueline slammed her chamber door closed behind her, then angrily threw herself onto her bed. She balled her hands into fists and pounded the mattress. It helped some, venting her anger, but not much. She would have had more satisfaction if it had been Terric she pummeled. The wretch deserved it.

She rolled onto her back as her anger was slowly replaced by hurt. Terric's announcement of his departure on the following day was completely unexpected. Jacqueline had known he would not be spending all the days leading up to the grand tournament at Carisbrooke, but she had not thought he would leave after only a few days. The training had just started. Plus, she had thought he was beginning to feel something for her.

That was what hurt the most. She thought the kisses they had shared meant as much to him as they did to her. She was a fool to think so.

The chamber door opened, and Beth walked in. She shut it, then walked across the room to the bed. Jacqueline refused to acknowledge her presence. She stared pointedly at the ceiling, but that didn't stop her friend from intruding. Beth calmly sat on the edge of the mattress and smoothed the skirts of her gown around her.

"You can act as if I am not here if you want, but I am not leaving, Jacqueline. You are upset about Terric going. I can see that, but I have only one question for you. Are you just going to stand by and let the man you are coming to love walk away without a fight?"

Jacqueline quickly sat up and looked at Beth. "What choice do I have? It is not as if I expected Terric to pledge his undying love for me."

Beth shook her head. "Jacqueline, the man is running scared. I am sure his feelings are a lot stronger for you than what he shows. He has probably never felt this way about another woman. So like the man he is, he is running away."

Jacqueline rolled her eyes at Beth's assumptions and snorted. "I think not. You are making Terric out to be a better man than he is."

"Is that so? All right, prove me wrong."

Jacqueline inched across the bed to sit beside Beth. "What do you mean? Prove what?"

A small smile played upon Beth's lips. "How else? Confront Terric. Tonight, before he leaves."

Jacqueline shook her head. "Are you mad? Mother would have my head for pulling such a stunt."

"So you are willing to let him walk out of your life, possibly forever? Because I can guarantee you, if he leaves without you making him face his feelings, he will not come near you again."

Standing, Jacqueline paced back and forth. She mulled over Beth's words. Admittedly, there were some very good points in what she had said, but how to arrange such a meeting would be the tricky part. Terric's chamber was right beside her mother's.

Having reached a decision, Jacqueline ceased her pacing. "Fine, I will do as you say, but I need your help.

Terric has to come to my chamber. His is too close to Mother's for my liking."

Beth gained her feet and shook out her skirts. "Leave that to me. Once your mother has retired for the night, I will devise a way to have Terric come to your chamber. That is the easy part. Yours, Jacqueline, will be the harder."

"What do you have in mind?"

Beth gave Jacqueline a sly smile and stepped to the chamber door. "Do not fret, he will come. Just be prepared...for his arrival."

After passing on that cryptic remark, she swept out the door, softly shutting it behind her.

* * * *

Terric was in a deep sleep when someone roughly shook him awake. Thinking it was Edwin who disturbed his rest, he brushed the offending appendage away and rolled onto his side. He was shaken once again. He rolled onto his back, ready to give Edwin a stern rebuke. Much to his surprise it was Lady Beth.

He propped himself up on one elbow and reached for the covers to make sure he was sufficiently covered since he slept every night naked. "Lady Beth, what do you here? Is something amiss?"

"Oh, Sir Terric, I am so sorry to disturb you, but I need you to assist me. Something is wrong with Jacqueline."

Terric sat up straighter. "Cannot her mother help her?"

Beth shook her head. "I am afraid not. Please, will you come with me?"

Terric glanced to where Edwin lay asleep on his pallet, and nodded. "Of course, just give me a moment to get dressed."

"I appreciate this, Sir Terric. I will await you in the hallway."

Once Beth softly closed the door behind her, he quickly donned hose and a tunic. Not bothering to awaken Edwin to tell him where he would be, he quietly left the chamber. Beth motioned him to follow her as she headed toward Jacqueline's chamber, which was at the far end of the hallway.

Beth opened the door, then stood aside so Terric could enter the chamber before her. Thinking she had followed him in, he turned to ask her what exactly was wrong with Jacqueline, only to find her shutting him inside. Before he could move to grasp the handle and try to open it, he heard her lock it from the other side.

"Sorry, Terric. I could not let you leave without speaking to you privately."

He spun around at the sound of Jacqueline's voice and found her standing in the middle of the chamber. "You did not have to go to such lengths, Jacqueline. All you had to do was ask."

She stepped closer. "Would you have come to me?" When he did not answer right away, she shook her head. "I thought not."

"Be that as it may, I am here now. What do you wish to say?"

*

Seeing the way Terric avoided looking at her even when she came closer, Jacqueline sensed he would not make this easy on her. "I want to know why you have decided you must leave on the morrow."

Jacqueline positioned herself so a few inches only separated them, and Terric fixed his gaze on the wall at the farthest end of the chamber.

"It is time for me to go. Tournaments are how I make my living. You know that. I must follow the circuit."

Jacqueline looked him up and down. He had his hands

clasped behind his back, trying to act as if her closeness had no effect on him, but she knew she stirred him. He could not hide how stiffly he stood.

"Is that so? If I were to offer to pay you to stay and complete my training, would you still leave?"

Terric opened and closed his mouth a couple of times, but in the end he said, "Nay, I would not."

He squirmed, and Jacqueline had to admit Beth had been correct. He *was* a man running scared, after all. Wanting him to squirm even more, she took another step nearer. Now she was toe-to-toe with him.

"If I were to pay you for your services, there should be no need for you to leave in such a great hurry. Unless there is another reason. One you have not mentioned."

He groaned and brought his gaze down to focus on her face. "Jacqueline, please do not do this. It is better for the both of us if I leave on the morrow."

"How so?"

"Because of this." Terric cupped her face in both his hands and lowered his lips to hers. He claimed them in an all-consuming kiss. Jacqueline wrapped her arms around his waist and held him closer. He lifted his mouth. "If we continue, I cannot promise you I will be able to end this before it is too late."

She ran her hands up and down his back and smiled. "What if I do not want you to stop?"

Her answer elicited another groan from him. "I have no right to touch you this way. You deserve better than a landless knight."

"The choice is mine to make."

"I cannot promise you more than one night. This does not change my decision to leave, either."

"Then make this night memorable for me. I choose no other."

Terric picked Jacqueline up in his arms and carried her to the bed. "God help me, but I am not strong enough to refuse you. I promise you will not regret this."

He laid her on the mattress and slowly followed her down. He claimed her lips again and seemed to give his passion free rein. Increasing the pressure of his lips, he urged her to open her own. His tongue gently entwining with hers brought a moan to the surface from deep down inside her. Jacqueline could not hold it back. As he ran his hands all over her, the sensations he caused took her over.

Gently cupping Jacqueline's breast, Terric took her pebbled nipple between his thumb and forefinger, rolling it between his fingers. Jacqueline moaned. He left her mouth and caressed the skin under her ear with his mouth. He nipped that sensitive area, then licked it. He moved lower on her body and took her breast into his mouth. Through the material of her tunic, he suckled her hard until she squirmed.

As if he found their clothes too much of a barrier, Terric divested them of the offending garments. The contact of bare skin against bare skin caused them to groan. Jacqueline gasped as they touched more intimately. Her senses became overwhelmed. Not wanting to lie still any longer, she tentatively ran her hands down his strong back. Much to her satisfaction, his muscles quivered beneath her touch. Growing bolder, she caressed his chest. Her fingers ran through his chest hair. She relished the feel of the thick padding of muscle to be found there. At his flat nipple, she pinched it between her fingers as he had done to hers. His harsh intake of breath was all she needed to hear to know he felt the same pleasure she had.

Terric took back control and caught Jacqueline's lips in a demanding kiss. He sucked her tongue into his mouth and battered her senses until she rocked her hips into his, demanding more. With a trail of kisses, he kissed and licked his way down her body until he reached her core. He settled between her thighs and forced her legs farther apart.

Coming out of the sensual fog Terric had wrapped around her, Jacqueline looked down, feeling self-conscious. "Terric, I do not think you should…" Her words trailed off in a moan as he showed her exactly what he planned to do.

He swept Jacqueline's sex with his tongue as she fell back in total surrender. He swirled it around the nubbin of hard flesh, the very center of her pleasure, then sucked it into his mouth. She buried her fingers into his hair, holding him in place as she arched. He gave her one last sweep, then pressed his tongue into her opening. He gave her no quarter and continued to stab into her, mimicking the act yet to come. Something built deep inside her, something she had no name for. She whimpered as he backed off and the sensations subsided.

Terric slid up Jacqueline's body, then slowly pushed himself into her. He groaned as he sank deeper. The feel of him entering her made her gasp in pleasure. Once he pushed past the barrier of her maidenhead, she could not stifle a small cry of pain. He stilled, allowing her time to adjust to his intrusion. The pain, though sharp, did not last long. The feel of him filling her so completely made her want something more. Something she had no idea how to obtain. Instinctively, she shifted her hips, sending waves of pleasure throughout her whole body.

Terric moved inside her. With each thrust of his hips, the pleasure build ever higher. It was like nothing she had felt before. Keeping a steady rhythm as he pumped in and out of her, he drove Jacqueline ever higher. She wrapped her legs around his waist and held him tightly. He pushed her over the edge when he reached down between their joined bodies, found the center of her pleasure, and stroked hard enough for her to drown in pleasure. Her inner walls squeezed his shaft, which made him thrust into her one final time. He threw back his head and groaned as he stiffened above her and a warm wetness filled her body.

Once he collapsed atop her, Jacqueline wrapped her arms around him, welcoming the feel of his greater weight. Their breathing slowly returned to normal. Terric rolled onto his back and pulled her up against his side. She placed her head on his chest and closed her eyes. The pleasure she had found in his arms had been like none she had ever felt.

* * * *

Just before dawn broke over the horizon, Terric carefully slipped from the bed. Jacqueline still slept. He gathered his clothes and then put them on.

Jacqueline rolled over and opened her eyes. She lifted her head and looked at him. "Did you plan to leave without saying goodbye?"

He went and sat on the edge of the bed next to her. "I told you this would not stop me from leaving."

"So that was it then?"

Terric reached out and gently brushed her sleep-tousled hair away from her face. "Hardly. What we shared this night, Jacqueline, has changed everything. I will not give you up so easily."

With a confused expression, Jacqueline sat up as she held the sheet against her chest. "Then why go?"

"Because if I do not, you will not be leaving this bed for quite some time."

She must have known what he meant, because she blushed. "Oh."

"Aye, oh. I do not think your mother would understand, either."

"Nay, I think you are right."

"You know I must leave, but it will not be forever. I will be by your side when you face your father at the grand tournament. After that, if you will still have me, I will speak to your mother."

Jacqueline only stared at Terric. She probably was not expecting him to say he would speak to her mother. After what they had shared, he did not want any man touching her but him.

She remained silent, and a wave of uneasiness washed over Terric. Would she reject him now? "Say something. I cannot offer you much, Jacqueline, but I will make you happy. You have my vow."

She quickly threw her arms around his neck and kissed him. "You have surprised me is all. I accept your offer, Terric. I know what you are, and I do not care whether you have lands or not. I accept you for yourself, nothing more."

Moved by her words, he pulled Jacqueline closer and kissed her thoroughly. Heedless of her nakedness, she pressed against him, returning his kiss. Although wanting nothing more than to press her back down onto the mattress and make love to her one last time, Terric resisted. He released her and quickly stood, putting much needed distance between them. It was impossible for him to think straight with her so near.

"I must return to my chamber before your mother awakens. I do not want you to suffer for my weakness."

Jacqueline pressed her hand to her lips, kissed her open palm, and then blew it in Terric's direction. "Then until the morn, my knight."

Terric returned her token in kind before he quietly stepped through the chamber door, which Beth must have unlocked sometime during the night.

CHAPTER NINE

W atching Terric ride away was not an easy thing for Jacqueline to accept, but she had to agree with his motive for leaving Carisbrooke. It would have been close to impossible for the two of them to act as if nothing had happened between them. It was just too risky for him to stay.

No sooner had he and Edwin disappeared from sight then Beth grabbed Jacqueline by her arm and towed her up to her chamber. After shutting the door behind them, Beth smiled at her.

"Well, tell me. What did you and Terric talk about last night? Or should I say *do*?"

Jacqueline felt herself blush to the very roots of her hair, and said, "I think you know very well what happened."

Beth laughed merrily. "Aye, I do, but I want to hear you say how it was. I can see you are no longer angry with Terric for leaving. So it could not have been all bad."

"Nay, it was not. It was wonderful."

"I hope you have not let him get away too easily then."

"Nay. He will meet me at the grand tournament. Once that is over, he wants to talk to Mother."

Beth embraced Jacqueline. "I knew Terric was the one for you. He just needed a little convincing."

"A little trickery on your part."

"Aye, and that too," Beth said laughingly. "I hope you did not mind me locking your chamber door. I figured Terric would have beaten a hasty retreat if he could have managed it."

Jacqueline shook her head. "Nay, I applaud you for your forethought in doing it." Growing serious, she asked, "How do you manage, Beth?"

"How do I manage what?"

"The loss of William. Until now, I really did not know what it must be like for you. I have only been able to think of how not having William here affected me."

The cheerfulness that had showed on Beth's face a moment before was now replaced with sorrow. "Sometimes I feel as if I cannot live another day without him. It is getting easier, not by much, but I can bear it now."

"I am so sorry that I have not helped you more. I love you as a sister. It has not been well done of me."

Beth wiped away a tear and gave her a small smile. "As I love you, Jacqueline, but you have helped me. You and your plan to face the earl have given me something to center my attention upon. I look forward to the day you give him the comeuppance he so richly deserves. It will give me the greatest pleasure."

"It is near at hand, Beth. I will do it for all of us. Most especially for William."

* * * *

After two days of rain, Lady Elizabeth decided to enjoy the now bright sunny day. She donned her cloak and stepped outside. She took a deep breath of fresh air. It was nice to be able to leave the hall without getting wet. There was another reason for her stroll. One she had been putting off for some time.

The pounding of hooves along with the sound of a breaking lance reached her ears before the training ground came into view. Lady Elizabeth stopped a short distance from the activity taking place there and watched her daughter.

Instead of going against a quintain, Jacqueline took runs at a shield, which had been mounted onto a thick wooden post. Even though she did not ride against a live target, she wore full armor.

Jacqueline took another pass, and Lady Elizabeth did not find it hard to believe it was her son she observed. Her daughter rode with all the confidence of any true knight. There was no hesitation or faltering in Jacqueline as her lance struck the shield. Lady Elizabeth felt a grudging pride in her daughter's ability. She had not expected to find her quite so skilled with a lance.

Sir Guy had kept her informed of Jacqueline's progress over the months, but she had presumed the praise he lavished upon her daughter was slightly biased. He loved Jacqueline as if she were truly his child, as he had William. Obviously, his words had been spoken in truth.

As Jacqueline prepared to make another run, Lady Elizabeth smiled. Her daughter trained as if the grand tournament were only days away instead of the weeks that separated them from it. Terric's leaving had precipitated these intense training sessions. Jacqueline had to be trying to distract herself, to make the separation from him more bearable.

It was after that last run that Jacqueline spotted her standing on the edge of the training ground, watching. Lady Elizabeth waved as Jacqueline rode her horse toward her. "I see you are trying to make up for the two days you lost to the rain."

Jacqueline unlaced her helm, then pulled it from her

head. She tucked it under her right arm and smiled. "You are the last person I expected to find here. I assumed you were keeping your distance from all this."

"So I decided to see how you are doing with my own eyes. What of it? I am your mother. It is my job to look out for you."

"And? What is your verdict?"

"Though I am reluctant to say it, I am impressed with your skill." She was more than just mildly impressed, but she was not ready to give that much praise to Jacqueline.

Bowing in the saddle, Jacqueline saluted. "I will take that as an encouraging thought."

Lady Elizabeth snorted. "I still do not approve. So do not get full of yourself."

Jacqueline smiled. "Whatever you say, Mother."

"There is one thing I wish to say before I return to the hall."

"That would be?"

"Relax a bit. Do not try so hard. It will not make the days go any faster. Just two short months, then you will be with him again."

It was obvious Jacqueline tried to act as if she did not know what she had meant, as she asked offhandedly, "Whom do you mean, Mother?"

Lady Elizabeth backed away as she smiled. "Terric, of course."

* * * *

The two remaining months before the grand tournament Jacqueline spent training, improving her skill. She would be more than able to go against the earl now. It helped to keep her mind off Terric too.

She missed him and looked forward to when they would be reunited in London. Even with her days occupied with training, her nights were filled with dreams of him. Now that he had fully awakened her body to passion, she craved his touch. She awoke wet and aching for him.

Once all the long months of training were complete, the true test would come. The day of the grand tournament quickly approached. The time had come for Jacqueline, her mother, and Beth to travel to London. Jacqueline could not wait.

* * * *

With the long, tiring days of travel behind her, Jacqueline was happy to finally see the city gates looming before her. She had only been to London once before when she had been a small child. Her mother had decided she and William had needed to experience the large city.

Once they had worked their way through the crowded streets and had reached their destination, Jacqueline, playing the part of William, directed the men-at-arms to set up her pavilion. The place set aside for the contestants was almost filled to capacity. It very much seemed as if a small city had been erected within the larger one of London. The positions of the pavilions caused a maze of pathways running throughout.

Hoping to see Terric's standard among the pavilions closest to where she was situated, Jacqueline scanned those nearby. Not surprisingly, she did not find it. Spotting his standard would be nigh impossible without knowing exactly where he was camped. There were just too many. Her mother called to her, and she gave up on her search. She stepped into the pavilion to find out what her mother wanted.

"Now, Jacqueline, I am going to your father. He requested I seek him out upon our arrival. You and Beth may stay here. I do not think it wise for the earl to see you up close."

"I agree. I intend to avoid him as much as I possibly can. What excuse will you give should he ask why William does not accompany you?"

Her lady mother casually waved away her concerns. "He will not ask, at least not yet. Besides, I know how to handle the earl."

"If you do not return before the feast, Beth and I will make our own way there."

With a nod, her mother motioned for the two men-at-arms to follow her as she walked out of the pavilion. Jacqueline and Beth were now left on their own.

"Well, Jacqueline, how do you feel? Now, after all the months of training, the day you have strived for is finally upon you," Beth said.

"I am ready, but I just want to have it over with. William has waited long enough for retribution."

"Then tomorrow cannot come soon enough."

* * * *

Her mother did not return before the feast that was to take place in the evening. So Jacqueline and Beth went on their own as planned. It was being held at a hall nearby.

Having waited for as long as they could, they found the hall filled with all the knights and those in their retinue when they arrived. It was with great difficulty that Jacqueline found two empty spaces at one of the many trestle tables. Once Beth was seated, Jacqueline took the opportunity to search the hall for Terric. Again it was futile.

She sat and accepted the food Beth passed her. She was being silly, but having not seen Terric since her arrival had made her concerned. Had he changed his mind over the intervening months? It was a possibility. She really had no hold over him and no betrothal to bind him to her.

An hour after their arrival, her mother and the earl

entered the hall. At the sight of her father, all the anger and resentment she felt toward him rose inside her. He led her mother to the raised dais where the higher nobles were seated. Her disgust in seeing him increased.

At the age of two and sixty, the earl still had the bearing of a much younger man. His shoulders were not stooped by age. His light brown hair that he wore closely cropped to his head was well sprinkled with gray. Jacqueline could see what had drawn her mother to him in the beginning. Even at his age, he still retained his fair face, and he was charming. Even now, he wielded his charm like a weapon, impressing all the nobles with who he paused to speak.

Beth leaned in closer and whispered into Jacqueline's ear. "I wonder if the earls realize how your father is manipulating them. They all seem so thrilled to be in his presence."

Jacqueline snorted in disgust. "It is very doubtful they do. The earl is cunning. He could charm a priest out of his robes if it furthered him."

Another hour passed, and Jacqueline felt a great need to leave the hall. If she did not, she would make a fool of herself in front of all present. The more she watched her father, the more she wanted to ram her fist into his face. His arrogance knew no limits. The way he treated her mother was inexcusable. He had reduced a strong-willed woman to a submissive possession. It was all too clear that the earl had only demanded his wife's presence to further his position amongst the other earls. How he had gained such control over her mother was a mystery. Seeing her only speaking when he spoke to her made Jacqueline feel physically ill.

She turned to Beth, and said, "I cannot take anymore. Let us leave."

Having surely watched Jacqueline scowl in the direction of the earl since his arrival, she agreed. "I do not think we will be missing much. The main entertainment here seems to be how much wine one can down."

Jacqueline took a closer look at those seated around them. Beth was correct. How some of the knights would be in any condition to joust the following day was beyond her. As they walked to the hall doors, Jacqueline had the distinct feeling she was being watched. She turned her head to look over her shoulder and found the earl staring directly at her. He in no way acknowledged that he knew she stared back at him. He just sat there with no expression upon his face. She turned back around once more and hurriedly ushered Beth through the doors. She was relieved to be able to close them behind her, separating herself from her father's unsettling regard.

All her tension she left her in a rush once inside her pavilion. She let loose a string of curses.

Beth, who had come in a step behind her, asked, "What is the matter?"

"Mother's trunk is gone. I do not think she will be returning, after all."

"I had a feeling she would not. The earl must have some need of her."

Jacqueline grumbled, "First, I cannot find Terric, now this."

Having poured them each a goblet of wine from the pitcher that sat on a small table in the center of the pavilion, Beth passed one to Jacqueline. "What is wrong? You do not think Terric would go against his word, do you?"

Jacqueline accepted the proffered goblet, then swallowed a large gulp from it. "Of course I do. It has been two months since I last saw him. Anything could have happened to make him change his mind. Including another woman."

"Oh, Jacqueline, Terric would not do that to you."

"How can you be so sure? I really have not known him all that long. He could have been lying, and I would not have been the wiser. He did not profess his undying love for me before he left."

Beth sighed. "He will be here for you. Terric is not the type of man to make false promises."

"You are quite right, Beth. I do not make false promises."

At the sound of Terric's voice, Jacqueline whirled around, causing some of the wine in her goblet to slosh over the rim and onto her hand. The first thought that came to her mind was, *He is here. He is actually here.*

Terric came to stand before her. He took the goblet from her and had a sip. He grabbed her hand and licked the wine from her skin. She uttered a small surprised gasp of pleasure.

Beth, whose presence had been forgotten, discreetly coughed. "I am pleased to see you again, Terric. Jacqueline was most worried."

Blinking, as if coming out of a trance, Terric turned to look at Beth. "I heard you trying to reassure her. My thanks for having such confidence in me."

"Do not think badly of Jacqueline. She has been under a lot of strain since our arrival."

"Well, I am here now. So she has one less thing to worry about." Terric released Jacqueline's hand, then reached for Beth's. After she placed it in his, he spoke once more. "If you agree, I would like some time alone with Jacqueline. Edwin is waiting just outside to escort you to my pavilion."

"I will leave you both alone, but I suggest you do not take very long. Who knows who might come to call when you least expect it." She looked pointedly at Jacqueline, who gave her a curt nod in understanding. Satisfied they had heeded her warning, Beth released Terric's hand and then stepped outside to where Edwin awaited her.

Seeing Terric again made Jacqueline realize how much she had missed him. She welcomed his embrace when he pulled her into his arms. The meeting of their lips was like a catalyst, and an explosion of flames engulfed her.

Their joining would be quick. The two long months of being separated from Terric had forced her to realize how much he really meant to her. She loved him. It was that simple.

He picked Jacqueline up into his arms and carried her to the cot in the corner. He dragged the furs from it and placed them on the ground. He laid her on them, then fell atop her.

Having dreamed for so many nights of being like this with Terric, Jacqueline once more relished the feel of him pressed so close. His kisses were not gentle, but demanding, almost as if he wanted to devour her. To know she had such an effect upon him increased her desire. She pulled at his tunic, wanting to be closer.

Terric leaned back and quickly shed it. As soon as his bared chest was exposed, Jacqueline rained it with kisses. He growled in the back of his throat. As she shoved him onto his back, she climbed on top of him. She straddled his hips and untied the laces on his hose. He silently watched as she pulled the garment down, exposing his full, erect member. He hissed with pleasure as she softly touched the tip.

Jacqueline circled the head of Terric's shaft with her finger. Finding a drop of fluid on the very end of it, she rubbed it into the soft skin. The first time they had made love she had not had a chance to get a good look at that part of him. She fully intended to satisfy her curiosity now.

She glanced down at Terric and found his eyes dark with desire. He made no move to stop her as she ran a finger down the length of him. She grew bolder, running her hand farther downward and then cupping his sac. At his groan, she wondered if he would like what he had done to her while back at Carisbrooke.

Before he could stop her, she shifted lower, took his

cock in her hand, and licked him from base to tip. He jerked and groaned with pleasure. Once she took him into her mouth and sucked, he moaned even louder. He let her have her way with him for a few seconds more before he seemed to reach his limit.

"If you continue what you are doing, this will be over even before it has begun," Terric gasped.

With a moan, Terric grabbed her and flipped her onto her back. He undid her hose and removed them after he roughly pulled her boots off. Once she was exposed, he pushed her legs apart with his knee and slowly worked himself home. They moaned. He surged into Jacqueline's body. She gasped. Her inner walls spasmed as she lifted her hips to meet his thrusts. He grasped hers, then thrust into her once, twice, before his release ripped through him. Out of breath, he collapsed on top of her.

Once their breathing slowed, Terric caressed Jacqueline's back. She nestled against his side with her head on his chest. She only wore her tunic, and his hose were pooled at his ankles. He still had his boots on.

"We have to get up, Jacqueline. Beth is right. We could have uninvited guests at any moment."

"I wish we did not have to. This feels too good. I could get used to having you as my pillow."

Terric chuckled. "I would not mind being used as one in the slightest, but your pillow is going to do what is best for you and get dressed."

As he slipped out from under her, Jacqueline groaned and put her face into the pile of furs. After he pulled up his hose and fastened the laces, Terric grabbed her hose and threw it at her head.

"Come now. Get up. Think of poor Beth. I am sure she wants to sleep soon, and she only has Edwin for company. I doubt she will be able to stomach his lovesick looks for long."

She pulled her hose from her head and smiled at the

thought of Beth having to fend off Edwin's admiring glances. "Then we had best rescue her. She is likely to smack him silly."

Finally accepting the fact he would not stay any longer with her, she hurriedly donned her hose. He was not totally unaffected by her. The evidence was there to see by the bulge between his legs. "Are you sure you have to leave, Terric?"

He nodded. "I must. There will be other nights."

"You promise?"

Desire showed in his eyes as Terric replied, "I promise, Jacqueline. You will not be rid of me so easily."

"Nor you of me."

"Until the morrow, my love."

Terric walked out of the pavilion. Had she heard him correctly? Had he just called her his love? Sighing deeply, she fell back down upon the furs. She looked up at the roof of the pavilion. She could not take the idiotic grin from her face.

That was how Beth found her upon her return. "I see Terric and you had an enjoyable...talk."

Jacqueline turned her head in Beth's direction and giggled. She acted like a fool, but she seemed unable to help herself. She was just so happy. "Very. I hope Edwin did not bother you much."

Beth laughed. "Nay, he was vastly amusing with his worshipping looks. I must admit I found his attention flattering, even though he is only a boy."

"That boy, as you call him, is the same age as you. Eight and ten."

"Really?"

Jacqueline shook her head in amusement. Maybe having her friend spend more time with Edwin would not be such a bad thing, after all. If he could help Beth handle the loss of William, he would be a blessing. Beth had suffered enough, and she was too young to act the widow for the rest of her days. Edwin could be the man who could make her put away her mourning for good.

CHAPTER TEN

The following day, Sunday to be exact, King Richard's grand tournament began. This day, the first day of the tilting, was called the Feast of the Challengers. It was to be the prelude to the real tournament. Around three o'clock, a parade through London's streets marked the start of the entertainment. The Tower of London was the starting point and it would end at Smithfield.

Sixty squires, atop barded coursers ornamented for the tournament, were the beginning of the parade. Behind them, sixty ladies of rank rode on palfreys. Each one led a knight, fully armored, by a silver chain. A number of minstrels followed in their wake. The whole group wound its way through the streets down Cheapside to the large square in Smithfield.

Neither Jacqueline nor Terric took part in the parade. They chose to watch from the sidelines. Beth and Edwin joined them. Already at Smithfield, they only saw the procession as it ended.

Jacqueline found herself in awe of those who participated, as the rest of the spectators appeared to be. The elegance of the richly dressed ladies and beautifully barded horses took her breath away. She had never seen anything of the like before. As each of the sixty ladies and knights entered the square, she noticed some wore matching livery.

Curious, she asked Terric, "Why do some have livery and others not?"

Terric took a closer look. "They must be the lords and ladies of the Garter. It is the king's livery they wear. I have seen it before."

As one of the ladies rode close by them, Jacqueline caught a better view of the badge she wore upon her gown. The king's livery was a hart with a golden crown that hung low on its body. It also wore a golden chain that encircled its neck. The livery appeared to be worn on coats, armor, shields, and even on the horses' trappings.

Once all the ladies had arrived in the square, their servants rushed to assist them in dismounting from their palfreys. They were then led away. The knights remained in the square, awaiting their squires who had also dismounted and were now leading their coursers to them.

After much discussion that morning, Terric convinced Jacqueline not to compete in this day's event. His reasoning behind it was her father would not be participating so why risk injury — one that could prevent her from joining in the jousting the following day. Reluctantly, she had agreed.

Now that the knights were ready to begin, Terric, Jacqueline, Beth, and Edwin slowly walked to the bleachers that had been erected specifically for the tournament. Since they were not the only spectators headed in that direction, it took much pushing and elbowing, mostly on Edwin's part, to obtain prime seating closest to the list.

As each knight thundered down it to meet his opponents with a resounding crash, Terric pointed out each weakness they had to Jacqueline. She had to admit there was an advantage in just watching, after all. With his help, she would be better prepared to face her adversaries on the morrow.

Just like the evening before, Jacqueline felt eyes watching her now that the competition had begun. It gave her an eerie feeling, being stared at so intently. It felt as if someone physically touched her. As casually as possible, she searched the bleachers, hoping to see whose attention she had gained.

Her gaze fell on the part of the bleachers where the king and queen sat, and she found her father sitting very close to the royal couple. It was he who stared at her. This time, his expression made her quickly jerk back around. His face was full of malice, almost as if he hated her. Almost as if he knew it was she and not William watching the tilting.

Leaning close, Terric whispered, "What is wrong? You are so tense I could bounce a pebble off you."

Speaking from the side of her mouth, Jacqueline replied, "My father. He is sitting near the king." Terric moved to turn and look back at the earl. She kicked his ankle. "Do not look at him. He is watching me."

Terric reached down to rub his abused ankle, but did as she had ordered. "All right, I will not turn to look. You could have found a less painful way to get my attention, you know."

The crowd roared as another pair of knights rushed toward each other. Using the noise to her advantage, Jacqueline spoke more loudly. "You will get over it. I have bigger problems than worrying about hurting your feelings. For some reason, I have earned my father's ire. He does not look at all pleased with me."

"I suggest when the tilting is through, you return to your pavilion. You and Beth."

"I agree. It will not be much longer. The day already grows late."

Once it became too dark to see, the tilting would cease.

The next hour stretched Jacqueline's nerves tighter and tighter. When at last darkness fell and the tilting was drawn to a close, she was up on her feet, leading Beth away. There was to be another feast this night at the bishop of London's palace near St. Paul's church, but she felt it prudent not to attend. Her father would definitely be present. The king and queen were lodged at the bishop's palace, and he would not want to miss any opportunity to gain their favor.

* * * *

Jacqueline stood at the entrance to her pavilion and looked at the bright, twinkling stars that studded the sky. She took a deep breath, then sighed. Her nerves were getting the better of her. On the morrow, she could very well be meeting her father in the list, but sleep was the furthest thing from her mind.

She glanced behind her. Beth was asleep on her cot. At least one of them would be well-rested.

Sighing again, she pulled the pavilion's flap closed once more. There was no help for it. She might as well accept that sleep would not come easily for her. Since she was going to be up half the night, she only wished she could spend it with Terric.

He had gone to the feast at the Bishop's palace. He had offered to stay with her and Beth, but she could not begrudge him that. He so enjoyed them. There was really no reason for him to be absent from it.

She crawled back onto her cot and tried to sleep once again.

* * * *

The hall at the Bishop's place was jammed packed full of people. Terric barely had enough room to comfortably

98

eat his meal. As if he needed a reminder of the cramped conditions, the person next to him elbowed him in the ribs.

Terric rubbed the area that had taken the hit and turned his attention to the upper table. Jacqueline's mother and father were numbered among the exalted company who sat there. The earl, as was his want, tried to ingratiate himself to the king. Lady Elizabeth, taking advantage of her husband's inattention, seemed more relaxed. She even conversed with the young queen from time to time.

After all had eaten their fill, the food was cleared away and the dancing began. It was during that time Lady Elizabeth caught his attention with a slight nod. She stepped out of the hall. Figuring she wished him to follow, Terric waited a few minutes, then headed from the hall as well.

She stood just outside the doors, waiting. "I do not have much time. The earl is ever watchful of me. Why, I have no idea."

Terric took hold of Lady Elizabeth's elbow and led her farther away from the hall doors. "How have you been treated?"

She waved his concern away. "With all the courtesy due me. My husband would never mistreat me in that way, most especially here. He would not want his name besmirched. Enough about me. How are they?"

Terric knew who she referred to. "They are fine." After quickly making sure no one was nearby, he continued. "Jacqueline is a bit nervous, which is to be expected."

"Aye, it is. I must return before the earl misses me and comes looking. Just promise to watch out for her on the morrow. I will be in the stands."

Bowing, Terric nodded. "I will."

"I wish you luck in the tournament as well, Sir Terric." Lady Elizabeth returned to the hall.

* * * *

"You missed a splendid feast last night, Jacqueline. You and Beth would have enjoyed it."

"It seems as if you enjoyed yourself, anyway."

Terric lounged in one of her camp chairs, lazily sipping wine from a goblet. Even though he tried to hide the smile he wore by holding the rim of it against his lips, Jacqueline still saw the mirth lurking in his violet eyes. She scowled at him.

Seeing the look she gave him, he said, "Are you worried I met another woman to while away my night?"

"Should I be?"

"Nay, I was true to you, but that did not stop them from seeking my attention. Poor Edwin had to sacrifice himself by offering his meager services."

Jacqueline laughed. "I am sure he groveled at their feet, more like."

"That is better. I made you laugh. Even if it was at poor Edwin's expense."

"Aye, you did. Now tell me what else happened at the feast. Besides you being swarmed by almost every female who attended."

"Fine, I will tell you since you insist. During the feast, they announced the winners of the tilting. The French count, Count de Saint Pol, was named the best knight of the tournament. The Earl of Huntingdon for the tenants. There was a last minute arrival as well."

"Who?"

"Count d'Ostrevant, William de Hainault, King Richard's cousin. He brought a large group of knights and squires with him. So there will be more competitors in today's tilting."

"I have no interest in the count. My main concern is my father."

Terric sat straighter. "Did you submit your challenge to him?"

Sighing, Jacqueline nodded. "I did. I have yet to hear if he has accepted it or not."

As if on cue, someone scratched on the other side of the pavilion flap. After opening it, Jacqueline found her father's squire standing there. He sketched a quick bow, then passed her the missive he held before leaving. Her hand shook as she broke her father's seal and read what was written on the parchment.

Terric came to stand behind her, placing his hands on her shoulders. "What does it say?"

She had to clear her throat before she answered. If she had not, her voice would have come out in a croak. "He has accepted my challenge."

"Congratulations, you now will be able to accomplish what you have worked so hard for."

Jacqueline nodded, unable to force a word past her lips. Terric was right. She finally got what she had striven so hard for, but instead of being elated, an overwhelming sense of sadness washed over her. The longer she looked at her father's missive, the more intense the feeling became. Soon the words blurred. Once a tear fell onto the parchment, smearing the ink, she could no longer hold back her sorrow. As her gut-wrenching sobs began, Terric turned her so she faced him. He wrapped her tightly in his embrace.

Gradually, Jacqueline's sobs eased. She hiccupped a few times and then fell silent. Terric loosened his embrace and placed a hand under her chin, tilting her head up. Her eyes had to be red and swollen from crying, but she felt more at peace. He brushed a gentle kiss upon her lips.

"Do you feel better?"

She nodded, and said hoarsely, "Aye."

"Now you can face your father with a clear mind."

She stepped back and wiped her eyes with the sleeve of her tunic. He was correct. Now, having released her pent-up sorrow, she felt remarkably calm.

She pulled herself up straighter. "I am ready to go against the earl now. Nothing will stop me."

* * * *

That afternoon the tournament truly began. King Richard entered Smithfield accompanied by dukes, lords, and knights. The king was to be the Chief of the Tenants of the list. Count d'Ostrevant arrived next, along with a large company of knights and squires, fully armed for the tilting. Count de Saint Pol, accompanied by the knights from France, followed.

Jacqueline sat in her pavilion, waiting for her turn in the list, when she heard the roar of the crowd. They equally cheered or booed, depending on which opponent they favored. There was no mistaking the sound of a knight being unhorsed. The resulting crash of armor impacting with solid ground was resounding.

Surprisingly, she still retained the calmness she had gained earlier. Even when Edwin came to help finish arming her, she felt no nervousness, no second thoughts. As the squire led her to the list, she felt as if she walked in a dream world. The people around her seemed move in slow motion, as if they were submerged in a heavy substance, which limited their movements. Even their voices were muffled.

Once she arrived at the list, the roar of the crowd fell away to nothingness. Her whole being focused on the knight at the opposite end. He held a shield, which bore the same coat of arms as hers — the Montacute's.

Jacqueline grasped the lance Edwin held out to her and placed it at the ready. Knowing what was to come, her steed stamped impatiently. The signal given, she set her courser into motion. Before her full attention was taken over by what she was doing, she silently said, *For William. I do this for you.*

Her steed reached a full gallop, and she flew down the list just as her father did. She braced herself and hit the earl's shield with her lance. It splintered into a thousand pieces. Her father's hit her shield with enough force to jar her almost out of her saddle, but she tenaciously held on. His lance also shattered on impact.

The second pass, Jacqueline's only skidded across the earl's shield, giving him the point. His lance hit her shield dead center, once again shattering.

She returned to her end of the list, accepted a new lance from Edwin and prepared for the final run. Her father was good, very good. After the two passes, she came to the conclusion she would not be able to unhorse him. She would be proving herself just by trying to keep her seat with each run.

She waited for the signal as she looked down the list at her father. She could not see his face with his helm on, but he must have noticed she watched him. He tipped his lance down in a salute. Jacqueline returned it in kind.

Once the signal was given for the final pass, their steeds barreled down the list at top speed. They met with a crash. Jacqueline felt the impact through her whole body. With both lances shattered, it marked the end of the jousting between her and her father. She turned around for the last time and passed the earl as he headed to his squire.

A moment before he passed her, he stopped. "Well done, William. I see your skill has improved since we last met in the list."

Jacqueline made her voice as deep as she could make it. "Thank you, Father. I have been training for this day."

"I must say your ability is better than I expected. We will speak later." He kicked his heels into his steed's flanks, leaving her to continue to the waiting Edwin.

Beth and Terric were at her pavilion, waiting for her return. Once she stepped through the entrance, they enthusiastically greeted her. Beth welcomed her first. "Oh,

Jacqueline, you were spectacular. William would have been so proud of you." She seemed to be crying and smiling at the same time.

Almost frantically, Jacqueline unlaced and then ripped off her helm. She took in great gulps of air once she was free of it. She looked at Terric and Beth. "He knows."

"Who knows?" It was Terric who had spoken.

"My father."

Beth gasped. "How could he?"

Jacqueline wiped the sweat from her brow, then shook her head. "I know not. All I do know for certain is he has seen through me."

Terric pulled her closer and unbuckled her armor. "What makes you think he knows? You and Beth have been careful not to be too close to your father."

She still felt the chill that had run down her back when the earl had spoken to her. "He talked to me after the final run. He said I surprised him."

"Jacqueline, that does not mean he knows. He could have just been surprised by your skill. Nothing more."

She shook her head once more. "Nay, Terric, you are wrong. He knows. He said we would speak again later. Nothing good can come of that."

Having divested Jacqueline of her armor as they had spoken, Terric rubbed her back. "Do not fret. I am sure it is nothing. Who knows, he might not even send for you."

She leaned against Terric's comforting warmth as a shudder ran through her. "I wish I could be so positive, but I cannot. The earl will not so easily forget. He knows."

* * * *

The earl roughly shoved his helm into his young squire's hands. He stepped into the shaded confines of his pavilion. After being divested of his armor, he impatiently waved his squire away. Left alone, he picked up the goblet of wine placed on the table for him.

He sat on one of the camp chairs and slowly sipped his drink. His brows furrowed in irritation as he replayed his meeting with his son in the list. It seemed William's skill had improved vastly. What bothered him the most was how quickly his son had recovered from his injury. The intervening months since their last meeting William should have spent healing, not improving his skill in handling a lance. William's armor seemed to be a smaller fit as well, though that could be easily explained. Being injured, William could have lost some weight.

He had thought of another explanation as well for all the changes in William, but he found it too ludicrous. The girl was dead and buried. Besides, no female would dare what he thought.

As his wife entered the pavilion, the earl broke off his musings about his son. Now would be the perfect opportunity to have her answer a few pointed questions in regards to William. He motioned for her to sit on the other camp chair across from him, then stared intently at her. Under his close scrutiny, she eventually lowered her head to look at her clasped hands on her lap. The earl smiled. He did enjoy seeing her cowed.

"Tell me about William. Did he recover from his injury without any complications?"

His wife kept her eyes downcast and squeezed her hands together so tightly her knuckles turned white. "Nay, there were no problems, though it was months before he regained his strength fully."

The earl nodded. "I noticed he has bettered his skill in the list."

"William has trained hard for this day," she replied dryly.

"Raise your head when you speak to me, woman," the earl snapped. "Why would our son train so hard, especially after receiving a grievous injury just to meet me here in the list?"

His wife lifted her head to look at him. "He only wished to please you. William wanted you to be proud of him. So when he recovered, he dedicated himself to improving his abilities."

Not wanting to pursue the topic any further, the earl stood. It was obvious his wife would only say what she thought he wanted to hear. "You may leave me now." Without a word, she got up and left his pavilion.

CHAPTER ELEVEN

In the evening another feast was to be held. Since she had participated in the day's tournament, Jacqueline attended. She did not want to give her father any more reasons to become suspicious of her.

Terric accompanied her and Beth, knowing how shaken Jacqueline had been by her confrontation with the earl. He still claimed she had nothing to worry about, and even went so far as to say that if her father knew her secret, he was almost positive the earl would have already acted against her. Still, hoping to lay her fears to rest, he planned to pay closer attention to the earl to see if he acted differently toward her.

The king and queen were present and seated at the table on a raised dais. King Richard was a young king, at the age of three and twenty, but the crown of England had been his since the age of ten. In his early years, John of Gaunt had acted as regent until Richard reached the age of majority. The regent had not been a favorite of the people. Their animosity had been caused by his oppressive government policies. They had been so intolerable the peasants had revolted in 1381.

That was all in the past. Richard now had full control over his throne. He was no longer king in just name, and he had chosen his queen. Queen Anne was the daughter of Charles IV, the Holy Roman Emperor and King of Bohemia.

Before the feast commenced, the winners from the day's tournament were announced. This time the ladies, lords, and heralds had been the judges. The winner of the tilting was Count d'Ostrevant, the king's foreign cousin. The tenants were given to an English knight, Sir Hugh Spenser.

Jacqueline was not particularly interested in who the winners of the tournament were. She had not been in the running for either prize, having only challenged her father in the end. She had accomplished what she had set out to do, and that was all that truly mattered.

As the evening progressed, Jacqueline allowed herself to relax. Her father acted as if she was not in the hall. He did not look her way. Not even once. She came to think maybe Terric was right, after all. No longer worrying about being summoned by the earl, she enjoyed the feast to its fullest. She ate and drank her fill, all the while talking and laughing with her companions.

She became quite startled to find her mother standing behind her seat when the feast drew to a close. Her first response was to quickly search for her father. He was no longer in the hall, much to her consternation. That did not bode well.

Jacqueline shifted her attention back to her mother and searched her face for any clues. Her lady mother's expression was passively bland. Her eyes, so much like Jacqueline's own, showed the strain she had been under since her arrival in London. There were prominent dark smudges under each of them. Jacqueline could only guess at what the earl had put her through.

"Is everything all right, Mother?"

Her mother nodded quickly. "For the moment. I must

return to the earl shortly. He sent me to deliver a message to you, to William."

Jacqueline's eyes widened in panic. Was her father going to summon her to him? "What message?"

Lady Elizabeth smiled. "He did not send me here for the reason you are thinking. He has no idea." She leaned closer and whispered for Jacqueline's ears only, "You did well. You know how I felt about all you had planned, but you have made me very proud of you."

Jacqueline had to blink back the sudden rush of tears that threatened to flow at her mother's praise. "Thank you, Mother."

Still smiling, Lady Elizabeth straightened. "Your father has instructed me to inform you that you are to depart London after the last day of the tournament at first light."

It was an order, Jacqueline knew, but it was one she would gladly carry out. "And you, Mother? Are you to leave with us?"

"He has allowed me to depart with you and Beth."

Jacqueline smiled brightly. "You may tell the earl we will be gone on the day he wishes."

"Until then." After taking a last look at Jacqueline, Lady Elizabeth left the hall.

A few moments of silence passed before Terric broke it. "It seems as if we will all be departing at first light on that day."

"Truly?" Jacqueline had hoped Terric would return to the isle with them. She did not think she could bear being separated from him again so soon.

"Of course. I have business to discuss with your lady mother. The isle is the only place where I can do it."

If they were not in a crowded hall where she posed as a man, Jacqueline would have thrown her arms around Terric and shown him how happy his words made her. Instead, she settled for reaching beneath the table and squeezing his thigh. He gave her hand a quick caress before she removed it. She wished they were someplace else.

Beth stood. "If we are to be awake for the events taking place in the early morning, I think it would be prudent to retire for the night."

Jacqueline tore her gaze from Terric's face, then stood as well and offered her arm to Beth. "Quite right." After nodding to the man who still sat on the bench, she led her "wife" from the hall.

* * * *

On the following day, it was the squires' turn to take to the list. They were to tilt in the presence of the king, queen, and all the nobles.

Since Edwin would be participating, Jacqueline and Beth joined Terric in the stands to watch. Edwin managed to acquit himself admirably. He did not win every match, but he had at least kept his seat throughout.

When it came for Edwin to finally face his last opponent, Jacqueline was about ready to jump up from her seat and run. As before, while being a spectator, she felt her father's eyes watching her. This time his gaze seemed to bore into her as if he tried to see what or who she truly was.

Once Edwin left the list, she grabbed Beth by the hand and pulled her to her feet. Beth did not question why Jacqueline wished to leave before the end of the tilting. The atmosphere was decidedly icy around the stands.

Terric followed. They separated when they reached the pavilions. Terric went to see to Edwin while Jacqueline and Beth retired to their own dwelling.

"I do not think I can last until the end of this tournament, Beth." Jacqueline sat heavily in a camp chair.

"You do not have much choice in the matter. The earl would become very suspicious if you left suddenly. Just a few more days. That is all."

"I keep telling myself that very same thing, but it is not helping any."

Beth took a seat in the chair next to Jacqueline. "You are safe."

"If the earl's behavior this day is any indication, I am not so sure of that. He looked at me as if he could see right through me."

Both of them let that topic drop as Terric and Edwin entered the pavilion.

Terric headed straight for Jacqueline. He pulled her from the chair and kissed her thoroughly. Having rendered her satisfactorily weak-kneed, he released her lips. She still clung to him when he whispered into her ear, "Just a taste of what is to come later."

Jacqueline's breath hitched. "I will hold you to that."

Terric reluctantly released her, taking a step away, and just in time since a visitor arrived unannounced.

A ripple of fear coursed through Jacqueline's body at the sight of her father standing just inside her pavilion. "Hello, Father."

The earl looked her up and down. Jacqueline hoped her face did not show any sign of the kiss she had received from Terric. She clenched her hands tightly at her sides and resisted the urge to wipe her lips with the back of one.

"I see you have company, William. Are you not going to introduce me?"

Needing further space between herself and Terric, Jacqueline went to stand beside Beth. "Father, this is Sir Terric Aubrey. This is his squire, Edwin."

Her father's gaze skipped over Edwin, having been deemed not worth of his lordly interest. "Sir Terric. I believe I have seen you before. At many a tournament, if I am not mistaken."

Terric bobbed his head at the earl in acknowledgement. "Aye, you are correct. I follow the tournament circuit each season."

The earl somehow managed to look down his nose at Terric. No small feat, considering Terric stood a few inches taller than her father, who was just slightly over six feet.

"How quaint, a tournament knight. I had not realized my son was acquainted with you. At past tournaments we attended together, I never noticed you in William's company, Sir Terric."

"William and I just became acquainted a few months past. At a tournament at Portchester Castle."

"How convenient," the earl said with a sneer. He turned his attention back to Jacqueline. "I came to make sure you attended tonight's feast, William. Your mother seems to think you would not."

Jacqueline stiffened. "I had not planned on attending."

The earl shook his head. "That will not do at all. I will not have my son hiding away in his pavilion. You and your wife will be present at the feasts. Do I make myself clear?"

"Aye, Father," Jacqueline answered meekly.

"I am glad we have rectified that. Now, I must return to the tournament. I will be watching for your arrival at the bishop's palace." With that said, the earl left the pavilion as suddenly as he had arrived.

Jacqueline trembled, and Terric fetched a goblet of wine. He made sure she had a large sip from it before he led her to one of the camp chairs. Taking another fortifying drink from her goblet, she looked at the others who hovered around her. "I have a very bad feeling about this. First, his comments at the list, and now this unexpected visit. It almost seemed as if he expected to catch me doing something I did not want him to see."

"Which is precisely what very nearly happened," Beth said.

Terric interrupted before she could continue. "It was entirely my fault. Do not blame Jacqueline for it. I put her in that position by kissing her. I will be sure to act with more circumspection in the future."

"See that you do."

After the earl's unexpected visit, Jacqueline found she was unable to enjoy the rest of the day. She felt nothing but dread every time she thought of that evening's feast. By the time they left for the bishop's palace, her nerves were wound so tight she jumped at the slightest noise.

Now, standing before the hall doors, Jacqueline took a deep breath, trying to steady her nerves. Beth squeezed her arm. "Steady now. You will be fine."

Jacqueline nodded jerkily, then pulled herself up straighter and opened the hall doors. Once inside, she kept her gaze from the raised dais. She spotted Terric, who was seated at one of the many trestle tables, and led Beth over to join him.

Terric shifted down on the bench, making room for them to sit. "About time you two showed up."

"Someone decided to take as long as she possibly could to dress," Beth stated flatly. She seated herself on the bench, leaving enough space for Jacqueline to slip in between her and Terric.

"I am sure we did not miss all that much." The other guests were already trying to get as much food and wine down their gullets as they could manage.

"You only missed the announcement made on behalf of the king."

When Terric was not forthcoming with any more information, Jacqueline asked impatiently, "Well?"

"The king has decided to leave London on the morrow with the foreign knights and counts."

Jacqueline felt as if a great weight had been lifted from her. The earl would not expect her to follow the court. Hopefully, neither would her mother have to. "That is most interesting news."

"I thought you would be pleased," Terric said

laughingly.

"I am more than pleased."

Now that her time under her father's rule would be drawing to a close, Jacqueline risked looking at the earl. Her father was deep in conversation with one of the foreign counts. He must have sensed her watching him, because he turned and looked directly at her. The smile that he had worn moments before disappeared. She refused to back down this time. She stared back at him, her gaze never wavering. The earl dipped his head in salute.

As the meal progressed, Jacqueline felt more relaxed. Forgetting about her father, she set out to enjoy what was to be her last night with the court.

Enjoy herself she did. After a few goblets of wine, she was able to completely ignore the earl's presence at the high table. Terric entertained her and Beth with the gossip that usually ran rampant wherever the court stayed. He told them everything from whose wives were having affairs behind their husbands' backs, to which of the courtiers padded their hose to create the effect of muscular legs.

In a small way, Jacqueline wished the night would not come to an end. Having Terric seated beside her, his leg plastered against her own, made her want more. After the earl's unexpected visit at her pavilion, Terric had decided not to come to her later that night. The risk was too great. She really could not, should not, complain about it, but she ached for Terric's touch, for the feel of him thrusting into her body. So, wistfully, she made do with what she could.

Once the dancing started, a young pageboy presented Jacqueline with a piece of parchment. After she accepted it, he bowed and left to continue with his other duties. She broke the seal on the missive and quickly scanned what was written inside. She smiled. "This evening is just getting better and better."

Beth peered over Jacqueline's shoulder, and asked, "Is

that from the earl?"

"Aye. We have been sent our packing orders. We leave at dawn on the morrow. Mother will join us as well."

Terric picked up his goblet and drained the rest of his wine before he stood. "If that is the case, I suggest we all retire for the night."

Following suit, Jacqueline got up from the bench and offered Beth her arm. "On the morrow then, Sir Terric," she said formally. Before quitting the hall, she once more looked at her father. She nodded in his direction, making it known she understood his wishes.

* * * *

They were greeted by Sir Guy when they arrived at Carisbrooke Castle. He anxiously searched each face in their party, waiting to see who would speak first. When he received no response, he took matters into his own hands.

"Well? Are you all going to leave me to guess what happened in London? Or are you going to give an old man peace of mind and tell me?"

Jacqueline took pity on him and linked her arm through his and led him toward the hall. "You are hardly an old man, and well you know it. I am parched from our travels so let me quench my thirst, then I will be happy to tell you everything."

"Just do not keep me waiting too long."

To ensure Jacqueline would not take any longer than she needed, he hurried her through the hall doors and then sat her in one of the chairs before the fire. He fetched a tankard of ale himself. Her mother and the others entered the hall at a more sedate pace.

Jacqueline sipped her ale and could not help but notice how Sir Guy hovered over her, impatiently tapping his foot. She said laughingly, "I can see you are not going to leave me be until I tell you."

"Nay, my girl, I will not. Now out with it," Sir Guy grumbled.

"You have not welcomed my mother properly as of yet. Should you not do that first?"

"She can wait. Talk."

"I guess I have tortured you enough. I challenged the earl at the grand tournament. As you can see, I am not the worse for wear from it."

"That is it? That is all you are going to say?"

Terric came to stand behind Jacqueline's chair. "She is being modest, Sir Guy. Jacqueline did more than hold her own against her father. She managed to keep from being unhorsed and scored a point on one of the runs."

Heedless of the tankard of ale she held, Sir Guy snatched Jacqueline from her chair and squeezed her in a bear hug. Her drink spilled into the rushes. The older man placed her back onto her feet. "I wish I could have seen you in the list."

"The grand tournament will be the last time I am to enter the list. I have done what I set forth to do."

Hearing Jacqueline's words, Lady Elizabeth came over and sat in the chair next to her. "Does that mean you will let your hair grow back and start wearing gowns like a proper lady?"

Jacqueline reached up and pulled on her cropped auburn locks. "I will let my hair grow back, but I will not give up wearing a man's attire."

"Not even after you wed? Terric might not want his wife going around dressed like that."

She once again found herself speechless by her mother's statement. Jacqueline had not known her mother knew how close they had actually become. She shot a look at Terric, who shook his head to let her know he was just as surprised as she.

Lady Elizabeth clucked her tongue. "Do you think I did not know what went on during Terric's previous stay? Just because I said naught of it does not mean I was oblivious to how you felt about each other."

Jacqueline felt herself furiously blush. "You knew all this time?"

"Of course I did."

"I thought you would be disappointed in me."

"If the circumstances were different, I might have reacted in another manner. What you did helped to protect you from the earl. If he had discovered your ruse, he would not have been able to use you to further his gains. You are no longer a maid, therefore, not so prized as you were in the past."

Her mother was canny, but she had not realized how intuitive she actually was. "What would you have done if Terric had no intentions of marrying me?"

"I would have not allowed what happened to take place. That is irrelevant now. Terric loves you. He will do all in his power to protect you."

Terric, having remained silent during the discussion between Jacqueline and her mother, acknowledged the older woman's praise by bowing his head in her direction. "I am glad to hear you find me acceptable, my lady. Then am I correct in assuming you will allow me to take Jacqueline to wife?"

"Aye, Sir Terric. You may have Jacqueline as your wife. The sooner the better."

The elation Jacqueline felt upon hearing her mother accept Terric quickly changed to concern. "Why the hurry, Mother?"

"Even though your father did not see through you, I still do not trust him. He is a sneaky, conniving man. He could be the one who fooled us all. Not the other way around. The sooner Terric puts a wedding ring on your finger the better I will feel. Even the earl cannot break the vows spoken before a priest."

Jacqueline felt a wave of uneasiness sweep through her.

She hoped her mother's fears would turn out to be unfounded. If it would save her from any malicious plans the earl might have in store for her, she would gladly marry Terric on the morrow.

CHAPTER TWELVE

"If you do not stand still, Jacqueline, I am likely to mortally wound you with these pins," Lady Elizabeth said exasperatedly.

"Sorry, Mother, but you have had me standing here for hours. All the while you have poked and prodded me."

"It has not been hours. You exaggerate. It only seems that way because you have done nothing but fidget. Either you hold still or your wedding gown will not look at all proper."

Jacqueline gritted her teeth and sighed in defeat. Her wedding day was two days hence. Her mother, along with Beth, had been frantically stitching her gown since their return from London the week before. She would have gladly worn a less elaborate one, but she did not have the heart to try to sway the two women into change their minds. They had enthusiastically started to work out the details the day after their return home.

The tight sleeved undergown was made from silk, dyed the color of a cloudless blue sky on a summer day. The looser overtunic was stamped velvet two shades darker blue than the undergown. The pattern was the Montacute coat of arms. The earl had sent the velvet to be used for Jacqueline's gown when she was to have wed the Earl of Somerset. Her mother had suggested they use it now. The reason she gave was that it really was exquisite and why should they not use it for what it had originally been intended. Jacqueline had agreed in the end.

Along with the undergown and overtunic there were tippets, trailing strips of cloth that fastened just above the elbow. They were also made from the same velvet. Around her hips, she would wear a girdle made from gold that had pearls set into each link. Upon her head, she would wear a sheer sky-blue veil, which would be fastened to a point at the center of her forehead.

The two women worked in the solar with the door firmly shut. Her mother did not want Terric seeing Jacqueline in her wedding gown before they were to exchange vows. So when a knock at the door could be heard, she nodded for Beth to see who it was.

Beth opened the door a half inch, then peered out. "Do not bother trying to come in because I will not let you."

Jacqueline heard Terric reply. "I have no intention of stepping into the solar. I have been warned off with dire threats to my person should I do so. I was just wondering if I could have a word with Lady Elizabeth."

Jacqueline's mother joined him at the door. "Sir Terric, I hope this is not a ploy to see Jacqueline's gown."

"I can assure you it is not," he said. "If I remember correctly, you told me you would drop me down that very deep well Carisbrooke is known for."

Lady Elizabeth chuckled. "I would do it."

"There is no need for that well today, my lady. I would like to speak to you, privately, if you can spare a few moments."

Her mother turned to look over her shoulder at Beth and Jacqueline, and asked, "Can you finish without me, Beth?"

The younger girl nodded. "Aye, of course."

"Then I am all yours, Terric."

* * * *

After slipping through the partially open door, Lady Elizabeth led Terric to the chamber next to the solar. It was not quite so large since she only used it to do the castle accounts. The space inside was mostly taken up by a large desk. She walked around it, then seated herself behind it and motioned for Terric to sit in the chair on the opposite side.

Once he had, she waited for him to speak. She had a feeling she knew what he wished to talk to her about. So she waited while he collected his thoughts.

Terric cleared his throat and seemed to force himself to begin. "With the wedding so close, I thought now would be appropriate to broach this subject with you, my lady. It is something I wish I did not have to ask."

Terric seemed on the verge of squirming. "Just spit it out, man. I do not bite, you know."

"Since I have no lands of my own, would you approve of Jacqueline and myself living here at Carisbrooke? I hope in a few years, while I follow the tournament circuit, to be able to purchase some land."

"I had assumed that after your marriage you both would be staying at the castle. It will no longer be necessary for you to follow the circuit."

Terric appeared slightly taken aback at her words. "Living off your good graces for long does not sit well with me."

"Do not worry. You will be earning your keep, Terric. With William now gone, there is no Lord of the Isle here. I wish you to take his place."

"Let me get this straight. You want me, a landless knight, to take over William's duties?"

"Aye, I do. As Jacqueline's husband, you are the only logical choice. It will not be an easy position to fill in the beginning, but I am sure you can learn all you will need to know."

"You do not want me to do the circuit anymore?"

"Nay, I do not. You may participate in a tournament or two, one that is close to the isle if you wish, but only for the sport of it."

Terric smiled and stuck out his hand. "I accept your offer, my lady."

With hands clasped, they shook. Terric stood, sketched a quick bow, then left Lady Elizabeth alone in the chamber.

* * * *

Terric took a deep breath and stared at the clear night sky. The stars flashed like so many diamonds. He still could not believe his good fortune. He had found the woman he had been waiting for to be his wife. Along with a woman who loved him, now he had a place to call home. To be part of a family. Something he had not had for so many years.

His father, Philip Aubrey, was a minor knight with a small holding and already married when Terric's mother, the fair Rosamond, caught his eye. She was the love of his father's life, but sadly, only a peasant. Her family farmed a section of land that belonged to Philip, and they paid him rent to work it.

At first, Philip's intent had not been to make her his mistress. Even though his marriage was a loveless one, it was not his way. Rosamond eventually won him over and they became lovers.

Terric was born a year later. He only had a few short months with his mother—a time of which he had no recollection being only a small babe. His birth had been too hard for her. She never fully recovered and finally succumbed.

Philip already had two sons by his wife—both much older than Terric. That being the case, it was not necessary for him to acknowledge Terric as his son, but he did. He was not able to bring his motherless son to live with him, though. Philip's wife would never have allowed it. So Terric had been raised by his grandparents.

At the age of ten, his father arranged for Terric to be fostered out. Knowing he could not offer much to the son of his love, he did what he could. He took steps to make sure her son became a knight, for which Terric was forever grateful. The life of a farmer had held no appeal for him.

Having made a complete circuit of the walls, Terric descended to the bailey below. He walked toward the keep in the direction of the hall and caught sight of a shadowed figure moving to intercept him. Once it became more discernible, he shook his head in disbelief.

"What are you doing out here so late?"

"I could very well ask you the same question," Jacqueline replied saucily. Before Terric could protest, she wrapped her arms around his neck and brushed a kiss across his lips. He placed his hands on either side of her waist, pulling her hard against him.

"Is it not bad luck to see me? We wed on the morrow."

"Just silly superstition. I needed to see you before I went to sleep. Come morning, mother will make sure we do not meet until the ceremony."

"We did see each other at the evening meal. It has only been a few short hours since we parted. Did you miss me so soon?"

"Of course." Jacqueline smiled seductively, then ran her hands through his hair. "I do not think I can wait until after the ceremony."

Terric groaned. "Are you trying to seduce me, minx?"

Jacqueline rocked her hips against his. "If I am?"

He unwrapped her arms from around his neck, then set her firmly away. "Tempting, but nay. We are going to do this properly."

She stuck out her bottom lip in a pout. "You will not change your mind?"

"Nay. Now go to your bed. Alone." Terric turned Jacqueline around, then pushed her in the direction of the keep, adding a swat to her rump to keep her moving.

Terric waited until Jacqueline disappeared within the building before he followed. He wanted to make sure she was safely in her own chamber. He needed the time to calm down the raging desire she had stirred inside him just by being in his arms. If she were to accost him again, he was not at all sure he could refuse her a second time.

Finally entering the hall, he found it deserted, which was a great relief. On the morrow he would make it up to Jacqueline since he had refused her offer. Once she was his wife, he might never let her out of his bed.

* * * *

The day of their wedding broke in a bright wash of sunlight. Jacqueline could not have wished for a better one. If the blue cloudless sky was considered a good omen for the start of her new life with Terric, then it portended good fortune.

Having followed her mother's strict admonishment of not seeing her intended before exchanging their vows, Jacqueline had not gone to the hall to break her fast. A servant had brought her a tray instead. Now she waited for the heated water for her bath to arrive. She did not have a long wait. Her mother, ever efficient, instructed the servants to prepare it once Jacqueline had sent down her tray.

With a knock, Lady Elizabeth opened the door and stood aside for the parade of servants lined up behind her.

Once the hip bath had been dragged into the room and then filled, the servants were dismissed, leaving Jacqueline and her mother alone. Jacqueline stripped off her robe, then immersed herself in the bath.

Lady Elizabeth went to stand behind her and washed her hair. "I never thought this day would come—the day I saw my daughter marry the man she loved."

Jacqueline wiped water from her eyes. "You no more than I, Mother. Especially after what we had done to stop my marriage to the Earl of Somerset."

"That odious man. With you wed to Terric, you will be safe. Our ruse will no longer be necessary."

Continuing to wash herself, Jacqueline knew her life could very well have been much different if her father had had his way. She would have been tied to a man she thoroughly detested.

Her bath finished, she stepped out of the tub and toweled dry. She donned her robe once more. All that was left to do was to dress in her wedding gown. Jacqueline's nerves were getting the best of her. She did not regret her choice in marrying Terric. If anything, she felt overjoyed by it, but she needed a few minutes alone to collect herself before the ceremony.

"Mother, is there enough time for me to sit by myself for a while?"

Lady Elizabeth smiled. "Not long, but we can work it in." She placed a kiss on Jacqueline's cheek, then left her alone.

Jacqueline sat on the window seat with her back toward the chamber door and looked out the window. Watching the normal goings-on down in the bailey helped to calm her. A warm breeze blew through the open shutters. She closed her eyes and took a deep breath.

At that moment, her chamber door opened. Thinking her mother had returned already, she did not bother to open her eyes. It was a shock to feel the cold blade of a dagger pressed to her throat by someone standing directly behind her. She inhaled sharply.

"Be a good girl and turn around."

Jacqueline felt all the blood drain from her face at the sound of that voice. How could he have gotten into Carisbrooke with no one knowing? Why today, of all days? Doing as she had been ordered, she turned to face her father.

He wore a hooded cloak, which partially hid his face. He pushed the hood back. His sharp gaze swept her from head to toe. "So, I was correct. It was you in London and not William. I did not think you were capable of doing such a thing. Especially since you have been dead and buried these past few years."

Jacqueline raised her chin a notch and gave the earl a defiant look. "You left me no choice."

"The choice was not yours to make. As your father, it was my right to arrange an advantageous match for you."

"You mean an advantageous match for yourself."

The earl reached out and painfully grabbed a handful of her hair. "I will not tolerate any disrespect from you, girl. I see your mother was too lax in her duty in the raising of her daughter." He released his grip and roughly shoved her away. "I want you to put on some clothes and then you are leaving with me."

Jacqueline rubbed her aching scalp, but did not move. "Nay, I will go nowhere with you. Today is my wedding day. I will not leave."

"I am afraid you will. I have plans for you." He picked up her wedding gown from the bed and threw it at her. "Put this on, and if you refuse, I have no compunctions about putting it on you myself if I must."

Her father would do exactly that. She turned her back to him and did what he had said. Once she had donned the gown, she faced him once more. He motioned her to where he stood next to her writing desk.

The earl placed a fresh sheet of parchment on top of it. He took up a quill and dipped it into the ink well. Holding it out to her, he said, "Write."

Jacqueline shook her head. "Nay."

He jabbed the quill at her again. "You will write a missive to your intended, telling him you have changed your mind and no longer wish to wed him." She still refused to comply, and her father forcibly placed the quill in her hand. "If you do not, I will have your mother removed from the isle. I will make her a beggar on the streets with no coin and no roof over her head. Do I make myself clear?"

Meekly, she nodded. Her father held all the power in this situation. She could not change that, but she had one barb in which to wound him. "You have not asked about William. Are you not interested to know why he did not go to London?"

"Anything you have to say about William is irrelevant. Sit."

Jacqueline pulled out the chair and seated herself behind the desk. "True it might be, but it will affect you greatly."

"Then tell me. Do not think I cannot see through this ploy to stall for time. We will be gone before anyone can stop us."

She looked up at her father, wanting to see how he would react to her news. "As you wish. You did more than wound William during the tournament at Windsor. You killed him."

The smug expression the earl wore slipped. Her words seemed to sink in. He appeared deeply affected by the news of William's death. She was certain he had felt no such sorrow when informed of her "death." To him, she was just a useless female—only good for furthering his position through a marriage to a nobleman.

Not able to look at her father's expression of pain any

longer, Jacqueline turned to the blank piece of parchment. The earl swallowed audibly, then said, "Write the missive and make it convincing. For if your lowly knight does not believe it and tries to come after you, I will gladly end his pathetic existence."

Jacqueline dipped the quill into the inkwell before she placed it on the parchment. As she wrote, tears filled her eyes. Terric would never forgive her for this.

CHAPTER THIRTEEN

Terric was nervous. He could face a fully armed knight charging down the list, but the thought of standing in front of a priest, reciting his vows to the woman he loved, was downright terrifying. Having Edwin fuss over him was not making matters better. The boy kept pulling at his tunic, trying to make it sit just so.

Having reached the end of his patience, Terric slapped Edwin's hands away. "Enough, Edwin. If you pull on my tunic any more, you will put a hole in it."

Edwin stepped back and gave Terric a thorough inspection. "I just want you to look perfect is all. You do not get married every day."

"You have done a fine job. Thanks to you, I will not shame Jacqueline by looking scruffy."

How he was attired on this important day was all Edwin's doing. As Lady Elizabeth and her daughter-in-law had labored over Jacqueline's gown, Edwin had been busy selecting what Terric would wear. Though he had few items of clothing, he did have outfits appropriate for the feasts after the tournaments he attended. His squire had gone through it all and personally mended and cleaned the items he had picked.

The tunic was black velvet, embroidered with gold threads along the cuffs, hem, and neck. Even though it was acceptable to have gems sewn onto it as well, Terric was never one to be so ostentatious. His hose was black, along with his boots. The belt strapped around his waist was plain black leather with a gold buckle.

Terric poured himself a goblet of wine, hoping it would help to steady his nerves. He resisted the urge to quaff it down in one large gulp and made himself take a small sip.

After knocking once, a very agitated Lady Elizabeth entered his chamber. The expression upon her face made Terric assume all was not well. He put his goblet down and then stepped closer to her.

"What is wrong, my lady?"

"It is Jacqueline."

Having only heard Jacqueline's name, a flood of worry washed over Terric. In his anxiety, he grabbed Lady Elizabeth by the upper arms and inadvertently squeezed. "What? Is she hurt? Tell me." The older woman cringed, he realized he was hurting her. "My apologies. I did not mean to cause you pain."

Lady Elizabeth rubbed her arms and nodded. "I know you did not. Jacqueline is not injured. At least I hope she is not. It is just...she is missing. She is not in her chamber, and I cannot find her anywhere."

"How can she have disappeared? Could she have gone to the chapel on her own?"

"Nay, I already checked. She was not there."

Unable to accept Jacqueline just having vanished into thin air, Terric brushed past Lady Elizabeth and went to his intended's chamber. Edwin and Lady Elizabeth followed. Seeing the empty chamber gave Terric an eerie feeling. Jacqueline was supposed to be there, happily preparing to pledge her love to him.

He searched her empty chamber, hoping to find a clue

as to her whereabouts. The others joined in the search as well. They soon realized Jacqueline's wedding gown was missing. Presumably, she had it with her. There was no sign of a struggle either. It looked as if she had calmly walked away. Feeling frustrated, Terric sat on the bed, leaving Edwin and Lady Elizabeth to continue the search.

Where could she have gone? He could not see Jacqueline leaving of her own free will. She knew how much he loved her. Now that he thought back on it, Terric sickened as he realized he had not once spoken those very words to her. He would have to rectify that error when they found her.

Leaning back on his arms, one of his hands slipped under a pillow. His knuckles brushed against what felt like a piece of parchment. He grasped it between his fingers and pulled out the folded missive.

Terric opened the stiff paper and read it. The more he read, the more his heart shattered into a million pieces.

His voice held no emotion when he asked, "My lady, is this Jacqueline's handwriting?"

Lady Elizabeth went to the bed and glanced at the piece of parchment Terric held. "Aye, it is. Where did you find it?"

"Under one of her pillows."

"What does it say?"

Terric wadded up the missive in his fist, then jerked to his feet. "More fool I for believing I would be able to keep her. It seems your daughter has had a change of heart."

He threw the balled-up parchment into a corner of the chamber, then stomped out the door.

* * * *

Something was dreadfully wrong, she just knew it. Hoping to get some answers, Beth went in search of her mother-in-law.

She had waited at the chapel after making sure the servants had everything under control for the meal to be served after the wedding ceremony. Sir Guy was the only person to arrive at the appropriate time, which concerned her. As minutes ticked by and still the main participants had not arrived, she decided to see for herself what caused the delay.

Encountering no one in the hall, the feeling that all was not well increased. Only after she entered Jacqueline's chamber and found Lady Elizabeth alone, holding a very crumpled piece of parchment, did she feel the full impact of uneasiness wash over her.

"She is gone, Beth."

"Who? Jacqueline?"

Wearily, Lady Elizabeth nodded in affirmation. "Aye, she has gone. How could she do that to Terric? I never expected her to act in this way. She seemed so happy with him."

"She was…I mean, is. How do you know Jacqueline no longer wants to go through with the wedding?"

The older woman held out the abused parchment for Beth to read. "She wrote this to Terric."

Beth took the missive and read:

Terric,

I cannot marry you this day. I thought I could go through with it, but I cannot bring myself to be tied to a lowly knight for the rest of my life. I do not love you. I never did. You were just a means to an end. Now I have reached that end, making you an inconvenience. Do not look for me. I will only spurn you.

Jacqueline

Shocked, Beth read the missive once again. Even though it was written in Jacqueline's hand, the words did not sound like her own. Jacqueline loved Terric. She would never hurt him so. There had to be a very good reason she would do that, one that made her act so rashly.

"Has Terric seen this?"

"Aye." Lady Elizabeth sighed deeply. "I am afraid it was he who found it. He did not take it very well at all."

The chamber door still stood open, and the sound of heavy booted feet descending the stairs could be easily heard. Beth raced into the hallway in time to see Terric disappear down the flight of stairs.

Edwin, who stood at his master's chamber door, looked crestfallen. He sadly shook his head. "He has ordered me to pack his belongings. We leave this day."

"Where has he gone?"

"To the stables to ready the horses."

Beth picked up her skirts and rushed down the stairs. She did not slow her pace until she reached the stables. She stepped into the building and waited a few moments for her eyes to adjust to the dim interior. Frantically, she searched for any sign of Terric. She did not see him at first glance. It was not until he walked out of a stall, leading his mount did she sigh with relief. He was still there.

He looked her way, but chose to ignore her as he adjusted his saddle. Not at all deterred, Beth went to stand beside him. "She did not leave you, Terric."

He snorted in disbelief. "Funny, but I thought that was exactly what she did. What do you take me for? An idiot?"

"She loves you. You have to believe that."

Terric pushed past her and led his horse into the bailey. Beth followed. She grabbed his arm and pulled him to a halt. "Do not leave. We have to find her."

None too gently, he plucked her restraining hand from his arm. "I have no intention of ever seeing Jacqueline again. She made her feelings perfectly clear in her missive. I am just abiding by her wishes."

"Forget the damn missive! Just answer one question. In any way, has she ever caused you to doubt how she feels about you?"

Terric gave Beth the full force of his anger. "Enough," he said with a snarl. "I will not listen to your nonsense any longer. She has made her choice." He swung a leg up and over his horse's back. "Tell Edwin to meet me at the ferry. I can no longer tolerate being at Carisbrooke. Give Lady Elizabeth my farewell."

After adjusting his reins, Terric walked his horse through the castle gates. Not once did he look back.

CHAPTER FOURTEEN

They had been traveling a few days now, and Jacqueline had no inkling of their destination. Her father had stealthily taken her out of Carisbrooke and then had deposited her into a covered wagon, one he had arranged to have waiting for him. The two men-at-arms who had been sitting atop it were the earl's men. They each wore his livery.

Once she was safely hidden from view, the earl had mounted his horse that had been tied to the back of the wagon. He had given a signal to the two men, and with a slap of the reins, it had lurched into motion.

Alone, Jacqueline had plenty of time to think—of what her father had forced her to do. She hoped Terric realized what she had written was a lie, but a small part of her knew he would not. Why would he? It was not as if she had ever said she loved him. Nor had he spoken those three simple words to her either.

The more time she dwelled on it, the more insecure she became about how Terric actually felt about her. Maybe he was happy she was gone. He could go back to the tournament circuit, free to flirt with all the available women who flocked to him wherever he went.

As the days went by and no one came to rescue her from the earl, Jacqueline felt her ponderings were more than just mere thoughts but actual truth. Terric was not coming. He was glad to be rid of her.

Feeling as if her worst fears were confirmed, Jacqueline grew morose. Where her father was taking her was no longer important. For if Terric no longer wanted her, life was meaningless. It mattered not what became of her. So when her father told her their destination, she could only feel it fitting. This would be the last humiliation. First, Terric's betrayal by not coming in search of her and now this. The earl was taking her to Nunney Castle, the home of Forwin De La Mare, the Earl of Somerset.

* * * *

The last night before they were to arrive at Nunney Castle, the earl led his party to an inn in a small market town. Since they would be reaching their destination on the morrow, he wanted Jacqueline to look presentable, which could not be accomplished by spending the night sleeping out under the stars.

Jacqueline, so deeply sunk in her own misery, barely noticed the inn into which her father escorted her. The only reason she spared it a passing glance was the name of it. The Happy Bride. She could not help but sneer up at it. She was anything but that.

The earl paid the innkeeper for the two rooms he requested, then the man led them to the inn's upper floor. The room to which she was taken was sparse, but it seemed clean enough.

After the innkeeper returned below stairs, the earl finally divulged his plans. "As you know, we will reach Nunney on the morrow. You will be respectful to Forwin. He is to be your husband. I want him to see what an obedient wife you will make him. He has graciously overlooked what transpired before."

Only half-listening to what he told her, Jacqueline sat on the bed. There was no point in responding to the earl's dictates so she remained silent. As the silence stretched between them, her father continued. "This door will be locked from the outside. I will be in the room next to this one. As well, one of my men will be standing guard just outside. So do not even bother to try to leave." He headed for the door, but added one last demand. "I want you ready at first light." He left her alone.

She had no idea how long she sat on the bed, staring at nothing. It only seemed a matter of minutes from the time of the earl's departure until someone knocked on her room door. Once she bid them to enter, it opened to admit one of her father's men, carrying a tray of food. He placed it on the small table next to the bed, then promptly exited. The lock turned on the other side.

She lifted the cloth that covered the tray and found a meat pie along with a couple of thick slices of cheese and a tankard of ale. She picked up the tray, then placed it on the bed before her and methodically ate.

The fare was simple but well-prepared. After finishing every last morsel, Jacqueline returned the tray to the small side table. She stripped off her gown to her chemise and looked at the state of her only garment. It showed the wear from days of travel. There was nothing she could do to remedy that, but she made use of the water provided in her room. She quickly washed some of the dirt from her body.

Jacqueline slipped between the bedsheets and hoped sleep would claim her. Surprisingly, it did come easily, and with it came a dream.

In it, Terric held her in his arms. He kissed her, holding nothing back. She kissed him in return with all the pent-up passion that had built inside her. She desperately clung to his muscular frame, afraid to let go. Afraid he would disappear and she would lose him forever. The dream shifted. One moment he was passionately kissing her, then the next he stood at a very great distance away. Jacqueline tried to reach him, but each step she took the farther away he seemed. In frustration, she called to him. He turned his back on her, moving into the thickening mist, which enveloped them. Before he disappeared completely, he spoke. His voice was muffled, but what he said turned her dream into a nightmare. He told her he could never love her. He could never forgive her for what she had done. With tears streaming down her face, she screamed his name, but it was no use. He still walked away, leaving her to mourn the loss of him.

Jerking awake, Jacqueline realized there were tears on her cheeks. She roughly wiped them away, then looked about the room, trying to get her bearings. Nothing had changed. She was still in the small rented chamber and Terric was not there to take her away.

She noticed the faint light seeping through the curtain-covered window. Dawn had come. The earl would be fetching her soon. Before this day came to a close, she would be facing her real-life nightmare.

* * * *

Forwin had been expecting them, which did not surprise Jacqueline in the least. Her father would have arranged this meeting prior to taking her from her home. If Forwin had not been agreeable to the idea of making a match with her, the earl would have left her alone. Until another prospect presented itself, that is. Why expend energy on a useless cause?

Standing in the hall of Nunney Castle, Jacqueline held herself stiffly while Forwin circled her. As he poked her here and there, she bit her lower lip until she tasted blood.

The urge to slap his face was great, but she was no fool. Any defiance on her part would be dealt with swiftly by the earl.

Forwin, seemingly satisfied with what he saw, nodded. "I find her acceptable."

Smiling, the earl said, "She is yours then. I presume you have made the proper arrangements?"

"Aye, all is at the ready. The priest will perform the ceremony on the morrow."

"Excellent." The earl rubbed his hands together, apparently very pleased. "Now all that is left to do is sign the marriage contracts. If you can arrange a chamber for my daughter, we can get down to business."

Forwin gave Jacqueline one last licentious glance, then clapped his hands. A young servant girl entered the hall a second later.

"Alice, take the Lady Jacqueline to her chamber."

Meekly, the girl nodded, then not waiting to see if Jacqueline followed, she crossed the hall to the stairway. Quite happy to be out of Forwin's presence, Jacqueline hurried to catch up.

The chamber was sumptuously appointed. A beautifully crafted writing desk was placed beneath the only window set high in one of the walls. The bed sat upon a raised dais. Its hangings were heavy velvet, colored dusty-rose. A matching cover was spread across the mattress.

The mental picture of what could possibly happen in that bed caused Jacqueline to shiver. If Forwin tried to consummate their marriage, she would fight him to the bitter end.

After making a full circle around the chamber, Jacqueline walked back to the waiting Alice. The young servant girl kept her gaze downcast. She was young. She seemed no older than three and ten, if that. Her fine brown hair was pulled back in a single braid, which fell to her waist. Her brown serviceable gown was made from homespun and looked as if it had been made for a much larger woman. It hung on her frame so loosely there was no way to determine the shape of her body.

The girl would not acknowledge her presence. Jacqueline asked, "Your name is Alice?"

Startled, the servant girl jumped at the sound of her voice, which did not go unnoticed by Jacqueline. "Aye, my lady."

"What are your duties in the castle?"

Still keeping her eyes adverted, Alice answered, "I used to work in the kitchen, but now I am to be your maid. If you find me acceptable."

There was a slight tremor in the girl's voice when she had spoken. It was not hard to guess what would befall Alice if she was found unworthy.

Thinking it best to lay the girl's fears to rest, Jacqueline said, "I will not reject you as my maid. It will be a learning experience for the both of us. You see, I have always made do for myself."

Alice lifted her gaze to meet Jacqueline's. Her eyes were hazel. "Thank you, my lady."

Jacqueline smiled and received a timid smile in return. She had an ally now in the form of this young girl. She would not have to be totally alone, after all.

* * * *

As dawn broke over the horizon, it heralded the end of her freedom. For after the short ceremony that would be performed in the chapel, she would no longer be her own woman. She would be classed as chattel, a possession Forwin owned and could use as he saw fit. The thought sickened her.

A soft tapping on the chamber door forced Jacqueline to come to grips with what would happen to her this day.

She sat up in bed and bade the person on the other side to enter.

Alice walked into her chamber with the gown her mother had made for her marriage to Terric. The servant girl had taken it away the evening before. She obviously had cleaned it.

"Time to get up, my lady. Your father will come for you soon. He bade me to tell you to wear this gown again."

Jacqueline easily guessed the motive behind his request. What better way to remind her of all she had lost? He hoped to hurt her, make it a punishment for choosing to live her life as she wanted. He failed, though. It would not hurt her to wear the gown. It would be her cross to bear. Her penance for writing all those hurtful words to Terric.

During the long night she had done a lot of thinking. It was her words that had pushed Terric from her. He had not seen past them, had not trusted her enough to call them false. Now she had to pay the price by being locked in a loveless marriage to a man she detested.

Accepting the inevitable, Jacqueline arose and let Alice help her prepare for her wedding. There was no feeling of joy as there had been when she was to have wed Terric. If it had been possible, she would have worn mourning clothes.

After her father came to fetch her, the rest of the day's happenings seemed to blur and run together.

During the ceremony, she stood beside Forwin and dutifully repeated her vows, not really paying close attention to the words. The feel of him sliding his ring upon her finger caused her a moment of clarity before she receded back into herself.

The wedding feast was a very small affair. The people present were Jacqueline, Forwin, and the earl. Forwin had no living family and was the last of his line. If, at his death, he produced no heir, his title and lands would revert back to the crown, hence, his need for a new wife after the death of each of the previous ones. He had tried to produce that elusive heir again and again.

The meal complete, Forwin summoned Alice to escort Jacqueline to her chamber. Jacqueline knew what was to come. With leaden feet, she followed the younger girl up the stairs, feeling as if she walked to her execution.

After helping Jacqueline remove her gown, Alice put her into bed and then left, leaving Jacqueline alone await her fate. She prayed it would be over swiftly.

CHAPTER FIFTEEN

The roar of the crowd echoed in Terric's ears. He let the sound wash over him. With a kick of his heels, he set his steed into motion. He barreled down the list, then had the satisfaction of his lance hitting his opponent's shield.

A loud clang came behind him. Terric peered over his shoulder to find the knight he rode against lying in the dust on his back. That would be another ransom he would collect this day. Having faced his last challenger, Terric headed to his pavilion. Edwin had run ahead and awaited him there.

Terric stepped into his pavilion. He gratefully unlaced his helm and pulled it free. He reached up and wiped the sweat from his brow. He noticed the cloaked figure of a woman who watched him. The hood of her cloak was pulled up over her head, shielding her face from view. An instant of excitement shot through him as he thought it was Jacqueline, but he soon realized this woman was not tall enough for it to be her.

"Whoever you are, leave." He turned his back on the woman and unbuckled his armor.

"I have no intention of leaving until you have listened to what I have to say."

Terric jerked back around as the woman pulled off the hood she wore and revealed her face. He shook his head in amazement. "Why am I not surprised?"

Beth closed the short distance between them. "You never gave me a chance to speak before you left Carisbrooke. I do not give up so easily."

"Obviously. What do you want from me?"

"For you to listen to me. That is all."

Terric threw back his head and groaned, then stared back at her. "There is nothing you can say that will change how I feel about Jacqueline. She made her choice."

"In that assumption, I think you are wrong. Jacqueline loves you. She told me so herself."

Terric intently searched Beth's face. Her expression said she meant every word she had spoken. "I once thought she did, but I am not so sure of that anymore."

"She does, I know it. Jacqueline looked at you the way I looked at William. I loved him with all my heart. Do not turn from her. You could come to regret this decision later."

"How do you explain the words she wrote?"

Pleadingly, Beth said, "You have to see past them as I did. She wrote them to protect you. To keep you away from something."

"To protect me from what?"

"Not a what, but a who. I believe the earl will be found at the bottom of all this. It bears his stench."

"I thought he had no idea it was Jacqueline in London."

"As far as we knew he did not, but that does not mean we were right. He is quite capable of letting us go on with our plans, all the while knowing the truth. Then at an opportune moment, he used it against us."

It was true, Terric realized. What he had seen and heard of the earl was not very awe-inspiring. The man was a snake, using all within his power to further his own gains. What Beth suggested could quite possibly have happened to Jacqueline. It was not too hard to believe.

If that was what really had happened to her, then he had already made a grave mistake. He had abandoned the woman he loved to the clutches of a man who could make her life unbearable.

"Will you help us look for her?" Beth asked.

Terric nodded. "Aye, you have convinced me. I can only hope when we find Jacqueline she forgives my stupidity."

* * * *

This trip to Carisbrooke Castle Terric faced with mixed emotions. Besides being the place where he'd last had seen Jacqueline and what had happened on what was to have been their wedding day, he felt some misgivings about seeing Lady Elizabeth. She had believed in him, and he had let her down.

He peered at Lady Beth, who rode next to him, and found her watching him while a slight smiled played upon her lips. The two men-at-arms who had accompanied her rode a short distance behind them.

"What?"

Beth shook her head. "I can practically hear you berating yourself. Stop it. You were hurting. You took what you felt was the correct course of action."

Terric grunted. "You mean I let my pride get the better of me and I ran away."

"That is not what I meant."

"I only wish I had listened to you that day. Jacqueline would be at Carisbrooke now."

"There is no point beating yourself up about it, Terric. You made a mistake, but you can redeem yourself."

Edwin, who rode directly behind them, broke into the

conversation. "You tell him, Lady Beth. I am sick and tired of his moping about."

Terric turned in his saddle and shot Edwin a quelling look. "That will be enough out of you."

Edwin chose to ignore the warning and edged his horse between Terric and Beth. "I told him we should return to Carisbrooke, but he would not listen to me."

Having heard enough of his squire's criticisms, Terric let his horse slowly fall back from the other two. With Edwin still off on his ranting, Terric gathered up his reins and slapped his squire's horse on the rump.

The horse shot off as if all the demons from hell nipped at its heels. The look on Edwin's face was quite comical. He had been in mid-sentence when his mount took off at a gallop. One moment he conversed with Beth, then the next he hollered as his horse shot down the road.

Terric moved his horse back up alongside Beth and smugly smiled. She wagged a finger at him. "Naughty, naughty, Terric."

"He had it coming. I did give him fair warning."

Beth laughed, then looked up the road. Edwin's horse was still in mad flight. "Should you not help him?"

"Nay." Terric said. "Trying to bring his mount back under control will keep him from wagging his tongue. Plus, it gives me a chance to speak to you alone."

"Well, you have me all to yourself. For the moment, at least."

"I just thought I would ask if Lady Elizabeth is upset with me. She has every right to be."

Beth reached over and reassuringly patted Terric's hand. "That is not the case at all. She will be most pleased at your return."

Terric breathed a sigh of relief. "I have much respect for that lady. I would not like to displease her."

They broke off their conversation as Edwin came pounding back down the road toward them. He seemed completely flustered and out of sorts. He pulled up in front of them and shot Terric a disgusted look.

"What is wrong, Edwin? All not well with your mount?" Terric asked nonchalantly.

"As if you had nothing to do with it," Edwin replied with a sneer.

Beth interrupted. "Edwin, why do you not ride on my other side? That way you will be safe from Terric. I suggest you be a little more circumspect with your comments."

Properly chastised, Edwin nodded and moved to where Beth indicated. The rest of the day he wisely kept his mouth shut.

* * * *

The following day they arrived at Carisbrooke. Terric felt as if he had come home — something he would not have expected. All the time he had spent there had not added up to much.

Sir Guy, who had been up on the castle walls, must have noticed their arrival and met them in the bailey. He hurriedly helped Beth dismount. "I see your quest was a successful one, lass." He gaze rested pointedly on Terric.

"Aye, very. It did take some doing to convince him, though. Now he is calling himself three times a fool for not thinking of it on his own. See to them and I will inform Lady Elizabeth of Terric's arrival."

Terric took up his mount's reins and led it to the stables. "So the time of reckoning has arrived."

Sir Guy chuckled. "Nay, lad, more like a time for rejoicing. My lady will be most pleased. Let us get these horses bedded down. We should not keep the ladies waiting."

* * * *

Sir Guy, Terric, and Edwin sipped from tankards of ale when the two women descended from the solar.

Coming to greet her guests, Lady Elizabeth gave Terric, and the startled Edwin, a kiss of peace on the cheeks. "I am so glad to see the both of you again."

Terric found himself deeply touched by the warm welcome. "As I am to see you once more, my lady. I just wish it was for better reasons that I returned."

"Nonsense," Lady Elizabeth said. "You being here gives me renewed hope. You will give us the added advantage we need to discover Jacqueline's whereabouts."

"That is my hope."

"I know so. You can go where we cannot. Finding where the earl is should be our first priority. Tournaments will be the perfect place for you to ascertain where to locate him as they are always rife with court gossip."

Terric nodded. "The next tournament is in a few days. I can start searching for the earl then."

While they spoke, the servants had laid out a light midday repast. Lady Elizabeth brought the conversation to a close. "I suggest you take advantage of your few days of respite from the list and rest." She motioned them toward the trestle table. "Now let us enjoy this meal. There will be time enough later to make all the necessary plans."

Allowing Lady Elizabeth to link her arm through his, Terric let himself be led to the table.

* * * *

Nunney Castle was built in the small Somerset village of Nunney some three miles south-west from the market town of Frome. From Sir Guy's teachings, Jacqueline knew the castle was designed in a French style rather than solely for defensive purposes. A tall four-story rectangular structure with large corner turrets surrounded by a moat made up the castle form. The moat was known for being one of the deepest ever made, which was a landmark for the castle as Carisbrooke's deep well was to it. As such, they had deemed it unnecessary to have a portcullis.

Jacqueline had been living at Nunney for a month. Surprisingly, she settled into her new life. She found she had a talent for the running of such a large household. Not all of her mother's lessons had fallen on deaf ears, or so it would seem.

Since her father's departure the morning after her marriage, she had been virtually left to her own devices. Her husband had nothing to do with her.

The wedding night she had so dreaded ended up being very uneventful. Forwin had not come to her chamber that night, or any since. For a man who had only married her so she could provide him with an heir, he was set on avoiding her. He kept to his chamber, even taking all his meals there.

On this morn Jacqueline walked to the ground floor where the kitchen was located. It was what she did every day. Not wanting to take her meals alone in the hall, she ate in the kitchen.

At first, the servants had been aghast that the countess would lower herself in such a way, but Jacqueline soon won them over. At Carisbrooke, she had never used her station in life to belittle those beneath her. Once the servants at Nunney realized she only wished to have their friendship, they readily welcomed her into their fold.

After reaching the kitchen, Jacqueline stood at the threshold and watched the bustling activity. The thirteen-foot fireplace was already roaring, heating the wall ovens beside it. Cook would have been awake for hours, preparing the bread to be baked for the day.

Jacqueline stepped into the warm room and took a deep breath, smelling the scent of fresh-baked bread. The cook, Mabel, was a large woman of middle years. She managed a well-run kitchen. Today, she had all those who worked under her moving at a brisk pace, which was not usually the norm.

"Mabel, why this flurry of activity?"

Mabel looked up from the worktable where she busily chopped vegetables and smiled warmly. "Your lord husband sent word down this morn. He is expecting a visitor. He wants a grand feast made for the evening meal."

Jacqueline was a little dismayed that Forwin expected a guest. He would, of course, be leaving his chamber now. "It must be someone important for him to order a feast."

Mabel snorted disgustedly. "Not likely. It is just a minstrel my lord has here to entertain him. He comes once a month. If you ask me, he is received better than a minstrel should, but my lord will have it no other way."

Intrigued, Jacqueline asked, "How long has this minstrel been coming here?"

"Ever since my lord's last wife passed. It must be four years."

Jacqueline pulled a stool up to the worktable and accepted the plate of bread and cheese Mabel handed her. Lost in thought, she started to eat.

When a minstrel arrived at a castle, it was usually marked as a festive occasion. Visits could be few and far between, but to have the same one come to a castle once a month was far from the norm. Jacqueline had to wonder if there was more to this visit than just a minstrel coming to entertain the lord of the castle. This evening could very well prove interesting.

* * * *

Forwin left his chamber shortly before his guest was due to arrive. Finding Jacqueline already present in the hall, he called to her. "Come to me, wife."

She gritted her teeth and stepped away from the table

where she had been overseeing the setting and walked to Forwin. He stood a few paces away, observing her. "My lord?"

Before he spoke again, he took the time to look at her. He nodded. "The guest I am expecting, I want you to treat with the utmost respect. I will not tolerate any mistreatment of him by your hand. Do you understand me?"

"Aye, my lord."

"Good. The man is Nicholas Talbot. He will entertain us after the feast, and then you may retire to your chamber."

"As you wish."

Forwin waved her away. Jacqueline eagerly complied. She had no inclination to be in his company any further than she had to be.

She saw to the last-minute details before the minstrel arrived as Forwin paced. His anticipation was palpable. She noticed something else. He had changed in the last couple of weeks, and not for the better.

His face, usually flushed and pasty, was now sickly white. Each breath he took seemed to rasp in his chest. Occasionally, Forwin would rub his left arm as if it pained him. It was all too apparent that her husband was a very ill man.

Nicholas Talbot made his grand entrance a short time later. He fawned over Forwin the instant he clapped eyes on him. Jacqueline found it as sickening a display of currying favor as she ever had seen. He went so far as to take Forwin by the elbow and assist him in sitting at the lord's chair. What surprised her the most, though, was that Forwin allowed this.

Being ignored by both men, Jacqueline used it to her advantage and took a closer look at their guest. The minstrel was exceptionally handsome. She had to give him that. He had blond shoulder-length hair and flashing gray eyes. He stood around six feet and had a well-toned body—broad shouldered and with enough muscles in his legs to show off the hose he wore. A well-defined jaw, straight nose, and nicely sculpted lips completed the package.

Now that he was comfortably seated, Forwin motioned for Jacqueline to come to him. "Nicholas, this is my new wife, Jacqueline Montacute. Her father is the Earl of Salisbury."

Nicholas took her hand and brushed a lingering kiss upon it. "An honor to meet you, my lady. I look forward to getting to know you better."

Jacqueline snatched her hand away and then wiped it on the skirt of her gown. She did not at all like the knowing smile the minstrel wore.

Not missing what she had done, Nicholas chuckled. "I see the lady has a mind of her own." He turned back to Forwin. "Do you think you can handle such a one as she, my lord?"

Forwin smiled. "Have no fear, my friend. I know how to control her. What do you think of her?"

Nicholas turned his attention back to Jacqueline and nodded. "You chose well, my lord. I find her very agreeable."

"Good, good. Now let us eat, then you can entertain us."

Not taking his gaze from Jacqueline's face, the minstrel replied, "As always, my lord. I will do my best."

Jacqueline shivered. She had a very strong suspicion the minstrel was not just talking about his planned performance that evening.

CHAPTER SIXTEEN

The evening left Jacqueline feeling even more confused as to what went on between Forwin and Nicholas. That there *was* something going on, she felt was a given. There were double meanings in most of the words that passed between them. A few sly looks sent her way by both men made the hairs on the back of her neck stand on end.

It was not until after she had been dismissed did she finally begin to relax. Sitting on her bed dressed in a nightgown, she brushed out her hair. Even though it was only shoulder-length, the strokes of her brush helped to calm her nerves. Something was afoot, and it was only a matter of time before Forwin made his move. Jacqueline just hoped it would happen soon.

Having expected something had been planned, it was no great surprise when her chamber door was thrown open by Forwin. Once he stepped inside, Nicholas followed in his wake.

Forwin's pallor was, if anything, worse. There now was a grayish tinge to his face. "The time has come for you to do your duty, my dear. I want an heir, and you are going to give me one."

Instinctively, Jacqueline inched across the bed until her back came up against the headboard. "I will fight you. I will not allow you to lay one finger upon me."

Her husband laughed. "Put your fears to rest. It will not be I who touches your lovely body, but Nicholas. Do you not find him appealing?"

Her gaze shot to Nicholas' face. He smiled. "What...what do you mean?"

"If I do not produce an heir, my lands could revert to the crown. I will be damned if I let that happen. So Nicholas and I have reached an agreement. He will do what I am no longer able to. I will claim the child he gets from you as mine."

"My father must not know of your plans. If he did, he would never have given me to you."

"Of course he does not. I am no fool. I let your father believe what he wanted. He thinks I will give my lands to him."

Shocked, Jacqueline quietly asked, "What did he ask you to do?"

"He had me sign a will bequeathing my lands to you. If I did not accept and do what he wanted, he would never have allowed our marriage to take place."

So that was what the earl would gain by her marriage to Forwin. The man's greed knew no bounds. "You have no intention of letting that happen, do you, my lord?

Forwin nodded. "Smart girl. Your father will never claim my lands as his. He thinks he has me under his boot, but he does not. I have drawn up another will. In this one, I leave all my lands to your child."

Jacqueline put her hand over her mouth, trying to hold back the laughter, which bubbled up inside her, but she could not control it. As she laughed uncontrollably, the two men in the chamber stared at her as if she had lost her sanity, which made her laugh all the harder.

Forwin took her by the shoulders and shook her until she ceased her outburst. "What is wrong with you, girl? This is no laughing matter."

Jacqueline broke free from Forwin's grasp. "Did my father promise you a maiden bride?"

Forwin narrowed his eyes. "Aye, he did."

She chuckled, the laughter once again threatening to rise to the surface. "Well, he lied. I am no longer a maid. My father stole me from the man I love on the day we were to wed. So you see, my lord, I could very well already be with child."

Forwin had not been expecting that bit of information. He appeared speechless. Nicholas looked equally shocked. Jacqueline bet he pictured all the wealth he was to gain turning to dust.

"I hate my father. Not only has he destroyed my only chance of happiness, he killed my brother. My twin. I feel nothing but revulsion for him. It makes me extremely happy to see he is finally going to be denied something he wants."

Forwin finally seemed to come to his senses. "What should we do about this? What if you are not with child?"

"Then I will submit to Nicholas."

Forwin reached out and grabbed her by the chin, forcing Jacqueline to look him in the eyes. "If you are not truthful, my girl, I promise it will not go easy for you. If you prove not to be with child and try to thwart me, I will personally hold you down as Nicholas has his way with you. For however long it takes."

After delivering his final threat, Forwin motioned for Nicholas to follow him and then he quit the chamber. Once the door shut tightly behind them, Jacqueline breathed a heavy sigh of relief.

That had not been an enjoyable experience, but she had gained valuable information. All had been revealed to her. Her father's well-laid plan was falling apart.

She crawled under the covers, thinking. She had been only trying to put Forwin off when she had told him she could be with child, but reflecting back to the last time she had been with Terric, she realized it could very well be a great possibility. She was late, something that had never happened to her before. So despondent about what her father had done to her, she had not been paying attention to the passing of weeks.

Jacqueline placed her hand on her belly and gave it a gentle caress. She prayed Terric's child was indeed growing inside her. She would have a part of him to cherish. It would be her salvation. Forwin would not be able to touch her then.

* * * *

Terric cursed the earl for his ability to cover his tracks so well. Each time he left the isle in search of the man, he came up against a dead end. The earl was not at any of his residences, nor had he made an appearance at any of the tournaments in which Terric had participated.

Lady Elizabeth was not happy with Terric's decision to still go to every tournament in the circuit. She had felt he wasted precious time that could be better used in searching for Jacqueline. He did not agree. Tournaments were the ideal place to hear the latest gossip, as they had agreed upon. Since the earl was a powerful man, he definitely garnered more attention from the gossip mongers. They had to find the earl first, and foremost, be absolutely sure he was the one who had indeed taken Jacqueline. Terric could not think of another way that would provide that information faster.

Though he was now convinced the earl was responsible, he still had some nagging doubts, but he kept them from Lady Elizabeth. She would be very disappointed in him if she ever found out.

He had yet again returned from a tournament with no leads whatsoever. Not relishing the idea of telling Lady Elizabeth of his failure once again, Terric slowly pushed open the hall doors. To his surprise, the hall was empty.

He walked to the stairs and detected the faint sound of voices coming from above. Figuring it was best to face the music now rather than later, he climbed the steps.

The voices came from the solar. Lady Elizabeth and Sir Guy seemed to be having a much-heated argument about something. As Terric entered the solar, they fell silent.

"I am sorry, my lady, but my luck has run out once more. I found nothing."

Lady Elizabeth sadly shook her head. "Sit down, Terric. We have had some news during your absence."

It was not good, Terric surmised. Hoping to allay some of his fears, he turned to look at Sir Guy. The older man jerkily shook his head.

Terric braced himself for the worst possible news and focused his attention upon Lady Elizabeth. "I think I will keep standing, if you do not mind. Tell me what you know."

"The earl has sent us a missive, informing us where Jacqueline is."

"And?"

"It seems my husband was not fooled by Jacqueline's performance in London, after all. As such, he took her and married her to Forwin, the Earl of Somerset."

An acute wave of pain washed over him. Terric should have expected this, but even if he had been, the pain he felt now, it would not be any less. "Then it is over."

Lady Elizabeth rose to her feet and adamantly shook her head. "I refuse to let this go. I want you to go to Nunney Castle and find out if what my husband says is true."

"Nay, send Sir Guy in my place."

Her voice rose in anger as Lady Elizabeth shot back,

"For a brave man such as yourself, Terric, you seem to run away when life is not to your liking. Are you going to leave Jacqueline alone again? I can only assume your feelings for my daughter were never true."

"What would you have me do? Is it not enough that I am already suffering from the loss of Jacqueline? Must you increase my pain by making me see her as the wife of another?"

Sir Guy spoke when they fell silent. "I think my lady is thinking more of what the lass must be going through, lad. If it is at all possible, I know Jacqueline would rather have you go to her than my old self."

Terric rubbed his hands over his face and sighed. "All right, I will go to Nunney, but I have a feeling I will not like what I find there."

"You might not, lad, but at least you will know if it is the truth or not."

CHAPTER SEVENTEEN

Much to Jacqueline's relief, her suspicions were correct. She was indeed carrying Terric's baby. The village midwife had confirmed it. Even though Forwin's plan did not go as he had exactly pictured, he was still quite pleased with the end result. Especially since he was running out of time.

Forwin was extremely ill, and it seemed unlikely that he would live to see her child born. That made Jacqueline fear greatly for the baby growing inside her, but her husband apparently had thought of every possible contingency.

Now that she was already with child, there was no need for Nicholas, or so Jacqueline had thought. Much to her dismay, though, her husband did not send the minstrel on his way.

The child she carried gave her a small measure of control over her life once more. She was left alone, Forwin only demanding she come to his chamber each afternoon. She assumed to make sure she had not run during the night. There really was no other reason for her to be there. She dreaded each sojourn she had to make to his chamber. Even though he was ill, she still disliked the man. They had reached an even accord, which was something more than they had had before.

One day, like every other day, Nicholas was with Forwin. Her husband was unable to leave his bed, and the minstrel had taken on the role of nursemaid. He was never far away from his charge.

Jacqueline pulled a chair close to the bed as Nicholas propped Forwin up with some pillows. "How are you this day, my lord?"

"How do you think, you silly fool? I am dying," Forwin answered grumpily.

Thinking the rest of her stay would progress the same way as all the other of her visits, Jacqueline did not expect Forwin to actually want to speak with her alone. He usually ignored her most days.

Forwin motioned Nicholas away from his bedside. "Leave us. I wish to speak to my wife." Nicholas stood his ground, and Forwin snapped, "Do as I say. Leave."

Nicholas hesitated for a brief second, but he left the chamber. Once alone, her husband enlightened her as to the new plan he had devised.

"I have been thinking about what steps can be taken to keep your child safe from your father," he said. "More importantly, to keep my lands safe."

Jacqueline braced herself, having a feeling it would not be at all to her liking. "What have you decided to do?"

"When I am gone, you will marry Nicholas. He will protect my lands, especially with you offered as the prize."

"I refuse."

Forwin's face turned an alarming shade of purplish red. "How dare...how dare you go against me? You will do as I order you."

Jacqueline shook her head. "Nay, I will not."

Her words worsened his condition. He wheezed and clutched his chest.

"I suggest you calm down, my lord. If not, you will

expire this very moment." After Forwin brought himself back under control, Jacqueline continued. "The days that I will allow myself to be coerced into another unwanted marriage are over. There is nothing you can do to me. Now or after you are gone. The only reason I stay is because it will hurt my father. If I need protection, I can easily attain it. In the form of the father of my baby."

Able to speak now without wheezing, Forwin asked, "Who is this man?"

"That, my lord, is none of your business. Let me just say he is a much better man than Nicholas."

Forwin scowled. "Nicholas will not be pleased. I have already given him my word."

Jacqueline laughed. "I cannot see such a powerful man as yourself letting a mere minstrel dictate to you."

His voiced laced with indignation, Forwin said vehemently, "He does not!" He spoke in a more thoughtful tone. "He does need to be rewarded for his loyalty."

"Give him a large amount of gold and send him on his way."

He seemed to take some time to consider what she had suggested. "I can see you are not some insipid miss. You will only do what you wish. I will give Nicholas the gold you have suggested, but he stays here until I am gone. Though he plays the part of being loyal to me, I still do not fully trust him."

She had to admit she was a little shocked by Forwin's admission. "You have taken an awful chance involving him in your plans."

He shrugged. "In a man of his caliber, it is expected. He can easily be bought." Forwin eased himself back down. "Leave me. I suggest you say not a word of this conversation to Nicholas. I would hate to see you come to harm."

Happy to be dismissed, Jacqueline left the chamber. She had much to think about.

* * * *

Nicholas grew impatient. Forwin was not expiring fast enough for his liking. The old fool just seemed to linger on and on. With each visit from the young chit who was his wife, he seemed to will himself to live another day. Nicholas did not like it one bit. The time had come to help matters along.

He looked down at Forwin's sleeping form. It could be so easy. If he wanted this over here and now, there was no one who could stop him. All he had to do was take one of the many pillows on the bed and place it over Forwin's face. The old man would be unable to dislodge him, but that would make the end come too quickly. It would not do to draw suspicion to himself.

Nay, that was not a possibility. Tonight, when Forwin's evening meal was brought up to him, Nicholas would make his move. He would increase the dose of the poison he slowly fed Forwin.

Of course the fools who lived there had no inkling of what he was about. They were all so trusting, or his acting abilities were better than he had originally thought. Even Forwin had been easily taken in by his charade. He did everything Nicholas suggested, even before he had married Jacqueline.

The woman was not so easily fooled, and Forwin seemed to listen to her more than he did to him these days. So far, she had changed the direction of his plans, but he would not allow her to mess them up any further. He had invested too much to let it slip through his fingers.

* * * *

Jacqueline had feared the worst when her father had brought her to Nunney, but this new life, though not one of her choosing, was tolerable.

She had found friendship and allies among the castle staff. The kitchen became the central hub of life at Nunney, at least for herself. She avoided the part of the castle where Forwin resided as much as she possibly could, except for her daily visits with him, of course. The ever-present Nicholas made her extremely uncomfortable. He had done nothing menacing, but having him watch her every move made her skin crawl. The man damn well knew it.

On this particular day, Jacqueline decided not to give Nicholas the upper hand. When she had to be in his presence, she would just simply ignore the man. Entering the kitchen, she received a warm greeting from Mabel.

"How are you this day, my lady?"

"Very well, Mabel."

The cook smiled and shook her head. "You are lucky. When I carried all of mine, I was sick as a dog in the beginning." Mabel had four sons, all working in various positions within the castle.

"I suppose I am."

Jacqueline went to the worktable and took some of the bread dough Mabel worked and kneaded it. "Has Nicholas been down yet today?"

The cook sneered in disgust. "Nay, which pleases me. I have had enough of that one's demands. The way he struts around here you would think he was master of Nunney."

Jacqueline could not agree more. Nicholas already acted as though Nunney were his. So much he knew. "Aye, he does, but for now, he is harmless."

Mabel shot her a questioning look. "What exactly do you mean by that? We all know there is more than one reason that knave is still here. He cannot be looking after our lordship out of the goodness of his heart. That minstrel does not own one."

Jacqueline punched the dough down with more force than needed for the task and remained silent. She hoped

Mabel would let the subject be, but the cook was not quite ready to give up just yet.

"My lady...Jacqueline, all of us who work in the castle know there is more going on. More than Nicholas' scheming, and that you are mixed up in it." Mabel placed her hands atop Jacqueline's, stilling her movements. "We know your baby is not your husband's as well."

Jacqueline clenched her hands into fists and brought her gaze up to look at Mabel. Worry was etched on the cook's face. "No fear, Mabel. The baby is not Nicholas'. I was already pregnant when I first came to Nunney."

"What happened?"

Jacqueline brushed the flour off her hands and seated herself on a stool. "It is a long story. To put it simply, my father stole me away on the very day I was to wed another."

"Oh, child." Mabel wrapped Jacqueline in a motherly embrace. "Men and their schemes. Well, once Forwin is gone, you can get your man back."

"Mabel!" Jacqueline said laughingly.

"I only speak the truth. As a widow, you will gain your independence. You can wed whomever you wish."

As Mabel returned to the task of bread making, Jacqueline mulled over what the cook had said. It was possible. She could marry Terric once Forwin left this earth, but there was only one hurdle she would have to face first. Would Terric believe her when she told him how she had been forced to write that missive? The chances were slim.

* * * *

Terric rode through the village of Nunney as he headed toward the castle. He studied his adversary's home as he drew nearer. The basic plan of the castle was one of four equal-sized large drum towers set at the corners of a rectangle. The south-west and north-east pair had a short connecting wall between them. While the north-west and south-east pair had a much longer one. He noticed the castle walls were finished in ashlar masonry of high quality.

As he approached the causeway, he glanced at the high conical roofs atop each of the towers. Terric crossed the wooden drawbridge and passed through the castle gate unchallenged. Apparently, Forwin did not expect any trouble, which marked him a fool. A man who left his castle open to attacks usually got one.

No one took any notice of his arrival until a servant came to the well, which was near the north-east tower. Once he was spotted in the bailey, the girl hesitated for a moment, then turned abruptly and went back inside the main building. Knowing Forwin would be notified of his presence, Terric dismounted.

* * * *

Jacqueline was in the kitchen when the young servant girl came rushing in, looking for her. "My lady, you must go to the bailey. A strange knight sits out there on his horse."

Her heart skipped a beat. Could it be Terric? She brushed flour from her hands, then headed for the bailey. She prayed it was not him. With everything she was embroiled in, he needed to stay as far away as possible from her, at least until Forwin made his exit from this world, anyway. Terric could all too easily fall prey to either her husband's or the earl's conniving plans.

Jacqueline stepped outside into the bailey and sharply sucked in a breath through her clenched teeth. It was Terric who stood waiting by his horse. He had his back turned to her and had not seen her.

Seeing him, as large as life, made all the feelings she

had for him resurface with a vengeance. She wished she could rush over to him, hold him in her arms, and beg him to take her away from all this. The need was so great within her it almost became an unbearable ache, but she would do no such thing. She loved him too much to risk losing him. Jacqueline took a deep breath for courage, then walked to Terric and did what had to be done.

Terric turned. Jacqueline stopped a short distance from where he stood. "What do you want, Terric?"

He ran his gaze over her. "When your father sent word of where you were to your mother, she wanted me to check and see if it was true. We have been searching for you, Jacqueline."

"You have found me."

He gave her a perplexed look. "What has happened to you?"

"All my father said is true. I am now Forwin's wife."

Terric frowned. "Why? You could have refused. No woman can be forced into marriage. It is church law."

Jacqueline shook her head at what he said. "That law means nothing, and you know it. My father does what he wishes. He can be very persuasive when he wants to be."

"Could you have not held him off for a time? You are a very capable woman. You could have thought of something to delay the marriage from taking place."

"What good would that have done?"

He ran his fingers through his hair. "I do not know. You had to have known I would come looking for you."

Jacqueline swallowed around the painful lump that had formed in her throat and shook her head once more. "Did you ride out searching when you found me missing that day?" His silence spoke volumes. She blinked back the tears that threatened to rise to the surface. "You did not, did you? You believed every word I wrote." Terric tried to take a step closer, but she did not allow it. She held out her hand to stop him.

"Your missive hurt, but I was a fool to take it to heart," he said.

"You must have known how I felt about you."

"I thought I did. The missive made me think you never really cared for me at all. You never said."

At his words, a single tear fell her cheek. He reached out and gently brushed it away. Jacqueline roughly shoved his hand from her face. "Just as you never spoke those same words to me. Now it is too late. The damage is done."

Terric grabbed Jacqueline by the arm and pulled her toward his waiting horse, but before he was able to take more than two steps, an all-too-familiar voice hailed them. Jacqueline caught sight of Nicholas heading in their direction with a smile and silently groaned. The man had perfect timing. She wiped her eyes with a quick swipe of her sleeve as she pulled herself together. She did not want to give Nicholas any indication of how she felt about Terric.

"Jacqueline, are you not going to invite our guest into the hall?"

She scowled at Nicholas. "He is not staying."

Nicholas' sharp gaze shifted from her to Terric, seeming not missing anything. "From the way you were conversing, I thought you were well-acquainted with each other."

Jacqueline caught Terric's gaze and stared intently into his violet eyes, hoping he would keep silent. Either he did not understand what she wanted him to do or he ignored her entreaty. He spoke to Nicholas.

"Lady Jacqueline and I are...were very close at one time. When I heard of her marriage, I came to pay my respects."

Nicholas smiled slyly. "I can see you two were very...close indeed. If that is the case, Jacqueline must have told you the good news."

Cringing, Jacqueline closed her eyes and swore under her breath, calling Nicholas every bad name she could think of. If she had had a knife in her hand, she would have happily stuck it into his gullet.

"What would that be?" Terric asked quietly.

"Why, Lady Jacqueline is carrying the next Earl of Somerset. Forwin's heir."

Terric looked at her. "Is this true, Jacqueline? Are you with child?"

Sadly, she nodded. "Aye, I am."

Terric silently turned and retrieved his horse. After mounting up, he turned his steed around and left the bailey. Not once did he look behind him.

Once Terric disappeared from sight, Nicholas said sarcastically, "He must not have been happy with your good fortune."

Jacqueline whipped around and slapped Nicholas across the face, leaving her handprint on his cheek. "How dare you? What right do you have to be involved in my affairs?"

Nicholas took her roughly by the arm and pulled it painfully up behind her back, forcing her against him. Anger flashed in his eyes, making them turn a stormy gray. "You will not strike me like that ever again. I see you have a lot to learn about being an obedient wife. I will take great pleasure in educating you once Forwin is gone. As mine, you will show me the proper respect I am due."

He thrust Jacqueline away, then returned to the hall. Rubbing her arm, a shiver of true fear caused her to shake uncontrollably. She needed help. Nicholas was a much bigger threat than she had realized. Once Forwin was gone, there would be no one to keep the minstrel in check. It was time to enlist the help of her mother.

* * * *

Now that she had made the decision to ask her mother for help, Jacqueline needed a way to sneak a missive out of Nunney. She was no fool. Nicholas watched her every move. She needed help from those within the castle. They were allowed the freedom she was not permitted.

Jacqueline read over what she had written to her mother and could not help but feel homesick. The isle had been the only home she had known. What bothered her the most was not being able to have her mother with her. She was the one steadying constant in her life. She was always there to help her through any troubled times.

Satisfied with the missive, she sanded it, then sealed it closed. She hastily shoved it into the bodice of her gown, then left her chamber to seek out Mabel in the kitchen.

As she walked past Forwin's chamber, the door opened, and Nicholas stepped into the hallway. He effectively blocked her way. "Is there something you want, Nicholas?"

He smiled, blatantly looking her up and down. "What I want is not yet mine to take. So instead, you can give me information I seek."

Jacqueline narrowed her eyes. "What information?"

He bestowed her with one of his most charming smiles. If she were easily turned by a man's good-looks, she would have fallen under the spell he tried to weave. Luckily, she knew what Nicholas truly was — nothing but a snake in the grass.

"That knight, the one who came to visit you. Who is he?"

"Just someone I know. If you will excuse me, I have other things to attend to." Jacqueline tried to step around him, but he blocked her path.

"Come now. You can tell me. He is the father of your baby. It was not hard to miss how you were panting over each other."

She glared at him, her disgust for him deepening. "Even

if I admitted that he was, it is still none of your business. I do not have to answer to you."

Nicholas' charming facade dropped. He took her by the shoulders and forced her against the wall. "Oh, but you will. Very soon."

He grabbed Jacqueline by her chin and roughly kissed her. She managed to bring her hands up to his chest and forcibly shoved him away. Nicholas sniggered as she scrubbed the back of her hand across her mouth, trying to remove all traces of his kiss. He gave her a mocking bow, then returned to Forwin's chamber.

Jacqueline patted the missive still concealed within her bodice as she hurried to reach the kitchen. How her future would turn out hinged on this single missive reaching her mother.

She safely arrived at the kitchen, sure her face was still red with indignation. Mabel, ever observant, placed her hands on her ample hips and questioningly looked at Jacqueline.

"What has the snake done now?"

"He cornered me outside my husband's chamber."

Mabel picked up the meat cleaver she had been using and muttered angrily under her breath. As she headed toward the door, cleaver still in hand, Jacqueline realized she intended to confront Nicholas.

"Oh no, you cannot, Mabel." Taking hold of the cook's arm, she steered her back inside the kitchen. She tried to stare sternly at Mabel, but found herself unable to do so. The very idea of the older woman chasing after Nicholas with her meat cleaver was highly amusing. Laughter bubbled inside her.

The more she conjured up the image of Mabel chasing a screaming Nicholas around the bailey with cleaver held high, the harder she laughed. At the perplexed look upon the older woman's face, Jacqueline managed to sputter, "The meat cleaver? Really now, Mabel? That would be a sight to see. You taking Nicholas to task with it."

Almost as if she had forgotten what she held, Mabel seemed mildly surprised to see the cleaver. She too laughed at the absurdity of it. "I guess you are right, my lady. That would be something, though."

Once their laughter dissipated, Jacqueline reached inside her bodice and withdrew the missive. "Mabel, do you recall the discussion we had pertaining to Nicholas? About how he is here for another purpose?"

"Aye." Mabel eyed the missive Jacqueline clutched.

"Well, you were right. I had thought I could handle him myself, but I know now that is no longer the case. I need your help."

"I would do anything for you. Tell me what has you so worried."

Jacqueline took a moment to collect her thoughts, then launched into the story of her life. She trusted Mabel implicitly. So, to better help the other woman understand her situation, she started her tale with the first betrothal arranged by her father to Forwin. From there, the rest just poured out of her. She left nothing out—the loss of her brother at the hands of her father, how she had assumed William's identity to meet the earl in the list, and she finally spoke of Terric.

Once Jacqueline reached the end, Mabel dabbed her eyes with the corner of her apron. "The knight who came here? It was Terric?"

Jacqueline nodded sadly. "Aye."

"Does he know you carry his babe?"

"Nay. Nicholas broke that particular piece of information to Terric before I could tell him."

"Just another strike against the rat," Mabel grumbled. "Well, if it is help you need, help you will get. What do you plan to do?"

Jacqueline placed the missive on the worktable. "It is time I call in the reinforcements. I need you to get this missive out of the castle and arrange to have it delivered to my mother."

"Consider it done, my lady." Mabel snatched up the missive and placed it in one of the deep pockets of her apron.

CHAPTER EIGHTEEN

Months passed, and Jacqueline's pregnancy progressed. Forwin, though still extremely ill, seemed to be clinging to life. He seemed determined to see her baby born.

She had not told Forwin about the incident that had taken place in the bailey on the day of Terric's visit, but she was much more guarded while in Nicholas's presence. Forwin was not a stupid man, though. He quickly noticed the change in her behavior. It was during one of her daily visits when Nicholas had briefly left them alone, something he very rarely did. Nicholas seemed to want to keep her and Forwin from ever being alone together.

Forwin gave her a simple warning. "We must tread carefully."

Jacqueline made sure the chamber door was shut tight by quickly glancing toward it before she spoke. "More than you know, my lord. Nicholas is not what he wants you to believe. I think he is capable of doing anything."

Forwin nodded gravely. "You have confirmed my suspicions. I think I have invited a viper into our midst."

"Then why keep him here? When he finds out you are

not going to keep your end of the bargain, he could retaliate."

"It is very simple really, my dear. It's better to have Nicholas here where he can be watched and contained."

Jacqueline still felt uneasy about that reasoning. "After you are gone? What then?"

Forwin gave her a wink and slyly said, "You, my dear wife, are quite capable of looking after yourself. I know from firsthand experience just what lengths you will take to save yourself. I have all confidence that you can protect your child from Nicholas."

He was right. She would use all within her means to keep her child safe. She had already taken the first step. With the help of Mabel, a missive was even now on its way to her mother.

As for Forwin's change of heart about Nicholas, it just meant he had come to see her as a more useful tool to keep his lands from her father. He had not once told her why he hated the earl to that extent, but Jacqueline did not really care. It was good enough that they had a common goal — seeing her father thwarted from getting what he wanted. She also knew why Forwin wanted to keep her at Nunney instead of sending her home where she would be safer. If she left, there would be no one to stop Nicholas from completely taking over.

Nicholas appeared a short while later. Where he had been, he did not care to share with them. The way his glance kept shifting between Forwin and herself made Jacqueline feel extremely uneasy being under his scrutiny. She stood and left the chamber.

* * * *

Lady Elizabeth read the missive she held once again. Jacqueline really had herself immersed in a fine mess. Most of it was not her doing. Damn the earl and his scheming ways. If only he could have just left them alone. Jacqueline and Terric would be happily wed and eagerly awaiting the birth of their first child.

Sighing deeply, Lady Elizabeth sadly shook her head. Her daughter had already suffered enough at the hands of her father, the greatest blow being the death of William. Now she had to suffer losing Terric as well.

Jacqueline was not going to have to go through this all alone. Her family would stand by her. When Forwin left this world, she would personally make sure Terric got his due—her daughter as his wife.

* * * *

"So you have given up. Just like that."

Terric scowled at Edwin, who sat next to him. "What would you have me do? She is wed to another and expecting a child."

Edwin shook his head. "I thought you were smarter than that."

"Just what, pray tell, do you mean by that?"

"I mean, how sure are you the child Jacqueline is carrying is not yours?"

Terric roamed his gaze over the other patrons of the inn where they sat and thought about Edwin's question. He had thought of that, but Jacqueline had had plenty of opportunity to tell him before that Nicholas had shown up.

"Nay, the babe is not mine," he said.

"You have to admit there is a chance it could be."

"A very slim one."

Terric drained his tankard of ale, then thumped it onto the table. He caught the eye of the buxom serving wench and signaled her to bring another round.

The woman sauntered over, seductively swinging her hips, carrying a pitcher of ale. She stood behind Terric and reached around him to fill his tankard. She purposely pressed her ample breasts against his back while she poured his drink.

"Anything else you would like, sir?" she asked in a seductive tone.

It was blatantly obvious what the wench offered. He looked at her. She would be considered pretty by some, but there was a coarseness about her. At one time, he would have seriously considered her offer, but now he found her not the least bit alluring.

Terric shook his head. "Nay, the ale is all I want."

The wench stuck out her bottom lip in a pout. "Well, if you change your mind, just ask for Lucy. I would be happy to...oblige such a one as you."

"Many thanks for the offer, Lucy, but I do not think I will change my mind."

Once the serving wench left their table, Edwin chuckled. "You have it bad."

"What do I have bad?"

"Love. Lady Jacqueline still holds your heart. There was a day when yonder wench would have found herself in your bed."

"Since when is my bed sport any concern of yours?"

Ignoring him, Edwin continued. "You love her. I know you do. So you should not give up hope. While you were at the castle visiting Lady Jacqueline, some of the villagers shared an interesting bit of information. More than one bit, actually."

Terric could see Edwin itched for him to ask what he had heard as he squirmed. He picked up his tankard and took a sip. He decided to see how long it would take for Edwin to break down and tell him without being asked. It only took a few seconds before the squire broke.

"Fine, do not ask. I will tell you anyway. They said Forwin is ill and near death. It is said he might not even live long enough to see his heir born."

It seemed Jacqueline felt it was unnecessary to relay

that information to him as well. "So Jacqueline will be a widow soon."

Edwin continued. "You see, there is more. Apparently, Forwin fell ill right after his marriage and has been practically bedridden ever since. So I feel Lady Jacqueline's babe is yours. How could a deathly-ill man father a child?"

Having heard enough of Edwin's assumptions, Terric stopped him from speaking further. "Shut your mouth, Edwin. The subject of Jacqueline is closed. I do not want to hear another word about it from you," he snapped.

Thoroughly chastised, Edwin wisely kept his mouth shut.

* * * *

Their small party of travelers entered the bailey of Nunney Castle. Beth was accompanied by Sir Guy along with four men-at-arms.

After dismounting, Sir Guy stepped to Beth and helped her down from her palfrey. He put the bailey and castle walls under close scrutiny. Obviously, finding them both lacking, he snorted in contempt. "This castle is just begging to be taken. No portcullis, only a simple wooden drawbridge operated by a manual crank."

Beth had to agree with what the older man said. The lack of defenses was appalling, to say the least. Allowing a party of strangers to enter the castle unchallenged made it even worse. "We must find Jacqueline."

"Aye, and quickly. The sooner we establish ourselves in the household the better."

Beth nodded as she picked up her skirts and headed in the direction of the hall. "Remember now, Sir Guy, what Lady Elizabeth wants us to do. We must not give our true reason for being here away."

"Fear not, my lady. I know exactly what has to be done. I will not put the lass in any more danger."

Beth pushed the hall doors open, and added, "Good. Now let us see what we are up against, shall we?"

The hall was just as empty as the bailey had been. Beth looked at Sir Guy, and he shrugged. It was midday. Usually, the hall would be filled with the occupants of the castle eating their first large meal of the day.

This was ridiculous. They could be left there all day before someone noticed their presence. Thoroughly disgusted, Beth decided to take matters into her own hands. She went in search of the kitchen.

After finding the stairs leading down to the bowels of the castle, she and Sir Guy descended to the kitchen. The sound of voices talking animatedly drifted up to them the farther they went. Beth recognized one of the voices amongst the others. Jacqueline was indeed down there. She entered the kitchen and found her sitting at the worktable, happily conversing with the kitchen help.

Clearing his throat loudly, Sir Guy made their presence known. "Is this any way to welcome guests, lass? By hiding in the kitchen?"

Jacqueline let out a squeal of surprise. She slipped off her stool, then ran to greet them. "I was not expecting you. Why did you not send word of your coming? I would have been better prepared."

Beth gave Jacqueline a quick embrace, then took a step back to take a closer look at her friend. "I must say you have widened a bit since our last meeting."

Jacqueline appeared not to know whether she should laugh or cry. "I am so glad you are here, Beth. You too, Sir Guy."

The older man smiled warmly. "Do you think your mother would leave you to face your time of trial alone? She sent us here to be of service to you." He stared intently into her eyes, then said pointedly, "To serve you in all matters, to the very end."

Jacqueline gave Sir Guy a quivering smile. "I will gladly

accept your help. Your presence brings me much comfort. You have no idea how much."

* * * *

Why did those two have to come? Nicholas silently gnashed his teeth in rage. All he had worked so hard to obtain was slipping through his fingers like so many grains of sand. The arrival of Lady Beth and Sir Guy marked the beginning of subtle changes within Nunney's walls. He could not prove either one was the cause of them, but he just knew they were.

All meals, which he was expected to attend, were now served in the hall. It seemed they tried to keep him from Forwin. What he found most disturbing was the now manned walls.

Sir Guy had been very unobtrusive about what he was doing. At first, the four men-at-arms who had accompanied him there took shifts patrolling the walls. Now, five more men had been added to their ranks. Where they had come from, Nicholas did not know and could not find out either. Those men were very close-mouthed and could not be easily drawn out in conversation. One thing that was true about all of them was that, to a man, they were all very well-trained. Sir Guy held daily training sessions in the bailey. Nicholas had watched one and observed how well those men handled their swords.

Having planned for the last few years to be the next owner of Nunney Castle, he was not prepared to just walk away. He would silently bide his time. Once Jacqueline bore her brat, then things would change. No one was going to stop him from getting what he had striven so hard for. Not the shrew Lady Beth, and not that old knight. He would show them all in the end.

CHAPTER NINETEEN

The time of Jacqueline's lying-in finally arrived during a cold and blustery winter night. It had been decided beforehand, amongst the three of them, to keep Nicholas ignorant as long as they could of what took place. At the very least, until after she had safely been delivered. She and the babe would be too vulnerable as she labored.

So with great stealth on Sir Guy's part, he secretly brought the village midwife up to Jacqueline's chamber when the time came. The older woman understood the motive behind it and was quick to reassure them she would not draw attention to herself in any way.

Apparently, the general opinion down in the village was one of hatred toward Nicholas. To see the back of him leaving Nunney would be a blessing to them. The minstrel would be a harsh master in their minds, if Nicholas was somehow able to find a way to claim the lands as his own.

As Jacqueline's labor progressed, Sir Guy left his post at her chamber door. He had only been tolerated in what was usually classed as woman's work because the women could not protect themselves against an attack. Now, he had to put into motion the next step in his plans to keep

Jacqueline safe.

Jacqueline clenched her teeth as another wave of pain hit her. The pains came faster, not giving her much time to rest before the next one took her over. Knowing it meant her baby was close to being born, she silently wished it to come quickly. Much to her relief, it did just that. A short time later, she began the job of pushing her child into the world.

With Beth holding her hand for support, Jacqueline gave one last push, and the child slip free of her body and into the waiting arms of the midwife.

At the muffled cries of her infant, she propped herself up on one elbow and expectantly looked at the midwife. "Tell me. What is it?"

Smiling, the older woman came to Jacqueline's side, then passed her the well-wrapped bundle of her child. "You have a fine, healthy son, my lady."

Seeing her child's face for the very first time was the most beautiful thing she had ever experienced. Jacqueline blinked back tears of happiness that threatened to fall. She pulled the blanket away from her son and checked every inch of him. He was perfect. The peach fuzz upon his head was dark brown. When the baby opened his eyes and looked at her for the first time, she found herself staring at a copy of Terric's own. They were a lovely shade of violet.

Hearing someone sniff, Jacqueline looked at Beth. She stood beside the bed, staring at the baby while silent tears dripped down her cheeks.

Beth gave her a watery smile. "Oh, Jacqueline. He looks so much like William."

Beth was right. Her son was a male version of herself. Exactly how William had looked. Jacqueline wrapped the baby back up again, then passed the infant to Beth. At first, she refused, but Jacqueline would not give in. Beth held the baby close.

"What are you going to call him, Jacqueline?" she

asked.

She had had names picked out long before this day had come, a boy's and a girl's. "He will be Jordan William." She almost added Aubrey to the end of her son's name, but that was not to be. Jordan would have Forwin's — De La Mare.

Though her labor had not been very long, tiredness slowly seeped through her. She needed to rest. For on the morrow, the greatest challenge would begin — ousting Nicholas and then securing Jordan's future as the next Earl of Somerset.

* * * *

Jacqueline had no idea why she awoke from her slumber. Maybe because she was now a mother and had come to possess that extra sense all mothers have when it comes to their children — the one that allows them to know when their child needed them without being told. Whatever it was, she sensed something wrong.

There was someone in her chamber. She knew that even before she came fully awake. Jacqueline reached under her pillow and grabbed the hilt of the dagger she kept at the ready. In one swift movement, she jumped out of bed, then held it against Nicholas' throat as he bent over her son's cradle.

"Move any closer to my child and I will cut a nice hole in your throat."

Nicholas slowly straightened. All the while Jacqueline kept the sharp edge of the blade against his throat. "Now, now, Jacqueline. Is this any way to treat your future husband?"

"The day I wed you will be the day hell freezes over. Besides, I still have a husband."

"I am sorry to give you grievous news, but Forwin is no more." After imparting those words, Nicholas laughed. A sinister laugh.

"What do you mean?" she asked.

"You are a widow. Once I dispatch your brat, you will be my wife."

Jacqueline tightened her grip on the dagger. Her top lip curled into a snarl. "Touch my son and you will die."

Nicholas laughed once more. "Really, Jacqueline. You just gave birth. I can feel you shaking. Do you honestly believe you can overpower me in such a weakened state?"

He was right. Her hand trembled. "I do not think it is wise of you to celebrate a victory you have not won yet." Jordan whimpered, which caused Jacqueline to nick Nicholas' throat.

Nicholas hissed in anger. "You will pay for that."

"I think not," Sir Guy said from behind them.

At the sound of his voice, Jacqueline turned to find Sir Guy standing just inside her chamber, flanked by two men-at-arms. The baby cried in earnest. Controlling the urge to pick up Jordan, she waited until both men-at-arms took hold of Nicholas. With him now safely in custody and no longer a threat, she put down her dagger so she could comfort her son.

Before Nicholas could be led from her chamber, Jacqueline spoke to him. "This will be the last time I see you so I am going to get right to the point. Whatever Forwin promised you, forget it. Nunney is now my son's, and no man will take it from him."

Nicholas' handsome face shifted into a mask of pure rage. "You might have won this time, but it will not be the end."

Sir Guy stepped in between them. "That is enough out of you. It is over. You will be escorted from Nunney, and you will not come back. On your way out, look to the walls. There are more men manning them. Men sworn to serve Lady Jacqueline." Coming to stand nose to nose with Nicholas, he said coldly, "If you decide to try to claim

Nunney Castle, which was never yours in the first place, it will be the end of you. Literally." With a swift jerk of his head, he signaled the men-at-arms to lead the minstrel away.

The encounter left Jacqueline completely drained. Still cradling Jordan close, she sat on her bed before her trembling legs gave out on her. "Nicholas said Forwin is dead."

Sir Guy sighed. "He is. With no small help from the minstrel."

Jacqueline gasped in shock. "Are you saying he killed Forwin?"

"Afraid so, lass. I would not be surprised to find out he had been at it for years. There are poisons that mimic symptoms of a serious illness. It would explain Forwin's inability to sire a child."

She had to agree with that assumption. Nicholas would have had no qualms about ridding himself of the man who stood in his way of gaining all he wanted. "We have removed the thorn from our side. Now what do we do to keep what we have gained?"

With all seriousness, Sir Guy said, "You must wed again, and quickly. Ideally, before your father finds out Forwin is dead and buried."

Kissing the top of her son's silky head, she nodded. "Terric. I will only have Terric. He deserves to be a part of Jordan's life. More importantly, this time I will only marry for love. I refuse to be used as a pawn to further a man's fortune again."

Sir Guy brushed a finger across the baby's soft cheek, then bent down to place a kiss on Jacqueline's forehead. "We knew that, lass. Your lady mother and I, that is. All the details will be taken care of. Have no fear. You will get your man."

"How long do I have?"

"A month to a month and a half. Then you will have

what you want."

"Nicholas? He knows about my father and what he hoped to gain. Will he not go to the earl and tell him what we have done?"

Sir Guy smiled a knowing smile. "I expect him to do just that, but he will have to find the earl first, then try to gain an audience with him. Nicholas is going to find out how a nobleman can really treat a lowly minstrel."

Jacqueline laughed. For once her father's disregard of anyone in the lower classes would work to their benefit. "Poor Nicholas. He will be shunned."

"Maybe not forever, but he will give you time to gain your strength back so you can confront Terric. You are going to need as much of it as you can get."

Confused, she looked at the older man. "Confront? How?"

Smiling, Sir Guy went to leave the chamber. "Why, you are going to face Terric in the list. What better way to gain his attention? After all, he is a tournament knight. So make your play for him in his territory. He can hardly ignore you then."

* * * *

It was not fair. All the years wasted catering to that fool Forwin and for nothing. Nicholas knew he should not have listened to him. Forwin's wife could have easily found herself rid of her child in the beginning. There were herbs that could have been slipped to Jacqueline without her knowing, but Forwin had not allowed it. He would have done it himself, but he had thought the risk too high if the herbs used were ever traced back to him.

He had lost it all and had been outsmarted by a woman, but the bitch would pay. He was going to make sure of that. Nicholas looked over his shoulder and found the two men-at-arms closely watching him. He snatched up his belongings and roughly shoved them into his bags. Once he finished, he brushed past the two waiting men. They closely followed him.

After reaching the bailey, Nicholas found Sir Guy there. "I will give you one warning, and one warning only. Should you ever return to Nunney, for any reason at all, I will be sure to give you cause to regret it." Nicholas didn't respond. "Your horse is saddled and awaits you at the stable. I suggest you leave now."

Nicholas walked past the older knight, then turned back around. "She might have won this time, but she has trifled with the wrong man. I will make sure she gets her own."

"I would expect no less from you. Try if you wish, but you are finished."

After giving one last snarl of rage, Nicholas stomped away. He was far from finished with them.

CHAPTER TWENTY

Beth pulled the hood of her cloak closer around her face and shifted from one foot to the other. Would he never leave?

She peered around the corner of the pavilion she stood behind, checking to see if Terric had left his. His horse was still picketed out in front of the pavilion. She groaned to herself. A quick second later, she shot back out of sight as the flap opened. After counting to ten, she stepped into the open. He was just disappearing from view.

Beth picked up her skirts and crossed the space between the two pavilions. Not bothering to announce her presence, she pulled open the flap, stepped inside, and pulled it back closed.

A look of shock crossed Edwin's face when he saw her. "What do you here, my lady?"

Beth shook off her hood. Edwin watched her every move. Not really sure why she did it, she reached up and pulled her unbound hair from beneath her cloak. The long, light blonde tresses tumbled down her back. His breath hitched.

"I need your help, Edwin."

"I thought..." His voice cracked, but Edwin cleared his throat and tried again. "I thought you were with Lady Jacqueline."

"I am." Edwin appeared to think over what she had said. Looking at him, really looking at him this time, she realized he was quite handsome. All the other instances she had been in his company, she really had never noticed his good-looks. Grief had overshadowed a lot of her senses.

"You mean Lady Jacqueline is here? At this tournament?" he asked, his smile widening while he spoke.

"Aye, she is. That is why we need your help."

He seemed not able to tear his gaze from her. "What exactly would you have me do?"

Beth smiled brightly. "Jacqueline is going to challenge Terric in the list. All you have to do is make sure he accepts."

"She what?" He furiously shook his head. "There is no way I can accomplish that. Terric will recognize William's name when he receives the challenge."

"She will not be using her brother's name. She will be keeping her name unknown."

"All right, then I can somehow manage what you ask." He frowned. "I thought Lady Jacqueline was with child. How can she ride in the list in that condition?"

Beth shook her head. "Jacqueline is no longer with child."

"She lost the baby?"

"Nay, do not be ridiculous. Jacqueline bore a healthy son, a month past." Beth paused to make sure she had Edwin's full attention. "Terric has a son."

Edwin let out a whoop. "I knew it. I knew the babe was his." He picked up Beth's hand and placed a lingering kiss upon it. With his lips hovering above it, he looked deeply into her eyes. "I am your servant."

* * * *

The start of the tournament circuit did not bring him much excitement this time around, not like previous years. It felt as if he were only going through the motions. The anticipation of meeting opponents in the list was gone. Nothing felt the same since he had lost her.

He had come full circle now. He was at Portchester Castle in Portsmouth where he had first met Jacqueline posing as William. He had not realized then that she would change what he wanted out of life. The dream of earning enough coin through tournament ransoms so he could buy land was not so pressing anymore. What good would the land be without Jacqueline? She was the one and only woman he wanted as his wife. Without her, owning property held no interest for him.

Edwin quietly helped him don his armor. Terric blandly accepted his assistance. "Who is my first opponent?"

Standing behind him, Edwin said, "I am not sure. This knight has chosen to keep his identity hidden."

Terric turned to look over his shoulder at his squire. "Who else did this unknown knight challenge?"

"Only you."

"Just me?" Terric found that surprising. Why him?

Edwin nodded. "Aye, just you."

Terric was curious as to the knight's identity. More importantly, why he had been singled out?

Edwin slapped Terric on the shoulder, signaling he was done arming him. Once they arrived at the list, the unknown knight was already waiting. A blank white shield was on the knight's left arm. With his helm in place, there was no way to tell who he was. Even the knight's young squire was unfamiliar to him.

Terric took to his end of the list, then accepted his first lance from Edwin. At the first pass, both lances shattered as they impacted against the hard surface of their shields. After the second pass, he found something vaguely familiar about his opponent's form. Why he did, he could not put his finger on.

After taking up his third and final lance, he closely watched as the unknown knight readied for the final pass. The sense of familiarity grew. Terric kicked his horse in its sides and started down the list. His opponent followed suit.

A quarter of the way down, Terric watched as the knight, who barreled toward him, adjust the aim of his lance. He cursed under his breath. With only a moment to spare before they met, he threw his lance away, forfeiting the match. He quickly turned his horse around as his opponent left the list with some hurry.

Edwin met Terric as he returned to his end. He gave his master a timid smile. Terric leaned down and grabbed him by an ear. Edwin danced on his toes, trying to escape his grasp.

"You knew all along. Did you not, Edwin?"

The squire started to nod, but then seemed to think better of it. "Aye, I knew."

"Why did you not see fit to inform me?"

"Well, you see, I figured no harm would come of it. They were so desperate, and I so much wanted to help them, and—"

"Enough!" Terric bellowed. He closed his eyes for a few seconds and took a deep breath, trying to keep his temper under control. "I believe you have stated your case, or should I say, buried yourself deeply enough. All I want to know is one thing. Where are they?"

Edwin swallowed audibly and pointed in the direction of the pavilions. "At the very far end. Out of sight."

Even before Edwin had said his last word, Terric released him and set off in the direction Edwin had indicated. Just as his squire had said, Terric found the lone pavilion not far from the main group of tents. It sat behind a small copse of trees that created a natural screen.

Terric picketed his horse next to the one already out in front, then roughly unlaced his helm. He pulled it completely free from his head as he stepped through the entrance.

She had only had enough time to remove her own helm. Terric stared at Jacqueline. Seeing her still dressed in her armor made his temper simmer all the more. Trying not to give it free rein, he punched out each word through his clenched teeth. "Just what in hell were you doing out there today?"

Jacqueline closed the distance between them. She pulled off one of her gauntlets and placed her palm on his cheek. "Getting your attention."

He grabbed her wrist in a vise-like grip, then pulled her hand from his face. "Why could you not seek it in the usual way?" He released Jacqueline and took a step away.

"I need your help, Terric. I could not afford to take the chance of you refusing to see me."

"You need my help," he said blandly. "What about your husband? Can he not do it?"

"Nay." Jacqueline stepped closer again. "Nay, he cannot. Forwin is dead."

All at once, his world right itself. Jacqueline was free, but there was still something that caused him to tread carefully. "What of the child? Forwin's heir."

"You left Nunney before I could explain."

"So you could tell me how you came to sleep with another man and bore his child?"

Jacqueline shook her head and smiled. "Terric, do you actually think I would give myself to Forwin? Well, I did not."

He wanted so much to believe her, but the child could not be so easily dismissed. "You have not answered my question, Jacqueline. I did not ask about our meeting at

Nunney. Changing the subject will not deter me."

"As you wish." Jacqueline put some space between them. "I gave birth to a son a month ago. Your son."

Terric shook his head in denial. "That is not possible."

"Why not? I was only married to Forwin for seven months. He died on the same day our son was born." He said nothing. "Terric, add up the months."

"If what you say is true, then you were already with child when—"

"We were to wed. Aye. It was the night at the grand tournament, I think."

Terric removed his gauntlets and set them on the ground next to Jacqueline's. "All right, I believe you. Now what? You are a wealthy widow able to be independent. You do not need me."

Jacqueline reached up, lacing her fingers through his hair at the back of his head. "How can you say that with all seriousness? My feelings for you have not changed. I love you, Terric. I always will."

With a clang, their armor met. Terric pulled Jacqueline into his arms and kissed her thoroughly. Waves of intense pleasure swept through his whole body. He had craved her touch for months. Groaning, he gripped the edges of her armor, hating the barrier it created between their bodies.

The sound of a babe crying caused Jacqueline to quickly pull away. He looked over his shoulder and found Beth standing inside the entrance, holding a babe that was making his displeasure known to all. She appeared to be completely frazzled from the baby's fretting.

"Sorry, Jacqueline, but he will not stop crying. I have tried everything. You are going to have to nurse him or he will not settle."

"What the little lord wants, he gets," Jacqueline said with a smile. "I just have to remove my armor, then I can feed him."

Before Terric could go to Jacqueline's side to assist her, Beth stepped around to face him and held out the crying bundle of baby. His first inclination was to back away, but curiosity to see what his son looked like won out in the end. Tentatively, he held out his arms to accept the infant. Beth gently passed him the small bundle before going to help Jacqueline in the removal of her armor.

Careful of the steel encasing his arms and chest, Terric pulled the blanket back to have his first look at his son. The baby's face was bright red. His eyes were tightly screwed shut with tears streaming down his soft cheeks. With hands fisted, he waved them in the air in indignation. Terric chuckled at the infant's display of displeasure.

"Come now, little man. It cannot be as bad as all that." At the sound of a new voice, the baby stopped crying and opened his eyes. Terric found himself looking into ones the same color as his own. Though their child had taken after Jacqueline in looks, the boy's eyes matched his. Terric felt a sense of connection with this small being he held, and a strong feeling of protectiveness. The baby whimpered, unhappy that Terric was not giving him what he wanted. He filled his lungs with air, then wailed once more.

Jacqueline touched Terric's hand. "This is your son, Jordan. Before he brings too much unwanted attention, I had better feed him."

With great reluctance, Terric allowed Jacqueline to take Jordan from his arms. Once she was comfortably seated in a camp chair, she put the baby to her breast. His cries instantly ceased. Enthralled, he could not pry his gaze from his son as he suckled.

"Tell me what could be so dire that you must enter the list to gain my attention, Jacqueline."

CHAPTER TWENTY-ONE

Jacqueline took a moment to collect her thoughts, then told Terric all that had happened since her father had stolen her from Carisbrooke. She did not leave out any details, even explaining why Forwin had brought Nicholas to Nunney. She also told him the lie she had given about already being pregnant, only to find out later it was the truth.

Replete, Jordan stopped sucking and fell asleep. Jacqueline switched him to her shoulder and patted his back. She continued her tale. "With Forwin gone, and Nicholas on the loose, my father will find out how he was tricked."

Terric was aghast at what Jacqueline had endured. If only he had stayed at Nunney long enough to have found out what was really happening, she would not be so vulnerable now. "I was a fool to leave you with those two."

"Do not blame yourself. You did not know. You are here now, and you can still save me."

"I will not abandon you like that again, I promise. Whatever it takes, I will do to keep you from your father's clutches."

"That, Sir Terric, is exactly what we had hoped you would say." Having been momentarily forgotten, Beth broke into the conversation. She breezed past Terric and went to the entrance of the pavilion.

She pulled the flap back and signaled to someone, who obviously had been waiting for just that. Terric was not at all surprised when Edwin stepped inside. What he had not expected was a priest closely following his squire. Terric looked at Beth, who smiled sweetly.

"If you want to keep Jacqueline safe, marry her. Here and now," she said.

Still holding their child, Jacqueline stood, watching for his reaction. Terric closed the space between her and himself. He went to her side, put his arm around her shoulders, and turned her to face the priest. "Well, Father, it looks as though you have a marriage to perform."

With Beth and Edwin acting as witnesses, the ceremony became a very simple matter. Jacqueline's mother had procured a special license so the banns could be overlooked. Beth had been given possession of it before she had left Carisbrooke with Sir Guy. Lady Elizabeth had known it would be put to use.

Once the priest pronounced them man and wife, Jacqueline kissed Terric. After their lips parted, she smiled lovingly into his eyes. His job now complete, the priest departed. Terric had to give him credit. He had not blinked an eye at the bride being dressed as a man.

A sense of euphoria wash over him. Jacqueline was his. "Now, wife, are there any other plans you have inside your pretty little head? Something I should know about?"

"Nothing too drastic, husband. We go home to Nunney. The longer we are absent, the more I worry."

"Then we leave within the hour. I can finally claim you as my own. No man will take you from me again." Seeing he had everyone's attention, Terric continued. "Once we all are behind Nunney's walls, we can breathe a little easier."

* * * *

He had not anticipated on it taking so long. He had assumed it would be no great feat to gain the presence of the Earl of Salisbury. Who would have guessed the man traveled around so much?

After a month of just missing the earl, Nicholas finally arrived in time to try to gain an audience at Castle Rushen on the Isle of Man, one of the earl's other holdings. After presenting himself as a traveling minstrel, he had gained entrance into the castle. To have speech with the earl proved to be no easy task. The man had no tolerance for those beneath him, and being styled the king of the Isle of Man did nothing to change the earl's attitude. He let no one forget that title.

The evening of his arrival, Nicholas had performed in the banqueting hall in the state apartments. The hall was the largest room in the castle. It had an enormous fireplace that was necessary to keep such a huge room heated during the winter.

After what Nicholas had thought was a perfect performance, he tried to speak with the earl. He had approached the raised dais, but the earl had in no way acknowledged him. Feeling like a fool standing there, he had finally given up.

His time was running out, though. He would be permitted to stay at Rushen for only a few more days, then he would have to move on. The Earl of Salisbury was not a man one could annoy and not expect to suffer some kind of consequences.

As the final notes from his lute faded into nothingness, Nicholas accepted the goblet of wine one of the pageboys offered him. It was welcome after his performance to wet his dry throat and give him the confidence needed to confront the earl. He swallowed all the drink in two large gulps, then wiped his mouth with his sleeve. It was time to face the dragon.

As before, the earl ignored him when he stood before the dais. Not wanting a repeat of the previous evening, Nicholas loudly cleared his throat. The earl glared at him. After executing an elaborate bow, which he hoped would impress the earl, he spoke. "My lord, I wonder if I can have a moment of your time."

Saying the earl was perturbed by Nicholas' impudence in addressing him personally was putting it mildly. He looked at Nicholas with complete revulsion.

"What could a lowly minstrel possibly have to say that I would deem of any importance?" With a negligent wave of his hand, he dismissed him. "Be gone, before I have you thrown into my dungeon."

Nicholas felt a moment of hesitation. He had heard much about the earl's dungeon during the short time he had been at Rushen. It was situated beneath the guardroom within the keep. Prisoners had to be lowered by ropes. Scarcely a ray of light penetrated the gloom in that miserable place.

Willing to take his chances, Nicholas persevered. "My lord, please do not belittle what I have to impart to you. It is of grave importance."

The earl surged to his feet and leaned upon the trestle table to stare at him. "Have you no sense? I thought I made myself perfectly clear."

Nicholas bowed submissively. "Aye, you did, my lord, but what I have to say will affect you greatly." He lifted his head and found the earl intently staring at him. "I have information in regard to your daughter and her husband."

The earl straightened, then motioned for Nicholas to follow. After leaving the hall, he pulled Nicholas into a dark corner outside in the bailey. A full moon high above provided limited illumination.

"Speak, minstrel, and if you are wasting my time, you will pay for disturbing me."

He adamantly shook his head. "Nay, my lord. I would never trifle with you."

"Then get on with it, man. My patience grows thin."

"Your daughter's husband, the Earl of Somerset, has died." Even with the small amount of light, Nicholas was able to see the earl flinch.

"When did this happen?"

"A month ago, my lord." Nicholas relaxed. It was quite obvious, judging by the earl's reaction, he had not known that.

The earl narrowed his eyes and questioned him. "How much do you know of my relationship with Forwin? I have the feeling you were closely acquainted with the man."

Nicholas let a knowing smile play upon his lips. "I know all, my lord, and other things you were never privy to."

When he did not continue, the earl snorted. "You will be rewarded." As he backed Nicholas farther into the corner, Nicholas couldn't hide the flash of fear he knew must have crossed his face. The earl calmly said, "Tell me all. Do not leave out anything. If you decide to ever come back once I am done with you to seek more coin for what you know, it will only end with you being one of my guests. In my dungeon."

The earl was shrewd, indeed. That thought had passed Nicholas' mind more than once before meeting him. Being in his presence, Nicholas knew he would be risking his very life if he tried such a thing. "I will tell you all, my lord. I was wronged just as you were. To see you exact retribution on those who cheated you will please me to no end."

CHAPTER TWENTY-TWO

E ven though they felt time was of the essence, Terric was ever mindful of his small son in their midst. Whenever Jordan cried, needing to be fed or have his bottom changed, he would find an appropriate place to stop.

At night both pavilions were set up, allowing Jacqueline and Terric a modicum of privacy. A place away from Beth and Edwin. The only other person who shared their pavilion was Jordan.

Their first night on the road, Beth took Jordan to stay with her and Edwin, giving Jacqueline and Terric the much needed time to get reacquainted, for which Jacqueline was very thankful.

That night Jacqueline felt as if everything would be all right in the world again. Being in Terric's arms did that for her. After such a long separation, and almost losing each other, consummating their marriage was all the sweeter for it. The bonds they had made in the past were reaffirmed.

Falling into each other's arms once alone, their lips met with burning need. That first time would be quick and desperate. Later, after they staunched their driving hunger, there would be time for a long, gentle loving.

Terric molded Jacqueline's soft curves to his body and rocked his erection against her. He pulled at Jacqueline's clothes and quickly peeled them off her body. Once she was naked before him, he stepped back and shucked his own.

Jacqueline skimmed Terric's body with her gaze. Finding his cock fully engorged and standing erect, she trailed her fingers down the length of him. His shaft jumped beneath her fingertips, causing her body to ache and weep with desire.

Terric took her hand off him, and said with a growl, "Enough. You do much more of that and this will end before we have even started."

He wrapped Jacqueline in his arms once more, kissing passionately. He sucked her tongue into his mouth and entwined it with his. He lowered her to the ground. Following her down, he ran his hands along her back until he cupped her bottom. He rubbed his cock against her. The wetness that pooled at her opening coated the very tip of him. He moaned.

Terric nudged Jacqueline's legs farther apart with his hips, then surged into her wet core. She groaned and clutched his back. She wrapped her legs around his waist and held on as he thrust into her. He was not gentle, but she did not want gentleness right now. She wanted him hot and hard inside her. Matching his pounding thrusts, her body clutched his hard cock as her climax washed through her. She moaned as he soon followed, filling her with his seed.

Lying in his arms, curled against his naked body, Jacqueline felt that if she were to die at that very moment, she would die a happy woman. Not that she intended to do any such thing.

She propped herself up on one elbow and looked at her

husband. Terric's eyes were closed, but she knew he was not asleep. Without opening them, he smiled, then asked, "Are you going to stare at me like that all night?"

"I would not find it a hardship. Just the opposite to be exact."

Terric opened his eyes and reached up to gently tuck her hair behind her ear. During the months of being apart, it had grown back. It was not as long as it once was, but it hung passed her shoulders. "Have I told you how much I love you, Jacqueline?"

She leaned down and kissed him on the chin, the stubble from the new growth of beard rubbed her lips. "Oh, just a few hundred times."

"Good. I do not want a day to go by that I do not tell you." As a smile faded from her lips, Terric pulled her back down to his chest, holding her close. "What is bothering you?"

"I hope I have not brought you into something you will regret later. Or get you hurt."

Terric held her tighter and shook his head. "Do not say that. Do not even think it. You have made me a very happy man being my wife. These past few months have been a living hell, not having you by my side. I never want to go through that again."

"Nor would I."

She had to try to get some sleep before Jordan woke up wanting to be nursed. Jacqueline let her eyes drift closed. On the morrow, they would continue their journey to Nunney. Once they reached the castle, she could lay her fears to rest.

* * * *

The days it took to travel to Nunney passed pleasantly. The weather held, and there was no rain to dampen their spirits. Having to contend with wet and mud would have made the trip extremely trying.

For their small group, the days on the road were euphoric. There were no pressing matters to deal with. No intrigues affecting their lives. Those were forgotten, at least for the time being. An old bond was re-established while a new one formed.

Each evening Terric and Jacqueline retired to one pavilion with their son, leaving Beth and Edwin to share the other. The first night had been uncomfortable for them. Beth trusted Edwin to act appropriately, but she still was a trifle uneasy sharing the pavilion alone with him. She was just not ready to face the emotions she felt while in his presence. Even though William's passing was over a year gone, she could not let go of him. She had a feeling she might never be ready. So the emotions Edwin engendered made her feel as if she betrayed William.

She tried to distance herself from Edwin. He immediately noticed the change. Therefore, knowing she would want more privacy, he had took to hanging a dividing sheet from one of the spokes on the pavilion roof supports, essentially creating a separate room for Beth to sleep in. The gesture was not lost on her.

With that one small kindness, Beth relaxed around Edwin. The second night she started the ritual of having a goblet of wine with him before retiring to her part of the pavilion. While they drank, they talked about a lot of things.

Edwin spoke of his childhood on the streets of London. How his mother had been a whore, and he had no idea who his father was. What affected Beth the most was hearing how his mother had abandoned him to the streets at the tender age of five. It made her heart break for the small, lost boy Edwin had been. Beth talked of her growing up with her three older brothers. How she had each one of them wrapped around her finger.

After this night, their final night on the road, their lives would return to normal. So they relaxed and enjoyed the last evening. The wine flowed a little more than previous nights. Barriers were weakened. When it came time to bid each other a good night, Edwin leaned toward her and kissed her. She allowed him that kiss, all too briefly, then jerked away.

"I am sorry, Beth," he quickly apologized. "I should not have done that."

Beth placed her palm along his cheek and gently caressed it. "If our situations were different…"

He stiffened. "Is it because of my lowly birth?"

"Nay, nay! Nay, that is not what I meant. It is all to do with me. I am starting to have feelings for you, but I feel as though I am doing something wrong. As if I am making less of William's memory."

"I understand. I will not push, but I want you to know one thing. If ever you need me, I am here for you."

His words caused her much relief. Alienating Edwin was the last thing she wanted. She valued his friendship. "Thank you, Edwin. I am here for you as well." After brushing a kiss across his cheek, she stepped into her sectioned-off sleeping area, alone.

* * * *

Jacqueline took a deep breath and filled her lungs with the spring air. She loved that time of year. Seeing all the trees sprouting new green growth after the winter months of dullness lifted her spirits. The air was laced with the smell of fresh vegetation.

Jordan squirmed against her, and she rubbed his small back to settle him. She smiled at her son. He was strapped to her chest with a blanket that she had made into a sling, then securely tied around herself. Since it was such a nice day, and they were not too far from Nunney, she had decided to ride on horseback for the last leg of their journey. It was a more comfortable way to travel than being bounced around in the baggage cart.

Terric had not been too pleased with her decision, but in the end, he relented. He had to know she was nearly at her wit's end tolerating the jostling in the cart. He had not been able to ignore the pleading look in her eyes.

Beth rode next to Jacqueline while Edwin and Terric rode in front. Two men-at-arms drove the cart at the rear.

As they approached the outskirts of Nunney village, a large party of men on horseback charged from the wooded area that ran parallel with the road they traveled. The men reached the slower-moving cart first. Realizing how much danger they were in when the armed men cut down the men-at-arms, Terric moved into action. He yanked violently on his mount's reins. The horse reared as he turned him quickly around. With sword drawn, he rushed to reach Jacqueline and Beth.

Before he rode past Edwin, he looked at the squire, and bellowed, "Take them! Do not leave their side, no matter what happens. Get them inside the castle."

Edwin shouted, "With my life."

Jacqueline made no move to follow Edwin and Beth in taking flight. Terric yelled, "Go!"

To make sure she complied with his order, he used the flat of his sword to slap her horse's rump. Her mount whinnied before taking off at a gallop. He let loose a battle cry and raced to meet their attackers.

They were getting closer. The sound of pounding hooves seemed to draw nearer no matter how hard Jacqueline urged her horse to go faster. She looked over her shoulder and found she was not too far off the mark. The two men, who had broken away from the main group to give chase, were definitely gaining on them. She set her heels into her mount's sides, pushing it for greater speed.

Edwin and Beth flanked her. They kept glancing behind them. As the gates of Nunney Castle came into view,

Edwin let out a whoop. They would make it. There were figures on the walls, running to man the drawbridge. Thundering across the causeway that spanned the moat, they cleared the drawbridge before it was once again raised behind them.

Once in the bailey, Jacqueline swiftly dismounted and unwound Jordan from the blanket keeping him secured to her. He seemed not at all perturbed with their mad flight.

Sir Guy ran to meet them. "Is anyone hurt?"

Jacqueline shook her head. "Nay, but Terric is still out there. You have to send out some men to help him."

"We cannot, lass," he said gravely.

With each second that passed, the feeling of desperation grew inside her. When Sir Guy refused to send out reinforcements to save Terric, Jacqueline panicked. "What do you mean? We cannot just leave him out there!"

Sir Guy gave her a sad look. "If we lower that drawbridge again, there will be no stopping them from entering Nunney. I told you before. The castle's defenses are totally inadequate."

She would not, nay, could not, accept that there was nothing they could do to help Terric. She would not abandon him. Not now. After quickly shoving Jordan into Beth's arms, Jacqueline ran toward the gatehouse where the mechanism for raising and lowering the drawbridge was housed. Before she reached it, a pair of strong arms snagged her around the waist from behind, lifting her off her feet.

Sir Guy pulled Jacqueline back against his chest and tightly held on to her as she fought to free herself. Once she yelled at him in frustration, he spoke to her sharply. "I will not allow you to put the castle at risk for just one man. Even if that man happens to be your husband."

His words penetrated through her frenzied attempts to gain her freedom. Jacqueline ceased her struggles. Sir Guy placed her back onto her feet, but she was not done yet.

Her elbow shot back, catching him squarely in his stomach. Groaning, he tried to grab her as she took off at a run once more. He was only able to grab a fistful of her cloak, which he held on to firmly.

He recovered his breath and turned her around to face him. He held her firmly by each of her arms. "Lass, if you do not desist this behavior, I will have you locked in your chamber."

Realizing she was unable to win, she broke down. She could not accept the thought of losing Terric after all they had endured. It seemed that was exactly what she was going to have to do. Tears poured down her cheeks unchecked.

Sir Guy gently pulled her to his chest, trying to console her. "If it were only the few men who gave you chase, then maybe I would have considered it, but there are a lot more than that. Too many. We are outnumbered. If they were to breach the walls, it would be over before you knew what was happening."

Jacqueline jerked her head up. Her cheeks were still wet from the tears she had shed. "What? How can there be so many? The men who first attacked us only numbered in the handful."

Sir Guy frowned. "They must have thought capturing you they would gain entry into Nunney more easily. Since that failed, they have resorted to a stronger tactic. There are a very large number of men outside the walls, preparing to lay siege."

Jacqueline roughly wiped the tears from her face and said gruffly, "Show me."

Sir Guy took her up the stairs to the castle walls, then pointed to the wide-open area situated in front of the causeway. The amount of men milling about made her realize how serious the situation really had become. It was a small army setting up camp.

Hoping to spot Terric in their midst, Jacqueline

searched the activity below. She cursed under her breath. Sir Guy echoed her sentiment.

"Aye, lass. It is your father who is responsible for this. Those men wear his colors. I knew I should have done away with that murderous minstrel."

"It matters naught now. The earl is here, and we must figure out what to do next. I only hope he has kept Terric alive. If he has not, nothing will stop me from putting an end to my father's life."

With that said, she turned her back on the troops preparing to lay siege to her castle and returned to the bailey below.

CHAPTER TWENTY-THREE

T erric tried to find a more comfortable position as he strained against the bonds that kept him restrained. With his hands tied behind him, there really was no comfort to be found either physically or mentally. Being taken as a prisoner was not the outcome he had thought would happen at the end of the day.

He had fought them to the bitter end, but being so greatly outnumbered had stacked the odds against him. He had only been able to bring down a few of the attackers before he was dragged from his horse. Terric just hoped he had kept them occupied dealing with him, allowing Jacqueline to make it to safety.

He was tied to the center post of the Earl of Salisbury's pavilion. Terric had not been too surprised upon learning whose men attacked them. He only wished Jacqueline's father had not come to Nunney so quickly.

Terric silently cursed the man who had tied his bonds. They were tight, causing him to lose the feeling in his fingers. He clenched and unclenched his hands, trying to force more blood into them, but it was futile. The strips of leather were too constricting.

Someone opened the pavilion's flapped entrance, and he ceased his struggles. The earl stepped inside. He came to stand directly in front of Terric and looked down. He put his hands behind his back and shook his head.

"Well, Sir Terric, tell me what I should do with you. I find myself in the midst of a quandary. On one hand, I should have you terminated, but on the other, I feel you are my best leverage to open Nunney for me."

Terric curled his lip in a snarl. "I will not allow you to use me to gain entrance to the castle."

The earl laughed. "My dear boy, in your present position, you really do not have much choice in the matter." He bent down and grabbed a handful of Terric's hair, then painfully forced him to look at him. "I am very sure my darling daughter would do just about anything to get you back." He released him as he slammed Terric's head hard against the post.

Terric tried to surge to his feet, forgetting he was bound. He growled in frustration. His hands itched to be around the earl's throat. "You can do whatever you wish to me, but leave Jacqueline alone."

The earl straightened to his full height and smiled. "Such display of emotion. How touching. So, you would be willing to endure anything in the name of love? If it would mean your life? What then?"

"Gladly would I give it." It was Terric's turn to smile. A disgusted expression crossed the earl's face. "Since you love no one but yourself, you cannot possibly understand."

The backhanded slap the earl delivered caught Terric on the corner of his mouth. A rush of blood entered it when his lip split. "Your devotion to my daughter might cause you to lose that very thing."

* * * *

209

A few hours after the earl's visit, Terric was moved to another pavilion. One that was used for storing the camp's supplies. Crates and casks haphazardly stacked.

His guards roughly shoved him through the entrance. He barely managed to keep his balance. If he had fallen, he would not have been able to catch himself. With his hands still bound behind his back, it would have been impossible, and well they knew it.

After depositing Terric in his new prison, the guards left, securing the pavilion flap. They softly spoke just outside the entrance where they stood guard.

He stepped to the centre of the pavilion, then sat on the floor. Night was slowly creeping in, and it was sure to be an uncomfortable one for him. Along with having no blanket to keep him warm, he had not been given any food or drink. His stomach rumbled, reminding him of the number of hours that had passed since he had last eaten. There was nothing for it. He would have to do without.

He dozed off and only came awake once the pavilion flap opened again. It was not the earl, but one of his guards, carrying a cloth-covered tray. Another man followed. Terric did not bother to pay close attention to either of them.

The tray was placed beside him before the guard roughly took hold of his bound hands and cut them free. Terric hissed as blood rushed into his numb digits. Barely given enough time to have the circulation fully restored, his hands were bound once more, this time in front of him. At least he would be able to use them to eat.

The guard left, leaving the other man behind. Still ignoring him, Terric lifted the cloth, then ate the bread and cheese he had been given. A pair of feet came into his field of vision, and he finally looked up.

The man was vaguely familiar. At first, he could not place where he had met him, but then it hit Terric who it was.

The man smiled. "Ah, I can see you finally remember me."

"Aye, I do."

"As I remember you. An *acquaintance* of Jacqueline's."

Terric tapped down his rage toward him, the minstrel, Nicholas. The one who had tried to end his son's life. The one who had been nothing but a thorn in Jacqueline's side. "What do you want?"

Nicholas sneered. "What do I want? Nothing from you. The earl is giving me everything I want. I just came to tell you not to worry what Jacqueline's fate will be. She will be left unharmed and well taken care of. By me."

Terric shook his head and chuckled. "Did the earl promise you Jacqueline?"

"Aye."

"You think he will keep his word?"

"Aye."

"You are a bigger idiot than Jacqueline described." Terric had the satisfaction of the minstrel's expression turning from cocky to uneasy. Finally, he became angry.

Nicholas kicked the tray of food beside Terric. He ground the bread and cheese into the ground with the heel of his boot. "The earl will not double-cross me. I was the one who told him of Forwin's duplicity. He said he would reward me with Jacqueline as my wife."

"If I were you, I would watch my back. I have a feeling you have outlived your usefulness."

Nicholas gave Terric one last dark look, then stomped out of the pavilion. Terric shook his head once more. The man was a stupid fool. He had put his trust in the maw of a viper.

* * * *

Jacqueline found no rest that night. Not knowing how Terric faired ate away at her. Finally, after fretting half the night through, she gave up. After giving Jordan his night feeding and then settling him back down to sleep, she went and sat at her chamber window. From that vantage point, she was able to look down at her father's camp. There were so many of them. She was not at all confident they could withstand an attack. Sir Guy was a very good strategist, but with such weak defenses, strategy would not be much of an asset. It could only work to a certain extent.

As dawn's light appeared over the horizon, the activity within the camp increased. Something was definitely happening. After quickly pulling on a tunic and hose, she checked to make sure Jordan still slept. She peered into her son's cradle and found him blissfully sleeping. She gently adjusted his blanket, then quietly left the chamber.

At the hall, Jacqueline found Alice preparing to light the fireplace. Once she lit it, she turned around. She jumped in surprise. With her hand on her chest, she said, "Oh, my lady, you gave me a scare. I did not see you come down."

"Sorry, Alice. I did not mean to give you a fright. What are you doing up so early?"

Alice brushed her hands on her apron and shrugged. "I could not sleep. All those men out there worry me."

"We are safe for the moment." Jacqueline hoped she sounded convincing, because that was not how she felt. Alice did not need to know that, though. "Now that you have the fire lit, can you sit in my chamber with Jordan? He is still asleep."

Alice smiled. "With pleasure, my lady. I will bring him to you once he awakens."

After Alice disappeared up the stairs, Jacqueline turned to face the newly-lit fire. Even though spring had arrived and the days were getting increasingly warmer, the castle still was chilly. She extended her hands toward the flames.

Sir Guy found her that way when he came in search of

her. "I am glad to see you are awake, lass. Saves me from having to wake you."

Jacqueline dropped her arms to her sides as the older man approached. "Something has happened. Has it not?"

"Aye. Your father is at the causeway, demanding to speak with you." Jacqueline moved to leave, but Sir Guy stopped her. "There is one other thing. He has Terric with him."

Her steps faltered for a moment, but she quickly regained her composure. With long, steady strides, she quickly left the hall and then climbed up to the top of the castle walls. Sir Guy followed her.

Just as Sir Guy had said, the earl stood at the end of the causeway. He was accompanied by two of his men, who acted as guards for their prisoner. Terric was between them, bound.

Anger boiled inside her. The earl looked so self-assured, almost as if he assumed his mere presence would open Nunney. She had no intention of handing the castle over to him. She walked to the parapet wall and stared down at her father.

"You requested to speak with me. Here I am," she said in a loud voice.

The earl looked up. "Ah, daughter. So you have come. Do you not think it would be better if you let me in? That way we could speak more freely."

"What do you take me for, Father? A woman without sense? If you want words with me, say them from there."

Even from the great distance that separated them, Jacqueline saw the earl's face turn red with ire. All pretences were gone when he finally found his voice once more. "You stupid girl! You know why I am here. Nunney is mine, and you are going to give it to me."

"Nay. I will not. Nunney is my son's birthright. It never was to be yours. It makes no difference what deal you made with Forwin. I wonder what the king would say if he found out about your underhanded ways."

"Enough!" the earl bellowed. He snapped his fingers. His men brought Terric to the end of the causeway. "Either you lower the drawbridge or you forfeit the life of your lover."

Jacqueline gripped the edge of the stone parapet wall so tightly her fingers turned white. Her gaze shot to Terric's face. He gave her a perspicuous shake of his head, telling her not to give in to the earl's demands.

The earl yelled, "Well? What have you decided?"

Sir Guy came to stand next to Jacqueline and spoke with hushed tones into her ear. "Ask for more time before you give him your answer. We need to think of a way to get Terric from him."

Jacqueline nodded, then said to the earl, "I need time before I can make my decision."

Below, Terric tried to pull free from the two men who held him. "Jacqueline! I am dead anyway. Do not let him take Nunney. It will make no difference."

Annoyed, the earl motioned to his men with a flick of his wrist. "Shut him up."

With the butt of his sword, one of the men slammed it onto the back of Terric's head. He crumpled into a heap on the dusty causeway as Jacqueline cried out.

"I will give you until dawn on the morrow. If you do not lower the drawbridge then, you can watch your lover die."

CHAPTER TWENTY-FOUR

Jacqueline felt sick as her father's men dragged the unconscious Terric away. She also felt helpless, which was exactly how her father wanted her to feel.

Before returning to his encampment, the earl had one final thing to say. "You might be my daughter, but that will not stop me from taking Nunney down a stone at a time if I must. Or from making you pay the price for trying to take what I want."

She stood at the wall long after the earl had gone. Sir Guy stayed by her side. "Time to return to the hall, lass. Standing out here will not be of any help to Terric."

Jacqueline pried her stiff fingers from the wall and looked at Sir Guy. "There is no hope for us. I cannot save him."

"There is always hope, Jacqueline. Do not give up the fight so easily. You are a fighter, girl. You cannot let him beat you. Now is the time to show that bastard he does not always get whatever he wants."

She meekly shook her head. "I am not strong enough. Too much is at stake here. How could I live with myself if I retain Nunney at the cost of Terric's life? I would look at these walls day in and day out and see his blood upon them. That is too much to ask of me."

"Come down to the hall. I am sure Beth and Edwin are now awake. We have a day. The four of us should be able to put our heads together and come up with some way of getting Terric from the earl's clutches." Sir Guy took Jacqueline by the arm and led her from the wall. "Remember, you are not alone. We will prevail."

* * * *

Surfacing to awareness, Terric groaned in pain. His head felt as if it were cracked in two. To make sure it really was still in one piece, he gingerly lifted it off the ground. It held together, much to his surprise.

After carefully rolling to his side, Terric tried to push himself into an upright position. The movement cost him greatly. Sweat poured down his face, and his world spun as dizziness overtook him. Closing his eyes seemed to help somewhat.

The picture of Jacqueline upon the castle walls rose to play behind his closed eyes. He had felt a moment of triumph, seeing that she was indeed safe, but he had seen the fear and helplessness she felt at facing the earl. Knowing it was he who engendered such feelings in her made Terric wish he could make this all disappear. She should not have to go through a situation like this. She already had been through enough hardship.

Around midday, one of the earl's men brought food and water for Terric. He silently placed the tray he carried beside him, then just as quietly left. Terric grasped the jug of water with his bound hands, then greedily drank. Figuring this would be all he could expect in the way of nourishment for the day, he made sure he left half the bread for later. He did the same with the water.

Once he finished his simple meal, there was only one

thing left to him — sit and wait to see what fate would deal him.

* * * *

"Can we come up with nothing?" she asked vehemently.

The hours of frustration wore Jacqueline down. Among the four of them, they had yet to come up with a feasible plan to free Terric. Many of the problems stemmed from the castle's own defenses. The moat being their only real barrier for safety, it extended all the way to the castle walls, and that made it as much of an obstacle as a defense.

At first, the only response Jacqueline received to her question was silence. Then Edwin cleared his throat and hesitantly said, "I have…have an idea."

Jacqueline immediately perked up. "What do you have in mind?"

"Well…what if I were to have someone lower me to the moat at the back of the castle. I could swim to the other side and sneak into the earl's camp to free Terric. I doubt they would expect someone like me to attempt anything like that. I know how to keep myself from being seen. I learned that lesson well before Terric found me in London." Having lived alone on some of that city's meanest streets from a very early age and survived, attested to his skill.

Sir Guy seemed to take what Edwin suggested into serious consideration, but eventually he shook his head. "Nay, sorry, lad, but it is too risky."

Edwin, who had been sitting by the hearth, shot to his feet and walked to the trestle table where Jacqueline, Beth, and Sir Guy sat. "It can work. I know it can. The earl does not have any of his men watching the back of the castle. I know, I looked. He thinks he has us where he wants us. He is too sure of himself."

Beth, who had silently listened as the others spoke, said, "Sorry to say this, Sir Guy, but I have to agree with Edwin. The earl would never expect what Edwin plans."

The older man threw up his hands in consternation. "I really have no right to stop you, Edwin, but I cannot help feel you do not know what kind of danger you will be putting yourself in."

Edwin chuckled, but without humor. "No more dangerous than what I lived with every day in London as a child. It makes no difference to me. Terric saved my life. It is my turn to pay back the favor. I have to try. I owe him that much."

Sir Guy nodded. "Fine, lad. We will give your plan a try tonight. Time is running out, and so far, you are our best hope."

* * * *

Jacqueline moved stealthily, keeping to the shadows as she headed to the back of the castle. After reaching the stairs that would take her to the top of the walls, she took them two at a time. She carried a long coil of rope over one shoulder.

As Sir Guy and Edwin had discussed the squire's plan to rescue Terric, she had been busily making her own. She decided she would take Edwin's place. So as darkness began to fall, Jacqueline made her move. She would cross the moat on her own, much earlier than Edwin was to make his attempt.

Once she gained the top of the stairs, she worked quickly. She tied the rope through one of the notches in the wall, then threw the length of it over. She slipped her dagger free from its sheath that hung at her waist and then placed the blade between her lips. She took hold of the rope and swung her legs over the wall before she slowly moved to the moat below.

Jacqueline sucked in her breath as she entered the water. The coldness was a shock. Setting off with smooth, even strokes, she clamped her teeth together, preventing them from chattering. Once she reached the other side, she quickly scanned the edge of the moat for any movement. Luck seemed to be on her side. She appeared to be alone. She pulled herself up and onto dry ground, then shook the water from her hair. Stealthily, she began the task of sneaking into her father's encampment.

* * * *

Sir Guy accompanied Edwin up to the wall. The sight of a rope already tied to the wall surprised him. Finding it hanging to the moat below sent a chill running down his spine.

He scanned the bank on the opposite side and found it deserted. Sir Guy swore under his breath and set off at a run. He took the steps down practically three at a time as he hurried to the hall. Edwin followed.

After throwing open the hall doors, both of them barreled through. Beth, who had been pacing before the hearth, let out a gasp of surprise as he searched every inch of the hall with his gaze. "What is wrong?"

"Where is she?" he asked.

"Who?"

"Jacqueline. Where is she?"

"Is she not with you? She is not in her chamber. I just came from there. Alice is the only one there, watching Jordan."

He let out a bellow of rage and headed for the chambers above. Mindful of the sleeping babe, he quietly opened Jacqueline's chamber door. Alice sat in a chair near the cradle, stitching. She looked up from her work as the door swung open. At Sir Guy's signal for her to join him outside, she put aside her sewing and came to him.

"Where is your mistress?"

Not looking him in the face, Alice said quietly, "I know not. She just bid me to mind the little lord."

He took the girl by the shoulders and gave her a little shake. "Do not play dumb with me, girl." Alice whimpered. "You know where Jacqueline went and you are going to tell me."

Alice whimpered once more. "She made me promise not to say. I will tell you, sir. She has gone to rescue her husband."

Sir Guy briefly closed his eyes and sent up a silent prayer, one to save him from headstrong women. "How long ago did she leave?"

"When it grew dark." Alice cringed.

He released the servant girl, then returned to the hall to break the news to Beth and Edwin. Both stood near the stairs, waiting expectantly. He shook his head. "The fool of a lass has gone over the wall by herself. From the amount of time that has passed, I would say she is at this moment working her way into the camp."

Silently, Beth walked to the trestle table and refilled her goblet of wine. She tossed it back in two large gulps. Sir Guy thought she had the way of it. They would all need some wine to fortify their spirits if they were to get through this night. He just hoped Jacqueline knew what she was doing.

* * * *

Nicholas savored the rich wine the earl provided to all who had been invited to his pavilion. They were celebrating the morrow's victory. The earl planned to walk through Nunney's gates and claim the castle as his own.

He had not spoken with the earl since their first meeting, but he expected he would soon. When he had received the invitation to join this impromptu celebration, it had said his attendance was mandatory. It was a command that had not really been necessary. It was not as if he would have turned it down.

Sipping his wine, Nicholas casually watched the earl conversing with the captain of his men. So far, his presence had not been acknowledged. There was nothing for it but to wait. As the evening progressed and still he had not been singled out by the earl, he wondered if he would be ignored, after all. After draining his fourth goblet of wine, he felt the pressing need to relieve himself. He slipped from the pavilion and found a secluded spot just behind it.

He loosened his hose before he did his business. Soon, he realized he was not alone. Two others were doing the same as he. Though he could not see them, he heard their conversation. What they said sent a chill running down his back.

"Did you see that minstrel in there? Acting as if he had every right to be among us," said the first man.

"Aye, but the earl promised to reward him," the second man replied.

"Oh, he is going to get his reward all right. The reward of meeting his maker." Both men laughed.

As their laughter faded as they headed back into the pavilion, Nicholas stood frozen. He was unable to move. Panic had seized him in its steely grip and it would not let go.

He broke out in a cold sweat and slowly backed up. There was no question of his returning to the earl's pavilion. He had to run before they realized he was gone.

Quickly as he could, he collected his belongings and then strapped them to his horse. Once more he had been cheated out of what was his due. He hoped the earl would get what he so richly deserved—his precious Nunney Castle barred against him.

* * * *

Jacqueline kept as low to the ground as she could and crawled around to the back of the pavilion inside her father's camp. She had donned her darkest tunic and hose before leaving the castle. With only a quarter moon covered by heavy clouds, she was able to move around virtually unseen. Not that there was anyone roaming about the camp to see her. The earl was indeed sure of his victory. No guards were posted, and the sounds of revelry could be heard drifting from the opposite side of the encampment.

Even in the darkness, Jacqueline easily distinguished the earl's pavilion midst the few others. His was the most lavishly adorned with his standard boldly before it. Hoping Terric was not being held in there, she decided to check the smaller pavilions at the very edge of camp. After reaching the first one, she used her dagger to cut a small slit in the canvas just big enough for her to peer through.

A meager light from a campfire on the other side of the pavilion filtered in through a small opening in the flap. At first, she only saw bundles of supplies spread haphazardly around the interior. Her gaze came to rest on the supine form of Terric. He lay off to one side, not too far from where she had made her peephole.

She used the tip of her dagger and cut a much larger slit in the canvas. She put her hand through it. Jacqueline stifled a scream as she was roughly yanked inside, ending up sprawled across Terric's chest. Doing what seemed the most natural thing to do in such a position, she took his face in both her hands and kissed him thoroughly.

At first, Terric enthusiastically returned her kiss, but he soon turned his head to the side and pulled free from her embrace. With eyes blazing, he looked at her. "What the hell are you doing here?" he whispered.

Jacqueline chose to ignore his ire and broadly smiled. She spoke in equally hushed tones. "I have come to rescue you, of course."

"Why did you not stay safely behind Nunney's walls? How could you have acted so rashly?"

Her smile slowly faded. "You cannot have expected me to idly stand by and let the earl kill you."

"If needs be, that is exactly what I wanted you to do."

Jacqueline slid from Terric's chest, then cut the strip of leather binding his hands before him. "Well, I could not live with myself if I had. It is because of me that you are here."

Terric pulled her back into his arms and kissed her deeply once more. "I will not say I am not happy to see you, Jacqueline, but you have taken a huge risk. If anything happened to you…"

Gently caressing his cheek, she gave him a half smile. "I too. You are a part of me now. I have already suffered greatly from the loss of William. Do not make me go through that again with you. I could not survive it this time."

"Then, lady wife, I suggest we get the hell out of here."

Jacqueline squeezed Terric's hand, then slipped out of the pavilion through the hole she had made. Once he joined her, she let him lead the way out of the encampment. She really had not thought of what would happen after she had freed him. All her attention had been focused on just finding him.

He took her by the hand and pulled her after him as he headed for the wooded area at the outskirts of the camp. The distance was great, but keeping to a crouched run, they reached it without being spotted. In the cover of the trees, they straightened and pushed through the thick brush.

"We need to find some place to hide. A thicket or some overgrown brush," Terric said, gazing around. "There is no question of us returning to the castle now. Once I'm found missing, the alarm will be raised, and being anywhere near the castle walls would be pure folly."

Fate seemed to be on their side. After walking for a quarter of an hour, what Terric had been searching for presented itself—a thicket surrounded by thorns. There was a small opening at the bottom. He squatting and peered through it. "It seems to be a rabbit run. There appears to be a clearing in the very center. It might just be big enough for you and I."

He stood once more. The top of the thicket was taller than Terric's six feet four inches, which was perfect. If anyone should walk by, she and Terric could remain undetected. The entrance would be a very tight squeeze, particularly for him, given the way it was now, but he must have thought of that. He motioned for her dagger, then went onto his knees and proceeded to push his way through, using the blade as he went. Once his feet disappeared, Jacqueline followed.

They did not escape the thorns completely unscathed. Both ended up with scratches. Terric suffered worse on his hands from having wielded the dagger. Jacqueline breathed a sigh of relief once she made it through. The clearing was a tight fit for the two of them, but as he pulled her into his arms, she found it mattered not.

Terric claimed her lips in a searing kiss. The feel of him on top of her felt like heaven. It was something she had not expected to experience ever again. She threaded her fingers through the hair at his nape. She was not ready yet to let him go, even though danger still lurked outside their hiding spot. He seemed to understand her desperation. He licked her bottom lip until she allowed him access to her mouth. The taste of him heightened her arousal. Moaning, Jacqueline lifted her hips to meet his, demanding more.

He broke contact with her lips, then rested his forehead against hers. He panted, as if he had run a long distance. Once he got his breathing back under control, he spoke. "I am just a man, Jacqueline. I cannot take much more of this.

We...I need to keep my wits about me. You are just too distracting."

Knowing Terric was right still did not make Jacqueline feel any better. Her body clamored for his. "When all of this is over, you better finish what you started here."

Terric smiled. "Your wish is my command, my lady. You should try to sleep while you can."

"What about you?"

"For whatever good it will do, I will keep watch. You rest."

Jacqueline yawned. The lack of sleep the night before was starting to catch up with her. "Fine, I will do as you say, but wake me up after a few hours so you can rest as well."

Terric moved to his back and pulled her to his side, holding her to his chest. It was not long before she relaxed and slipped into sleep.

* * * *

The morning was not going as he had expected. When the earl retired the night before, he knew he had won, but much had transpired during the darkness.

Firstly, his association with the minstrel had not been brought to an acceptable close. The sniveling man must have gotten wind of what was in store for him. The earl shook his head. He disliked loose ends such as Nicholas running about. Enemies tended to hold grudges, but the problem of the minstrel was minor compared with the other.

The earl sat in one of his camp chairs and cursed his daughter once more. He knew she was partly responsible for freeing her lover. He had once again underestimated her. In some small way, he felt a growing respect for Jacqueline.

The loss of William he still felt keenly, but not out of

any feeling that one gets at the death of one's child. Nay, he did not feel that way. What he felt was the loss of an heir. With William gone, all his holdings would now go to one of his cousins upon his death. If only his wife could have born twin sons instead of bearing a worthless daughter.

A scratch came on the outside of his pavilion, and the earl bid the person to enter. One of his men stepped inside. "Well? Have you found any trace of him yet?"

The man shook his head. "Nay. We have looked all around the perimeter of the camp. There is no sign of him."

The earl leveled a steely gaze upon the man and said very slowly, "I suggest you further your search. Did it not occur to any of you to search farther than just the camp? Like in the forest next to it." The man-at-arms mumbled something unintelligible. "For god sake, man, speak up!"

The man cleared his throat. "Most of the men are afraid to go in there."

"I want that forest searched. Now!" the earl roared.

Bowing, the man-at-arms backed out of the pavilion. The earl ground his teeth in ire. He was surrounded by idiots. No wonder his best-laid plans were falling apart.

* * * *

The feel of bright sunshine beating on her, along with the birds singing to the dawning of a new day, brought Jacqueline out of her sleep. Blinking, she tried to get her bearings. Being wrapped in the arms of her still-sleeping husband helped her to recall all the events from the previous night.

Jacqueline turned her head to look at her husband. She smiled at the sight of him. Asleep, his face seemed softer. She extended her hand and softly brushed a finger across his lips. Terric opened his mouth and nipped it.

"I thought you were supposed to wake me."

Terric stretched. "I did not have the heart to disturb you. I managed to get a few hours of rest."

Jacqueline sat up and stretched the kinks out of her back. "Still, you should have."

"Be that as it may, we had an uneventful rest. We should head to the castle. Though this was a good hiding spot at night, in the light of day it loses some of its merits. I think it would be prudent to leave."

Jacqueline had to agree. She would not relish the idea of being trapped within these thorny confines, unable to flee quickly. She gladly followed Terric through the wicked barbs. She had managed to just safely get her head through the thorns when he slammed a hand down onto it and pushed her back in. He was totally clear of them and stood just outside the opening.

"Stay there!" he whispered harshly.

Before she could question why, he took off at a run, heading deeper into the woods. The sound of voices moving closer to her hiding spot caused her heart to jump into her throat. It was not long before a couple of men stood directly in front of the run where she lay. Jacqueline stiffened, afraid to move even slightly, not wanting to draw their attention. Her heart thudded in her ears so loudly she was sure it would give her away.

After what seemed an extraordinarily long time, the men moved off to carry their search elsewhere. She let her breath out in a loud gasp. She fought the urge to burst from her hiding place and search for Terric. Instead, she lay there for a few minutes longer, then pulled herself free.

In a quandary as to what she should do, Jacqueline fought a silent battle. She could either try to find Terric in the woods or her own way out of them. She had not really been able to see in which direction he had headed. If she tried to follow, she risked the chance of meeting the earl's men as well.

Jacqueline hit her fist on her thigh and cursed. There really was only one option. She had to work her way to the castle without Terric.

* * * *

Edwin stretched his stiff back. He had been standing way too long. As the hours ticked by and no cry came of Jacqueline or Terric returning to the castle, he had climbed the stairs to the walls. Sleep would be an impossible task with those two still somewhere out there near the earl's camp.

On the walls, watching the camp below, made him feel a little bit better. As long as no hue and cry rose, Jacqueline and Terric were safe. If it did occur, he was prepared to try something, anything, to help.

At some point during the night, Sir Guy had come to share his vigil. Worry lines were etched into the older man's face. "Still no sign of them?" he calmly asked.

Edwin shook his head. "Nay, nothing. As long as there is no activity below, I take that for a good sign."

"I agree. I should still wring the lass' neck for pulling this stunt, though. I think she has aged me another twenty years this night."

Beneath the gruffness, Edwin heard the deep concern Sir Guy had for Jacqueline. "She can take care of herself. She will find a way to set Terric free."

Sir Guy grunted. "Aye, I know she will. I just wish she would not take such risks. She has a son to think about."

They fell silent. Not long after, the sound of footsteps ascending the stairs at the far end of the wall brought them out of their silent reverie. Both of them turned as Beth stepped onto the walkway. Edwin couldn't stop himself from staring hungrily at her.

Before Beth reached them, Sir Guy said, "I will leave you two alone." He turned to Edwin. "Do not give up on her, lad. The time will come when she will be ready to accept you." Edwin stared at him in shock. Sir Guy smiled and winked. "I might seem old to you, but I am not dead yet." With that said, he left him and Beth alone.

Beth paused on the walkway as Sir Guy took the stairs down to the bailey. She looked questioningly at Edwin once they were alone. "Where is he off to?"

Edwin sheepishly answered, "He is giving us some privacy."

Beth came to stand beside him and smiled. "Sir Guy is cannier than I thought."

Even though dawn was closely approaching, the chill of the night still could be felt. Beth wrapped her arms around herself. Edwin noticed what she did, pulled her to stand in front of him, and took her in his arms. She allowed it.

They stood in that position, in silence, for a few minutes. Beth was the first to speak. "You are worried about him. Terric must mean a lot to you. Am I right?"

"Aye. He is like a brother to me. If not for Terric, I doubt I would be alive today. I owe him so much."

*

Beth leaned farther back into his embrace and realized how much she missed this, being held tenderly by a man. "Everything will be all right, Edwin."

Edwin kissed the top of her head. She fitted nicely under his chin. "I have told myself that very thing time and again." He turned Beth in his arms so she faced him and stared at her. "I know right now I have nothing to offer you, but Terric has promised to knight me soon. Do you think, after I am knighted, you could consider me worthy of you?"

A wide range of emotions flitted across his face. She knew this cost him much. His feeling of uncertainty could be easily read in his eyes. She loved those green eyes. She would always love William, but Edwin had wormed his way, slowly albeit, into her heart.

Sending up a silent pray of forgiveness, if William watched over her, Beth smiled. "Aye, Edwin, I would happily accept you." To show him how she felt about him, she went on tiptoes and placed a kiss on his lips.

Edwin crushed Beth against his chest and greedily kissed her back, as if he poured his heart and soul into the kiss. She reciprocated in kind. As it continued, the dawn's sunny rays reached the castle walls. The bright light washed over them.

CHAPTER TWENTY-FIVE

The time it took to return to Nunney was more than it had taken to enter the woods. Afraid to come across the men searching for her and Terric, Jacqueline stopped every few minutes to listen for sounds of movement. A few times, she heard a snap of a twig coming from behind her or in front. The trees distorted the sounds, making it hard to judge the exact location.

By the time she reached the edge of the trees, the sun was high. Sweat ran down her back, making Jacqueline wish she could have a bath. Her breasts ached from a buildup of milk, reminding her that she had to get to Jordan very soon. It would not be at all well to have her milk dry up now.

From the corner of her eye, she spied a group of men exiting the woods about twelve feet from where she stood. Jacqueline quickly took a step back inside the tree line.

There were four of the earl's men, and they had Terric with them. She did not think and only acted. She ran after them. They did not see her at first so she was able to reach the last man of the group and throw her full weight against his back. Unprepared, the man fell to his knees.

Using the momentary confusion, Terric slammed his fist into the jaw of the man at his side. He dropped like a stone.

Unarmed, Jacqueline jumped onto the back of one of the two still standing and placed her hands over his eyes. Unable to see, he tried to shake her off. She tenaciously hung on until Terric finished taking care of the final man. She jumped off before Terric's fist met the man's face.

With three down and one still struggling to gain his feet against the weight of his armor, Terric grabbed Jacqueline's hand and took off at a run. They ran straight into the earl. Her father was not alone. He had at least a handful of men with him. Terric valiantly tried to get them through, but sheer numbers won out. He was roughly subdued by the earl's men, leaving Jacqueline by herself to confront her father. The earl stared at her, trying to intimidate her. She lifted her chin in defiance and boldly glared back.

The earl took her arm in a steely grip and led her toward the castle. "I admire your boldness, daughter, but on a woman, it is an unseemly trait. It seems I have misjudged you."

Jacqueline did not respond. Instead, she looked behind her to see if Terric was still with her. He was being held by a man on either side of him with a third bringing up the rear. That one used his sword to jab into Terric's back to urge him on.

Her father did not miss her show of concern. "You love him. I can see it. Shall we test your love for him? How far will you go to save the life of a mere landless tournament knight?"

"He is more than that. He is my husband," Jacqueline said through gritted teeth.

The earl pulled her up short, almost jerking her off her feet. "Has the marriage been consummated?" Jacqueline defiantly refused to answer, and he gave her a hard shake.

"Answer me, girl! Has it been consummated?"

She put a sweet smile on her lips. "Aye, well and truly."

Her father pulled her once more into motion and marched her to the castle causeway. "You just signed your husband's death warrant. Nunney is mine, and nothing will stand in my way of claiming it."

In a load roar, the earl yelled up at the castle, making their presence known to those within. A minute later, Sir Guy appeared at the top of the wall. His face fell when he saw Jacqueline beside her father.

"Lower the drawbridge or I will be forced to take drastic measures." His threat engendered no response from the man above. He hissed at Jacqueline. "Order that old fool to do as I say."

She shook her head without meeting the earl's gaze. "Nay."

With a snarl, the earl ordered Terric brought to them. "I will ask you one more time. Give the order."

Terric caught Jacqueline's gaze. He gave an infinitesimal shake of his head. She knew what he was asking her to do, but she did not know if she could follow through.

"I see your decision is made. So be it." Her father turned to his men. "Kill him."

Jacqueline clenched her hands into fists. Her nails bit deeply into her palms. She felt ill. As her father raised one of his hands to give the signal, the feeling intensified. She closed her eyes, unable to watch what would happen next.

The blast of a horn reverberated throughout the encampment, causing all the participants in the grisly tableau to freeze and search for the source of the sound. Desperately, Jacqueline scanned the surrounding area, hoping their luck had changed.

At the sight of a large party of mounted riders, a renewed sense of hope surged through her. Their numbers were much larger than the men her father had under his command. There was something about one of the lead riders she found very familiar. Once the party grew nearer, it became easy to discern that a woman rode in front.

Squinting, Jacqueline peered closely at her. When she recognized her, she let out a loud whoop of joy. The earl flashed her a quelling look. She laughed. "It seems you have lost, after all, Father. If I am not mistaken, my mother leads that large party of soldiers approaching."

The utter fury that crossed the earl's features was terrible to behold. Spinning around, he grabbed the sword aimed at Terric's chest from his man. With a growl, he drew it back to thrust it through her husband's heart.

"Nay!" she yelled. She threw herself at her father and barreled into him, pushing him away from Terric. The instant the touch of a cold steel blade rested against the base of her throat, breaking into her awareness, Jacqueline froze.

"You have made my life very burdensome of late, daughter. Once I am through dealing with your husband, I will make you regret ever crossing me."

"I think not, William." Jacqueline's heart thrilled at the sound of her mother's voice. Her mother swung a leg over her horse's back, dismounted, and went to her husband. "Lower the sword, William. It is over." He did not quickly comply with her order, and she stepped closer. "I suggest you take a good look at the soldiers I have brought. They are the king's men and wear his colors."

The earl's face blanched quite white. She had brought a large force of the king's men with her. He slowly let the sword fall from Jacqueline's throat.

The knight who had come to stand next to her mother took the earl by his arm, and said, "By order of the king, you are to quit Nunney and return to London, my lord. The king commands your presence there."

Defeated, the earl allowed himself to be led to the encampment. His men were escorted with him. Jacqueline, unable to stay away any longer, threw herself into Terric's outstretched arms. She desperately clung to him. He held her equally tight.

"Tell me. Do I have a new son-in-law?" her mother asked.

After releasing Terric, Jacqueline embraced her mother. She stepped back and reached for her husband's hand. "Aye, Mother, you do." Looking at the now overflowing encampment, she asked, "How...how did you manage all this?"

Lady Elizabeth chuckled. "I am not completely useless, though your father thinks I am. During the grand tournament, I decided to make some connections of my own. While you were off playing knight, I gained the queen's favor. Let us just say, I pulled some strings and was able to speak with the king and queen. The earl is going to have to do some quick talking to explain his actions here. The king is displeased with him at the moment."

The frightening episode at an end, all three relieved the tension by laughing at what the earl would have to endure to gain the king's favor once more.

The sound of a baby's wails drifted over the castle walls. Jacqueline cringed. "I think I had better get myself to the hall. Beth must be ready to pull her hair out." As if on cue, the drawbridge lowered and there stood her friend with a very distressed Jordan in her arms.

"Do you think, Jacqueline, now that you are no longer busy, you could please feed your son? He has made his displeasure known about having to take the cow's milk we gave him."

Jacqueline took pity on her and laughingly shook her head. She went to retrieve her son. "Of course, Beth."

* * * *

With Jordan happily fed, Lady Elizabeth claimed her grandmotherly rights and spirited him to the hall, leaving Terric and Jacqueline alone in the lord's chamber. Both had bathed, changed into fresh clothing, and now sat on the bed feeding each other from the tray of food Alice had brought to them.

Jacqueline could not get the smug smile to leave her face. Everything was now as it should be. Terric was her husband, and the earl had been put in his place. On the morrow, the king's men would take him to London.

Having had her fill, she sighed and lay back. Terric removed the tray and then fell into her outstretched arms. His lips greedily covered hers. After making her completely breathless, he pulled away and worked on unbuckling the belt that circled her hips. Impatiently, Jacqueline shoved his hands away to remove it herself. He smiled.

"I hope you never tire of me, wife."

Jacqueline tossed her belt to the floor and then worked on Terric's tunic. "Never. You will not be rid of me so easily. I do not give up on things I have to fight so hard to keep."

Terric reached for the hem of her tunic and eased it up her body. "I am pleased. No more talk. I have waited long enough to make love to you properly. There will be time later. Much later." He claimed her lips once more.

Jacqueline groaned with pleasure. There would be more than enough time for talk. A lifetime of it. Her tournament knight was now hers. Nothing could break them apart. The last coherent thought she had before pleasurable sensations took her over was to send up a prayer of thanks.

She pushed Terric onto his back, then slowly stripped away each piece of clothing he wore. When he tried to help, she only slapped his hands away. "You will lie there and behave yourself. I want to have my way with you."

Terric groaned. "Do you not think I have had enough torture? Do you really want to send me to an early grave?"

Jacqueline smiled saucily. "No, I do not. I just want to give you pleasure."

He spread his arms wide. "Then I give my lady wife permission to pleasure me any way she sees fit."

She straddled Terric's thighs and ran her hands across his hard chest and then trailed her fingers to his engorged shaft. She grabbed it and gently squeezed, then pulled down before sliding back up to the tip. He lifted his hips as she worked his cock.

Becoming just as aroused as Terric by what she did, Jacqueline released him and inched forward so the tip of his shaft nudged her slick opening. She shifted her hips at the right angle and pushed down, fully sheathing him inside her body. They moaned.

Terric grabbed Jacqueline by the hips, lifted her slightly, then pushed her back down onto him, showing her how to ride him. She moaned at the feel of having him so deep inside her. Doing as he had shown her, she slid up and down on his cock. As her climax inched ever closer, she increased the pace. Once it hit, her head fell back and she groaned with her release. He pushed up, hard, once more, then emptied himself into her, filling her with his cum.

* * * *

It was some hours before Terric and Jacqueline joined the others in the hall. The need to reaffirm their bond had not been something they could easily ignore. With that desperate need fulfilled, at least for the moment, they emerged from their chamber.

Lady Elizabeth, who held Jordan in her arms, was the first to notice their arrival. "So you have finally come up for a breath of air I see."

Jacqueline felt the heat as she flushed to the very roots

of her hair. "Mother!"

Her mother laughed. "My marriage to your father might not be made from the stuff of dreams, but I do recognize true love. I see it in the love you and Terric have for each other. It is nothing to be ashamed of."

Jacqueline kissed her mother on her cheek, then noticed Jordan was fast asleep in his grandmother's arms. "Let me take Jordan to his cradle. Alice will not mind watching him until he wakes up."

"You will do nothing of the sort. He is perfectly fine here. He is content, and so am I."

"Very well, have it your way, Mother. I want to hear exactly how you managed to acquire some of the king's men."

Lady Elizabeth smiled slyly. "I used my time in London to my advantage, as I said before. Your father assumed I was properly cowed." She paused as Jacqueline burst out laughing. Once she brought herself back under control, her mother continued. "Hmm, as I was saying, the earl thought I was firmly put in my place. As all men of his ilk forget, we women can be very resourceful when pressed. So when your father allowed me to join the queen and her ladies, I took advantage of the situation."

Jacqueline shook her head. The earl was a fool. He knew not what his wife could do. If he had taken the time to know her better at the start of their marriage, he would have realized her mother was an asset to him. She would have been able to help in furthering his status.

"However you did it, Mother, I applaud you. If not for your propitious arrival, I would now be a widow once more."

Terric came and wrapped his arm around Jacqueline's waist, pulling her close. "I agree with Jacqueline, my lady. You could not have picked a better time."

Sir Guy broke into the conversation. "Aye, you put the earl in his place quite nicely, my lady. There appears to be one loose end in all this."

Lady Elizabeth arched a brow at him. "What loose end?"

"I had a little chat with one of the earl's men. As we predicted, Nicholas was the one who informed the earl of Forwin's double dealing. He also joined the earl when he marched on Nunney."

"Are you saying Nicholas is right now down in the camp?" Jacqueline asked.

"Nay, lass, but he was. Apparently, the earl had decided to end his association with Nicholas, permanently. Somehow the minstrel caught wind of that and beat a hasty retreat."

"I knew Nicholas was in the earl's camp. He came to see me, but I did not know about his leave-taking," Terric added.

Jacqueline looked at her husband. "What did Nicholas want with you?"

Terric shrugged. "I think mostly to lord it over me that I was the captive and he was in the earl's good graces, or so he thought."

The conversation switched to the earl's departure on the following morning. Jacqueline, lost in her own thoughts, did not pay very close attention to what was being said. One part of her felt safe and secure now that her father could no longer hurt her or her family, but another small part of her felt uneasy. The others might assume Nicholas was no longer a threat, but she did not. The one thing she had learned about the minstrel during the months of his living under the same roof was that he did not give up easily. Though the chances that he would attempt something on his own were slim, she could not dismiss the persistent feeling that he would.

CHAPTER TWENTY-SIX

Life finally took on some normalcy for Jacqueline. She settled into the role of chatelaine once more, but what she found most rewarding was being a wife and mother.

Lady Elizabeth and Sir Guy stayed at Nunney with them for a month. That was as long as her mother wanted to be absent from Carisbrooke. It was a sad leave-taking on the day of her departure, but her mother had promised to return soon. She did not want to miss too much of Jordan's growing.

The earl had definitely been put in his place. A missive arrived at Nunney shortly before her mother left. It told how the earl had been ordered to leave Nunney alone. The king also recognized Jordan as Forwin's heir and the new Earl of Somerset.

A new love bloomed as well. It grew more apparent as the days passed. Edwin and Beth were falling for each other, which pleased Jacqueline to no end. Beth was far too young to stay a widow for long, and Edwin was perfect for her.

Knowing what the end result would soon be, Jacqueline

and Terric decided a talk with the young couple was in order. One evening, after Jordan had been put to bed, the four of them sat in the hall and discussed the future.

Terric was the one who started the topic. "Edwin, I would like to know what your intentions are toward Beth."

Edwin choked on the wine he was drinking, causing him to cough. "My intentions?" he asked hoarsely.

"Aye. Since Beth has no male relations present, I feel it is my place to act in their stead. So, are you going to give me an answer?"

Nervously, Edwin shot a quick glance toward Beth. "Well...um...you see..."

Terric shook his head at his squire's hesitancy and interrupted. "Spit it out, Edwin, for god's sake. We know."

"All right then. I love Beth and intend to make her my wife once I become a knight, that is. If she will still have me."

Beth, who had been sitting beside Jacqueline, got up and walked around the trestle table until she stood next to Edwin. "Of course I will still have you. I told you I would wait, no matter how long it takes for you to get your spurs."

Jacqueline had come to stand at Terric's side while Beth had spoken. She gave her husband a nudge. He looked at her, and she cocked her head toward Edwin.

Terric cleared his throat to get his squire and his lady love's attention before he continued. "I am glad to hear your intentions are honorable. That being the case, Jacqueline and I have discussed this at some length. Since you wish to become a married man, your waiting for your spurs is over. A day from now I will knight you."

Edwin's reaction to this news was quite comical and in keeping with the squire. His jaw dropped, but when it really seemed to sink in that he was to be knighted, he lost control.

He jumped up from his chair, then wrapped Terric in a bear hug. "Oh, thank you, Terric. I will never forget this."

Then it was Jacqueline's turn. Edwin kissed her on both cheeks. With much enthusiasm, he took up her hands and rained kisses upon them. Finally, he picked up Beth and spun her around in circles, laughing all the while.

Edwin brought himself back under control and put Beth onto her feet. Still holding her close, he asked, "Will you make me a happy man and accept my offer of marriage?"

Blinking back tears, Beth nodded. "Aye, I will."

As the newly-betrothed couple sealed their promise to each other with a passionate kiss, Jacqueline and Terric quietly left them alone in the hall, giving them some much needed privacy.

* * * *

The next day was spent preparing for Edwin's knighting. Bright and early that morning, Terric and Edwin went to the village blacksmith to have the final pieces of the squire's armor completed. This left Beth and Jacqueline alone for most part of the day.

Using the time given to her, Jacqueline decided to have a serious talk with Beth. She knew her friend was happy, but there had not been any opportunity for her to really talk with her without Edwin being around.

They sat in the solar. Beth worked on a tapestry while Jacqueline nursed Jordan. "Beth, may I ask you something?"

"Of course." She put down her needle, then sat next to Jacqueline. Seeing Jordan still nursed, she smiled at him and gently brushed a finger across his silky cheek. "What is it that you want to ask?"

"Do not take this the wrong way. I beg you."

"I promise not to get upset. I think of you as a sister. You know that. You can say anything to me."

Jordan released her nipple, and Jacqueline looked down at him and found her son asleep, replete. She moved him to her shoulder to burp him. "You will always be a sister to me, Beth. So keeping that in mind, I have to ask this. Are you truly happy?"

Beth smiled brightly. "Aye, I am."

"What of your family? Edwin is of low birth. Will they accept him?"

Beth did not answer right away. Her smile faded slightly. "Well…that is another matter entirely."

"You have not told them, have you?"

"Nay," she said sadly. "I am afraid my father would never understand. They do know of William's passing, though. They assume I am still in mourning. So my father will not be arranging another marriage for me any time soon. Given our station, he would try. When that day does come, it will be too late. I will already be married to Edwin and hopefully have a child of my own."

Jacqueline felt sorry for Beth. She only wished there was something she could do to help her, but there was nothing. "Well, never mind them. We are your family now."

* * * *

Terric and Edwin returned to the keep in the late afternoon. It had been decided that the knighting would take place just prior to the evening meal. Since it would only be the four of them attending, the ceremony would be simple. Edwin hadn't wanted a big celebration.

After preparing himself, Edwin arrived at the hall. Terric, Jacqueline, and Beth waited for him there. He was dressed in his best tunic and hose. He nervously tugged at the hem of his tunic in agitation. Beth smiled reassuringly at him.

Terric motioned him to where he and Beth stood.

"Come, Edwin. Let us do this."

With a quick nod, Edwin complied. Once he reached them, he gave Beth a kiss and then stepped back. "I am ready."

Terric turned to Beth and took the first piece of Edwin's armor from her. Normally, it would have been a male relative from Edwin's family who would help with the arming, but since that was not possible, Beth had stepped in to fulfill that role.

After placing each piece where it was to be worn, all that remained were the spurs. Terric motioned Edwin to kneel, then pulled his sword free of its scabbard. With it, he tapped the blade first on one of Edwin's shoulders and then the other. "You may rise, Sir Edwin." Once the younger man gained his feet, Terric took the spurs from Beth. He buckled them onto Edwin's boots.

Beth flung herself into her intended's arms. "Oh, Edwin! I am so happy for you."

Jacqueline, who had been off to the side, now came forward to kiss the new knight's cheek. "Congratulations, Edwin. Now, let's celebrate, shall we?"

As if on cue, the servants came from the kitchen bearing platters of food. There was roasted capon along with a haunch of venison. Small baby potatoes, peas cooked in a cream sauce, and a salad of fresh greens rounded out the meal. They partook of each dish, eating as much as they could hold.

The remnants of the meal were cleared away, leaving the wine they drank behind. They were all content to just sip on their goblets and talk. Jacqueline was the one who brought up the subject of the up-coming wedding.

"Well, Beth and Edwin, when do you want to be wed? There is nothing stopping you now."

The betrothed pair looked longingly at each other. Edwin clasped Beth's hand in his. "If it is not too soon for Beth, I was hoping in a week's time."

Beth nodded. "That is not too soon for me. I would happily marry you on the morrow."

Before Edwin could accept Beth's suggestion, Jacqueline interrupted. "Nay, that is too soon. Beth needs a new gown. Every bride deserves that much."

"You did not even get that, Jacqueline," Terric said.

"Aye, but I am different. I have no need for such things." To prove her point, she stood and motioned to the tunic and hose she wore. Looking meaningfully at Terric, she added, "All that really mattered in the end was getting you."

If they had been alone, Terric would have grabbed his wife and shown her how much he loved her. They were not, so he settled for intently staring at her, letting her know what to expect later that night.

Edwin cleared his throat. "Can a gown be made in time?"

Jacqueline tore her gaze from Terric. "Aye, Edwin. Though I am not as skilled with a needle as some, I am passable. I am sure Alice will help Beth and me as well. All we have to do is buy the fabric. Tthe best place to go for it is Frome."

* * * *

The market town was well known for its wool and that once a year it had a fair. Even though a market was held every week, the fair was a major event. People would come from all over Somerset to buy and sell there. As it happened, the day the trip to Frome was planned was the first day of the annual fair.

This was the first time Jacqueline had been to Frome. Even though she had lived a year at Nunney, such a trip as this had not been allowed. So this was a thrill for her, especially being able to attend the fair.

They arrived early in the morning, planning to make a

day of it. After stabling their horses at an inn, they headed to the fairgrounds. There were crowds of people milling about, too many to count. The noise they made could be heard even before reaching the fair.

"Well, ladies. What shall we do first?" Terric asked.

Jacqueline settled Jordan better in her arms. "The question is what do we not want to do?"

Terric chuckled. "All right. Since you are undecided, how about we just wander around until you see something you like?"

"Agreed."

There was everything imaginable offered for sale. The proprietors of each stall loudly competed with each other, shouting their wares. Edwin was the first to stop at a stall. That one sold jewelry of all kinds.

He pulled Beth over to look and motioned for her to pick something. She hesitated. "I want to get you something. Choose what you like." Hopeful of a sale, the owner separated a few pieces for Beth to look at.

"I do not know, Edwin."

"Please. Think of it as a betrothal gift." He beseechingly stared at her.

Beth shook her head and laughed. "How can I say nay to those puppy-dog eyes. You win." She scanned the table of goods offered, then finally settled on a simple silver link bracelet.

Happily, Edwin paid for his purchase and then placed it around Beth's slender wrist. With that purchase made, they moved on to the next stall.

This one sold bolts of material. Jacqueline and Beth gave them a cursory glance, finding the goods offered not what they were looking for. After the third such rejection, the men were decidedly losing interest.

Noticing how Terric and Edwin lagged behind, Jacqueline elbowed Beth. She cocked her head toward the men. "Shall we give them a reprieve and let those two find something else to occupy themselves?"

"Aye," Beth said laughingly. "I think we have tortured them enough."

Once the two lag-behinds caught up with them, Jacqueline turned to face them. "You may both go. It is obvious you are bored to tears."

"Are you sure?" Terric asked.

"Aye, go. We can meet again later."

"All right. Edwin and I had planned to look at the horses for sale. Edwin needs a better mount now that he is a knight."

"Then go. Beth and I will meet you at the inn when we have finished our shopping."

Terric kissed Jacqueline on her cheek, then motioned for Edwin to leave her and Beth to their browsing.

* * * *

His life could not sink any lower than it already had. This past year had just been one disappointment after another. He had drunk deeply from the cup of despair and found it a bitter brew.

Nicholas took a large swig from his tankard of ale, then wiped his lip with his sleeve. Ideally, he should be out plying his trade. After all, market fairs were where entertainers such as himself made the most coin, Frome's was no different from any other, but a lethargy had claimed him, and he had no wish to change it.

Of course all his troubles stemmed from one person and one person only—Jacqueline Montacute. He wished to god he had never set eyes on that witch. He hated the woman with every fiber of his being. Just the thought of her made his blood boil.

He sipped again from his tankard and happened to glance out the open inn door, then froze. Unbelievably, the one woman he never wished to see again stood in the yard, and she was not alone. Her haughty friend, Beth, was next to her.

Unsure of exactly what he planned to do, Nicholas stood. Cautiously stepping closer to the open door, he searched the yard. The two women appeared to be alone and seemed not to be interested in entering the inn.

He could only surmise they had come because of the market fair. Beth held a cloth-wrapped bundle in her arms, more than likely some purchase she had made. Jacqueline, he noticed, carried her brat. She was scandalously dressed in man's attire, much to his shock.

Nicholas inched even closer to the door and searched again for any sign of an escort. There was none that he could see. Satisfied they were indeed alone, he pulled up the hood of his cloak over his head. He stepped into the yard.

* * * *

"Do you think we should fetch them, Beth?"

"Let's give them a little more time. They cannot be too much longer. It has been a while since they left."

Jacqueline nodded. Beth was right. Besides, it would do no good to be wandering the fair, looking for Terric and Edwin. In all probability, they would miss finding them and just cause much confusion.

She glanced toward the entrance to the inn's yard and hoped to catch a glimpse of their errant men folk. She barely glanced at the hooded figure coming up behind Beth. It was not until her friend gasped in surprise did she turn her attention to who it was.

The man—she could tell it was a man from his attire peeking through his half-open cloak—held a knife at her throat. As Jacqueline took a step closer, the man pressed the blade nearer, causing Beth to whimper. Jacqueline stilled.

KNIGHT OF HER LIFE

"If it is coin you want, I will gladly give it. Just release my friend. It is not necessary for you to use such extreme measures."

The man shook his head and laughed. There was no humor in it. "Oh, but I must disagree. There is every reason for me to use extreme measures."

That voice. Jacqueline knew it, but it could not be him. No man was that stupid. "Who are you?"

Their assailant reached up and pulled back his hood, revealing his face. "You wound me, Jacqueline. Have you forgotten me already?"

Jacqueline stiffened. "What is it you want, Nicholas."

"Nothing much really. Just to make you suffer as you have made me."

"Hurting Beth will not change anything."

"Maybe not, but it will give me some satisfaction in doing it."

Nicholas was a man who no longer cared what happened to him. Jacqueline easily read it in his eyes. She had to do something to get Beth from him. There was no telling when Terric and Edwin would arrive at the inn.

"Let Beth go. It is me you really want."

"Are you offering yourself in her stead?"

Seeing the desperate, pleading look in Beth's eyes, she knew there was no turning away. "Aye, I am. Release Beth and I will go freely with you."

Nicholas took some time to consider her offer. In way of an answer, he roughly shoved Beth from him. "I accept."

Before Nicholas could grab her arm, Jacqueline quickly passed Jordan to Beth. Under her breath, she quietly whispered, "Watch where he takes me. Terric will want to know."

Nicholas forcefully took hold of her arm and pulled her away. After shooting Beth a last glance, Jacqueline allowed herself to be dragged from the deserted inn yard.

249

* * * *

A short time later, Terric and Edwin arrived at the inn. An extremely distraught Beth pounced on them. She talked and cried at the same time. Most of what she said was unintelligible, but Terric managed to pick out Jacqueline's name and *gone*.

He took Beth by the shoulders and tried to calm her. "Slowly now. What happened to Jacqueline?"

Beth swallowed back tears, then took a deep, steadying breath. "It was Nicholas. He was here, at the inn. He has taken Jacqueline."

Having picked up on Beth's distress, Jordan wailed. Terric took his son from her and quieted him by rocking him. "Start from the beginning and tell me how this happened."

* * * *

Jacqueline dragged her feet as Nicholas proceeded to pull her through the fairgrounds and then the town streets. She had a feeling he really had no idea where he was taking her. Not once, but twice, he had steered them into a dead-end alley. He did it for a third time, pushed her against a wall, and brandished his knife. She held her breath, expecting the worst to happen. She closed her eyes and waited for the blow to fall, but it never came.

One minute Nicholas had her pinned, then the next, he was gone. Jacqueline cracked open one eye and found Terric standing over the fallen minstrel. He held the point of his sword to Nicholas's chest.

Rage emanated off Terric in discernible waves. Jacqueline placed her hand on his arm. "He is not worth it, Terric. Let him go."

"He can always come back to hurt you again," he said through gritted teeth.

"Aye, but he will not. Look at him, sniveling in fear. He is too much of a coward to try again."

To prove her correct, Nicholas whimpered. Terric snarled. "Since my wife has asked me so nicely, I will do as she says and let you go, but the next time, I will not be so forgiving." Terric turned his sword and cut a shallow cut across Nicholas' chest. The minstrel whimpered again.

Nicholas jumped to his feet and raced off. Terric pulled Jacqueline into his arms and held her tight. She allowed it for a few seconds, then smacked him on the back, trying to get him to ease his hold.

"I am fine, Terric. He did not hurt me."

"It would have gone much worse for him if he had."

"How did you find me so quickly?"

"Beth sent me in the right direction. It was pure luck that one of the people I asked happened to see you pass by."

"However you did it, I am happy to see you."

Terric pulled her close again and claimed her lips in a demanding kiss. After he softened it, he released her mouth. "Come, we should return to the inn. Poor Beth had worked herself into a state before Edwin and I arrived. It would be cruel to keep her waiting."

"Aye. Now maybe we can have a normal life."

Jacqueline accepted the arm Terric offered and placed her hand atop it. The sun was beginning to set. The sky was painted in shades of blue, mauve, and pink. A beautiful ending for a somewhat calamitous day. She truly hoped their lives could be like every other person's now. She had everything she could ask for—a husband and child.

Looking lovingly at her tournament knight, Jacqueline thought her life could not get much better than that. She was complete.

The End

About the Author

Marisa Chenery was always a lover of books, but after reading her first historical romance novel she found herself hooked. Having inherited a love for the written word, she soon started writing her own novels.

She now writes young adult books and erotic romances.

Marisa lives in Ontario, Canada, with her boyfriend, Steve, four children, four grandchildren (she's a young grandma in her fifties) and rabbit and dog.

www.marisachenery.com